T0044224

Karolinum Press

MODERN CZECH CLASSICS

A World Apart and Other Stories
Czech Women Writers at the Fin de Siècle

Selected and Translated by Kathleen Hayes

KAROLINUM PRESS 2022

KAROLINUM PRESS
Karolinum Press is a publishing department
of Charles University
Ovocný trh 560/5, 116 36 Prague 1
Czech Republic
www.karolinum.cz

Copyediting by Pavlína Píhová
Image of Beneš Knüpfer's Soumrak (ca. 1890) courtesy
of National Gallery Prague
Graphic design by Zdeněk Ziegler
Set and printed in the Czech Republic by Karolinum Press
Second edition

Cataloging-in-Publication Data is available
from the National Library of the Czech Republic

ISBN 978-80-246-4733-3
ISBN 978-80-246-4804-0 (pdf)
ISBN 978-80-246-4805-7 (mobi)
ISBN 978-80-246-4806-4 (epub)

CONTENTS

ACKNOWLEDGEMENTS

I would like to express my thanks to those who took the time to read through drafts of the translations. Their suggestions were invaluable: Ivan Gutierrez, Linda Hayes, Radek Honzák and Deborah Michaels. Robert Pynsent gave advice regarding the selection of the stories and help with the translation of obscure words. David Short was kind enough to read and make corrections to the translation of 'Gazdina roba.' I would like to thank Mary Hawker in particular for the time and effort she took helping to prepare these texts. The errors and awkward phrases that remain are my own responsibility.

CONCEPTIONS OF WOMAN AND THE 'WOMAN QUESTION' AT THE FIN DE SIÈCLE

Few works by Czech women writers have been translated into English; Kovtun's *Czech and Slovak Literature in English* (1988) lists nineteen women whose works have been translated since the first known translations into English in 1832 up to 1982.[1] Most of these translations are of poems and short stories included in anthologies. From the paucity of translations, one might conclude that there were few women writing. Yet Czech women writers were published, widely read and admired. Karolina Světlá (1830–1899) may serve as an example. In her lifetime she was considered one of the greatest Czech writers of the century, yet only two of her short stories and one novella have been translated into English.[2] Some volumes published recently have tried to correct this imbalance.[3] Writers from the *Fin de siècle*, however, have not received much attention from translators, despite the amount of scholarly research concentrating on the period.[4] The present volume includes a selection of short stories by Czech women writers who were well known in their own era, although not necessarily at the time of the publication of the stories included. Several of

1 George J. Kovtun, *Czech and Slovak Literature in English,* Washington, 1988.
2 *Poslední paní Hlohovská (Světozor,* 1870), translated as *Maria Felicia* (1898); 'Nebožka Barbora' [1873], translated 'Barbara' by Š. B. Hrbková, *Czechoslovak Stories* (1920), and as 'Poor Dead Barbora' by William E. Harkins, *Czech Prose. An Anthology* (1983); 'Hubička' was translated as 'A Kiss' by M. Busch and Otto Pick, *Selected Czech Tales* (1925).
3 For example: *Daylight in Nightclub Inferno,* selection by Elena Lappin, North Haven, CT, 1997.
4 Two fascinating studies are: Mark M. Anderson, *Kafka's Clothes: Ornament and Aestheticism in the Habsburg Fin de siècle,* Oxford, 1992; and Jacques Le Rider, *Modernity and Crises of Identity: Culture and Society in Fin de siècle Vienna* [1990], translated by Rosemary Morris, Cambridge, 1993.

the writers represented here are more famous for their post-war works.[5] I have chosen material from the last decade of the nineteenth century up to World War I.

It has become conventional to describe the *Fin de siècle* as a period of change, and for women in Central Europe it certainly was that.[6] Before World War I, it was illegal for women in the Bohemian Lands, as in all of Austria, to join political organizations.[7] They did not have the right to vote. Their rights within the household were also restricted. For example, at the turn of the century, the husband's status as the head of the family was codified by law; his wife was obliged to be obedient to him; the father alone had the right to chose an occupation for his offspring, while they were still minors.[8] Even after the war, women, like minors, criminals, members of religious orders and foreigners, were not supposed to become legal guardians. In the event of the death of the father, the paternal grandfather, rather than the mother, would become the guardian of the children.[9]

---

5   Benešová, for example, for *Don Pablo, don Pedro a Věra Lukášová* (1936); Tilschová for *Stará rodina* (1916) or *Synové* (1918).

6   Catherine David provides an overview of the history of the women's movement in the Bohemian Lands in her study 'Czech Feminists and Nationalism in the Late Habsburg Monarchy: "The First in Austria"', *Journal of Women's History*, vol. 3, 1991, no. 2, pp. 26–45. Wilma A. Iggers has selected and translated autobiographical writings and letters by women from the period in *Women of Prague: Ethnic Diversity and Social Change from the Eighteenth Century to the Present*, Providence, RI, and Oxford, 1995. The work also includes a useful introduction. Pynsent examines the works of women writers more generally in his 'The Liberation of Woman and Nation: Czech Nationalism and Women Writers of the *Fin de siècle*', *The Literature of Nationalism*, Houndmills and London, 1996, pp. 83–155. See also: Marie L. Neudorflová, *České ženy v 19. století*, Prague, 1999.

7   Katherine David, 'Czech Feminists and Nationalism in the Late Habsburg Monarchy: "The First in Austria"', p. 27.

8   Alois Hajn, 'Hospodářská reforma manželství' [1909], *Ženská otázka v letech 1900–1920*, Prague, 1939, p. 110.

9   Alois Hajn, 'Nutnost další reformy manželského práva' [1919], ibid., pp. 127–128.

Yet despite these restrictions on the lives of women, in 1912 Czech political parties cooperated to bring about the election of the first woman deputy to parliament in Central Europe: Božena Viková-Kunětická (1862–1934), an author of novels, short stories and plays who was well known for her feminism.[10] A municipal secondary school for girls (Městská vyšší dívčí škola) was founded in 1863. A technical school for girls was founded in Prague in 1884 (Městská pokračovací dívčí škola průmyslová), and similar training schools for girls appeared elsewhere in the Bohemian Lands. Minerva, a private grammar school (gymnázium) for girls preparing them for a university education, was founded in 1888; teaching began there in September 1890. From March 1897, women were able to enroll at the Faculty of Arts of Charles University (then named the Czech Charles-Ferdinand University). Women began to study at the Faculty of Medicine in 1900. The educational reforms opened up new employment opportunities; this meant that women did not have to depend on finding a husband to ensure their financial security.

Fashions were changing as well. The social reforms and even the new clothing trends reflected changing ideas about woman's 'nature' and role in society.[11] This discourse was manifest, for example, in contemporary publications like Otto Weininger's (1880–1903) notorious *Sex and Character* (Geschlecht und Charakter, 1903) and Freud's (1856–1939) *Three Essays on the Theory of Sexuality* (Drei Abhandlungen zur Sexualtheorie, 1905).[12] It was also manifest in contem-

10   She was elected to the Bohemian Diet. Viková-Kunětická, like those who voted for her, regarded her election as a victory for the Czech 'nation' rather than for the woman's cause. On the election, see: Jiří Kořalka, 'Zvolení ženy do českého zemského sněmu roku 1912', *Documenta pragensia XIII: Žena v dějinách Prahy*, edited by Jiří Pešek and Václav Ledvinka, Prague, 1996, pp. 307–320.
11   Eva Uchalová, *Česká móda 1870–1918: od valčíku po tango*, Prague, 1997.
12   See the useful introduction in: *Freud on Women. A Reader*, edited by Elisabeth Young-Bruehl, London, 1990.

porary art work, both graphic arts and literature.[13] One can find many examples of literary meditations on the changing roles of the sexes: Ibsen's (1828–1906) *A Doll's House* (Et Dukkehjem, 1879), Henry James's (1843–1916) *The Portrait of a Lady* (1881), Oscar Wilde's (1854–1900) *Salomé* (1894). Relations between men and women were a topic of great interest to Czech writers. The two most famous Czech women writers of the nineteenth century, Božena Němcová (1820–1862) and Karolina Světlá, had written about issues related to the 'woman question'.[14] At the *Fin de siècle*, both male and female writers treated this theme. A selection of the women writers is presented in this volume. Of works by male writers, one thinks of Josef Svatopluk Machar's (1864–1942) *Magdalena* (1894) and Karel Matěj Čapek-Chod's (1860–1927) *Kašpar Lén the Avenger* (K. L. mstitel, 1908), both of which concern prostitution.[15] Matěj Anastazia Šimáček (1860–1913), in his novel *The Soul of the Factory* (Duše továrny, 1894), writes about a factory worker who is torn between her devotion to the factory and her ties to her husband and child. Czech Decadents also

13   The depiction of woman in the graphic arts is treated by Bram Dijkstra in *Idols of Perversity: Fantasies of Feminine Evil in Fin de siècle Culture*, New York and Oxford, 1986. Robert Pynsent discusses conceptions of women in the writings of the Czech Decadents in 'Conclusory Essay: Decadence, Decay and Innovation', *Decadence and Innovation: Austro-Hungarian Life and Art at the Turn of the Century*, London, 1989, pp. 111–248. More general studies of conceptions of women in the period concerned have also appeared; one thinks of Elaine Showalter's *Sexual Anarchy: Gender and Culture at the Fin de siècle*, London, 1990; and Nina Auerbach's *Woman and the Demon: The Life of a Victorian Myth*, Cambridge, MA and London, 1982.
14   See, for example: Němcová, 'Čtyry doby' (1855); Světlá, *Frantina* (1880) and *Konec a počátek* (1874).
15   Machar was a feminist, whereas Čapek-Chod was not. Čapek-Chod's conception of woman, however, was in some respects unconventional. On the theme of prostitution, see: Kathleen Hayes, 'Images of the Prostitute in Czech *Fin de siècle* Literature', *The Slavonic and East European Review*, vol. 75, April 1997, no. 2, pp. 234–258.

wrote about the nature of the female outsider, for example, the courtesan in Miloš Marten's (1883–1917) *Cortigiana* (1911), or Salomé in Jiří Karásek's (1871–1951) 'The Death of Salomé' (Smrt Salomina, 1911). The Czech Decadent Arthur Breisky (1885–1910), however, displayed the characteristic Dandy disdain for women in his essay 'The Quintessence of Dandyism' (Kvintesence dandysmu, 1909). Perhaps the most famous Czech feminist of the period was Tomáš Garrigue Masaryk (1850–1937), who became the first president of Czechoslovakia. He frequently reflected on the woman question in his writings;[16] his American wife, Charlotte (1850–1923), translated John Stuart Mill's (1806–1873) *The Subjection of Women* (1869) into Czech.

In this introduction, I shall consider the changing perceptions of woman and the woman question in this period as these are reflected in several contemporary sources.

THE KREUTZER SONATA

In 1890, the first Czech translation of Tolstoy's (1828–1910) *The Kreutzer Sonata* was published (Kreitserova sonata, 1890, English translation 1890). The copies were confiscated, as the work had been banned in Austria-Hungary.[17] Before World War I, six more Czech translations of the work were published.[18] The number of translations indicates not only the renown of the Russian writer, but also the impor-

16   See, for example: T. G. Masaryk, 'Moderní názor na ženu', *Ženská revue*, July 1905. See also: Marie L. Neudorfl, 'Masaryk and the Women Question', *T. G. Masaryk (1850–1937)*, vol. 1, *Thinker and Politician*, edited by Stanley B. Winters, Houndmills and London, 1990, pp. 258–282.
17   The work had also caused a scandal in Russia. In 1890 Tolstoy wrote the postscript to the short story to try to clarify his views and intentions in writing the work.
18   1890, translation by Antonín Hajn; 1890, L. F.; after 1900, Ferdinand Kraupner; 1909, Vinc. Červinka; 1903 and 1910, J. Zvolský; 1912, Frant. Husák and Jaroslav Janeček. It was translated into Slovak by D. Makovický in 1894.

tance of the subject of the work – marriage and the woman question – at the *Fin de siècle*. The issues Tolstoy touches on were debated during the entire period under consideration: the education of women, the double standard of sexual behavior for men and women, prostitution, the 'marriage market'.[19]

The Kreutzer Sonata is narrated by the character Pozdnyshev, who murdered his wife in a fit of jealousy. During a train journey, he describes his marriage to a fellow passenger and explains why he killed his wife. He criticizes the education of young men and women of his class, the landed gentry. Men, he argues, are brought up to believe that it is perfectly natural and healthy to turn to prostitutes for sex before they are married. They learn to regard women as objects of sexual desire, and they see their wives in the same light. The enslavement of women, he asserts, is due to the fact that men use women as instruments of pleasure.[20] Pozdnyshev claims that marriage is nothing more than a form of prostitution. Girls are raised in a state of ignorance about sex. They enter into marriage innocent, morally superior to men, and are degraded by sexual contact with their jaded husbands. Girls are practically sold to their husbands: the introduction of young women to society is nothing more than a marriage market; that is, they are taken to balls and parties where they might meet prospective grooms. The role of mothers is to set traps for these men, using their daughters as bait. The education of women is directed towards teaching them how to please men. It is unnatural, Pozdnyshev claims, to marry off girls to such

19   In his 'Epilogue', written after the first publication of the work, Tolstoy states that his intention was to argue in favor of the ideal of chastity. His ideals did not coincide in every respect with those of the Czech women's movement.

20   See: Leo Tolstoy, *Sonata Kreutzerova,* trans. V. Červinka, Prague, n. d., p. 54.

immoral older men. The brides are shocked to learn about the sexual desires of their husbands; they do not enjoy sex themselves, and only tolerate it because they want to bear children. In marriages that are contracted in this manner, the husband and wife have little in common and their estrangement from one another is to be expected.

Pozdnyshev's interpretation of the debased relations between the sexes and the difficulties of a woman's position in society corresponds to the analysis put forth by supporters of the women's movement in the Bohemian Lands. The similarity of views is manifest in the review of *The Kreutzer Sonata* written in 1890 by Tereza Nováková (1853–1912), a Czech writer and supporter of emancipation for women. Nováková does not agree with all of the opinions expressed in the work or the epilogue; she does not share Tolstoy's belief that all sexual relations, even those within marriage, are debased. She rejects Tolstoy's contention that a mother's love for her child is animal and selfish. Nonetheless, she states that 'the principles expressed in the "Sonata" and in the "Epilogue" are profound, truthful and noble; they seem to be, and indeed they are, bitter, like a radical medication for a serious illness; they seem impossible because they are new and completely unlike anything proclaimed before now.'[21] Nováková suggests that if the work were not written in such a 'Naturalist' style, it would be advisable to recommend it as educational reading for young men and women.[22] She writes: 'There, where the first awareness of erotic passion slinks into a young heart, unspoiled by the tales of comrades – slinks in through rosy dreams, through

21   Tereza Nováková, 'L. N. Tolstého "Kreutzerova sonáta" a její "Doslov" ze stanoviska ženského', *Ze ženského hnutí*, Prague, n. d. [1912], pp. 13–32, see p. 14. Nováková notes under the title that the essay was written at the end of 1890. In this collection of essays Nováková outlines her views on a wide range of issues related to the woman question.
22   Ibid, pp. 19–20.

all of the most beautiful impressions of life, through art and the delight of nature – there one must point out where that passion leads. One must point out how one day it will be a humiliation, a bond that, according to Tolstoy, will prevent the rendering of "service to humanity and God". There one must offer support so that reason will prevail and not stray from the ideal of purity under the pressure of the powerful feelings set by nature in the human breast.'[23] She agrees with Tolstoy that most girls are preoccupied with finding a husband, stating that this is because they have thus far been dependent on marriage as a means of providing for their existence. If women are to pursue the ideal of chastity that Tolstoy extols, other opportunities must be made available to them; the view that the most appropriate position for a woman in society is that of wife and mother must be changed. Tolstoy's ideal of chastity cannot be achieved, not even partially, until women have educational opportunities comparable to those available to men. She agrees with Tolstoy that many women consider sex unnatural, are disillusioned by marriage and would rather live in a state of absolute chastity. She concludes her essay with the remark that, with a few reservations, women will agree with the theses expressed in Tolstoy's work, and in particular his sharp criticism of the double standard of sexual behavior. Nováková's understanding of the position of women and the relations between the sexes is echoed in both fiction and non-fiction written by supporters of the women's movement at the *Fin de siécle*.

MODERN WOMEN

The publication of a translation of Laura Marholm's *Modern Women* (Das Buch der Frauen, 1895) in 1897 indicates

23   Ibid., p. 20.

that a more traditional conception of woman was still prevalent.[24] In this work the author presents portraits of 'dysfunctional' women who tried to imitate men by pursuing careers and in doing so sacrificed their femininity. The work argues with feminist demands, yet inadvertently awakens the reader's admiration for the women described. It presents a perception of woman that was widespread in the period, one that was informed by anxiety over the changing roles of the sexes. The portrait entitled 'The Tragedy of a Young Girl' (Tragedie mladé dívky) gives an account of Maria Konstantinovna Bashkirtseva (1860–1884), a woman who tries to develop her artistic talents: she is a gifted writer, singer and painter. Her pursuit of an artistic career is presented as the result of her disappointment in love and subsequent desire to find a sense of self-worth in her own achievements.[25] She dies at the age of twenty-four; the author implies that this is the fate that awaits a woman with such unnatural desires. The author states that women are not interested in knowing themselves; they do not have an inner life.[26] Woman is, mentally and physiologically, an empty shell; she is completed by a man.[27] Women are incapable of reason, and they cannot create art because they are 'empty'.[28]

In the portrait 'Pioneer', the author describes the Swedish writer Anne Charlotte Leffler (1849–1892). The depiction illustrates the author's point of view: woman at the end of the 19th century wants to be independent of man, but really the life of a woman begins and ends with a man; man is

24 Laura Marholm, *Kniha žen. Podobizny časové psychologie*, translated by Olga Mužáková, Prague, 1897.

25 Marholm, 'Tragedie mladé dívky', ibid., p. 21.

26 Ibid., p. 9.

27 Ibid.

28 Ibid., pp. 10, 25. Weininger, influenced by Wagner's anti-Semitic ideas, made the same claim about women and the Jews.

the 'contents' of a woman.[29] A woman who wants to write without the support of a man is an unhappy and divided creature.[30] The author describes the change in relations between the sexes as a kind of feminization of the times.[31] Women have not gained anything, however, as a result of this change. On the contrary, woman 'means' less than she did before; she has lost her importance as an individual.[32] Men and women no longer understand one another; relations between them are cold. In this portrait, the author suggests that women can be writers; their writing, however, is not 'rational', but rather 'temperamental'.[33] She expects a woman writer to manifest a 'mobile, nervous life'.[34] In his introduction to a collection of travel essays by Božena Viková-Kunětická, the feminist Machar also expresses the view that works written by women will be fundamentally different from works written by men because the former will express a woman's mind.[35]

In the portrait of the writer George Egerton (1859–1945), 'Nervous Basic Tones', the author describes the 'New Woman' who neither imitates nor seeks equality with man. The New Woman is refined, sensitive, feminine; she is independent. New women perceive one another in an entirely new manner.[36] As an utterly subjective being, woman can only present herself, her own ego, in her writings. This is what she contributes to literature, the expression of her

29 Marholm, 'Průkopnice', Kniha žen, pp. 38–39.

30 Ibid., p. 43.

31 Ibid., p. 35.

32 Ibid., pp. 34–35. Božena Viková-Kunětická makes this point about individuals generally in the increasingly mechanized society at the turn of the century. See her novel Vzpoura (1901).

33 Marholm, 'Průkopnice', Kniha žen, p. 40.

34 Ibid., p. 43.

35 J. S. Machar, 'Paní Božena Viková-Kunětická', Božena Viková-Kunětická, Švýcarské scenerie, Prague, 1902, pp. I–VIII, see pp. III–IV.

36 Marholm, 'Nervosní tony základní', Kniha žen, pp. 95–96.

female personality.[37] The author does not entirely rule out the possibility that women can produce art, but does insist that the only valuable new writing by women will express a woman's soul.

A PROGRESSIVE VIEW ON THE WOMAN QUESTION

Pavla Buzková (1885–1949) was a writer and feminist activist in the pre-war and inter-war period. In her collection of essays *A Progressive View on the Woman Question* (Pokrokový názor na ženskou otázku, 1909), she rejects the view of woman as victim. 'Mere violence does not give rise to slaves. I cannot be enslaved unless I allow myself to be enslaved,' she writes;[38] 'mental slavery is impossible, unless it is willingly accepted'.[39] Buzková accuses women of being morally weak: 'Woman allowed herself to be enslaved because it was pleasant for her to cast off the burden of responsibility'.[40] Woman's passivity confirmed man in his belief that she was an inferior creature, something half-way between a child and a man.[41] Buzková contrasts the oppression of women and the institution of slavery in America, and asserts that women had always had greater, but unrealized, opportunities for educating and liberating themselves.[42] She agrees with the harshest criticisms of women: 'If women are accused of shallowness, carelessness, lack of self-discipline, there's 95% truth in the accusations. How these flaws developed is another ques-

37   Ibid., p. 92.
38   Pavla Buzková, *Pokrokový názor na ženskou otázku,* Prague, 1909, p. 4.
39   Ibid.
40   Ibid., p. 5. Buzková's assertions remind one of Masaryk's philosophy of personal responsibility.
41   Ibid., p. 6.
42   Ibid., p. 7.

tion, but they do exist, that is a fact.'[43] Women are 'drowning in pettiness'.[44] 'It is not the fault of men,' she writes, 'but the fault of the superficiality and weakness of women in earlier eras, that we are where we are today.'[45] It is women, rather than men, who must fight for equal rights. Men are not the enemy; she states, 'one hears that only from public speakers or those who don't want to look at the root of things; women are the enemy, unconscious, uneducated women, and, of course, uneducated men.'[46] Buzková supports the idea of equal rights for women; she believes, however, that it is not a question of a struggle between men and women but rather a struggle between progress and backwardness.[47] She accuses women of being politically conservative, in particular because they are susceptible to the influence of the Roman Catholic Church (a view that was widespread at that time).[48] Nonetheless, she believes that women should be granted the vote even if a conservative political reaction will follow. Buzková expresses a widely held view when she asserts that men should raise women to their level so that, as equals, women can help them in the struggle for the rights of the nation.[49] She links the freedom of women (understood in terms of the right to vote) with the future of the nation, which cannot consider itself cultured or free

43   Ibid., p. 9.

44   Ibid.

45   Ibid., p. 10.

46   Ibid., p. 12.

47   Ibid., p. 13.

48   Ibid., pp. 14–15. Pynsent also makes this point. Pynsent, 'The Liberation of Woman and Nation', p. 116. Buzková's anti-clerical views were typical of the Czech nationalism of the period. Nováková also expresses this view in 'Ženy pro svobodnou školu' (written 1905), *Ze ženského hnutí,* pp. 222–224, 228.

49   Buzková, *Pokrokový názor na ženskou otázku,* pp. 22–23. Pynsent comments: 'For Viková and Buzková every politically aware patriot should be a feminist.' Pynsent, 'The Liberation of Woman and Nation', p. 85.

unless there is equality between the sexes.[50] She considers political participation to be the moral duty of women as members of the nation.[51] Her view on relations between the sexes is characteristic of Czech 'progressive' thinkers of the period:

Only a mutual intertwining of relations between men and women will remove the unhealthy [brand of] feminism from society, that incorrect understanding of the women's movement, which does not [actually] consist in the emancipation of women from men and men from women, but [rather] the emancipation of women from their laziness, shallowness, unconsciousness, and men from their frivolous perception of woman and their overvaluation of their own masculinity. Both sexes should then be liberated on the one hand from their animal nature, and on the other hand from demoralization, as Professor Masaryk put it so well in his *The Social Question*.[52]

She criticizes the contemporary upbringing of women. Girls are still educated as their mothers had been; they are prepared for marriage and motherhood, and this suffocates all talent and encourages frivolity. Society cannot expect anything from women until the entire system of education for girls is reformed.[53] She believes that every girl should be raised to become financially independent; she should also be obliged to devote a year of her time to serve the state.[54] She attacks middle-class women in particular. She asserts that: 'If bourgeois women would help themselves, a great act of social work would be achieved,

50   Buzková, *Pokrokový názor na ženskou otázku*, p. 23.
51   Ibid.
52   Ibid., pp. 26–27.
53   Ibid., p. 32.
54   Ibid.

because nothing poisons society so much as their rotting.'[55] Women from the working class are morally superior to middle-class women.[56] The woman question is most pressing for the middle class because at this social level there is the greatest difference between the position of man and that of woman. The higher the social class, she claims, the more women are enslaved: 'or rather, her inferiority is more obvious because her interests diverge from the interests of men, and because her economic worth declines and there is nothing with which to replace it'.[57] Woman suffers because she is destined, by social conventions, to be fulfilled by marriage and motherhood; she has no civic or political duties to fulfill. She is limited to the sphere of the home and has nothing with which to occupy herself but her husband and children. It is no wonder, then, that she is unhappy, dulled, unbalanced.[58] Buzková even goes as far as to state that marriage represents a kind of prison for women, and love a kind of slavery.[59] She claims that 'female' characteristics – gossiping, mysticism, sentimentality, shallowness – will only disappear when women are educated, when they are integrated in society as individuals with an interest in that society, when they become engaged in political and public activities.[60] Buzková also claims that the participation of women in public life will bring about a greater morality in the life of the society: 'The removal of prostitution, the spread of abstinence, the fight against militarism and against great capitalism [...] can certainly be expected of them.'[61] This was another common theme in the

55   Ibid., p. 33.
56   Ibid.
57   Ibid., p. 34.
58   Ibid., p. 36.
59   Ibid., p. 38.
60   Ibid., p. 41.
61   Ibid., p. 44.

writings of supporters of the women's movement. Equality in all areas of life is necessary if the lives of women – and thus the life of society – are to be reformed.

THE WOMAN QUESTION

Some of Buzková's views on the woman question are echoed in the writings of a male supporter of the women's movement, the journalist and Social Democrat Alois Hajn (1870–1953). A selection of his newspaper articles on the subject was published in *The Woman Question, 1900–1920* (Ženská otázka v letech 1900–1920, 1939). He also criticizes the character of contemporary women. In an early article ('The Precious Legacy of the Czech Woman' [Vzácný odkaz české ženy], 1901), he states that most Czech women are 'sunk up to their necks in mental backwardness and cultural ignorance'.[62] Despite his support for reform, his perception of woman is in some respects rather traditional. In 'The Equal Worth of Woman and Man' (Rovnocennost ženy s mužem, 1910–1912), crediting his views to Havelock Ellis (1859–1939), Hajn states that woman is more determined by her sexual characteristics than man is.[63] Woman is also not as developed physically as man; she resembles 'younger' beings (the child, the adolescent) in her lack of body hair, height and voice.[64] In terms of character, women are more interested in their immediate surroundings; they have a sense for the decorative, for the individual and the concrete. Men are more interested in things that are useful, general, abstract.[65] Women are receptive, sensitive, perceptive, but also more conservative and more inclined to profess a religious faith.

62 Alois Hajn, 'Vzácný odkaz české ženy' [1901], *Ženská otázka v letech 1900-1920*, p. 53.
63 Hajn, 'Rovnocennost ženy s mužem', ibid., p. 13.
64 Ibid., p. 14.
65 Ibid., pp. 16–17.

Hajn states that if woman is not equal to man, she is of equal worth (rovnocenná), rather than inferior to him.[66] Hajn is convinced that with woman's entry into public life, a new culture will develop, one that is more perfect and beautiful than that which men have been able to create.[67]

In 'Woman and Public Life' (Žena a veřejný život, 1913) Hajn reiterates that women will have a positive effect on public life.[68] He writes about the 'social meaning' of motherhood; that is, woman as mother is crucial to society and the nation (elsewhere, he adds 'the race'). Society has a moral obligation to protect mother and child, and to enable the mother to perform her important social role, enriching the state and nation with a strong, healthy offspring.[69] In 'The Protection of Motherhood is the Foundation of the Culture of Childhood' (Ochrana mateřství základem puerikultury, 1913), he claims that the highest function of woman is motherhood.[70] A politically aware and culturally 'mature' woman can also strengthen the nation when she plays an active part in public life.[71] No distinctions should be made between single and married mothers, or between legitimate and illegitimate children.[72] This view was unconventional, but not original. Božena Viková-Kunětická had asserted that single mothers were due respect as mothers in her novel from the turn of the century, Medřická (1897).

Like Masaryk, and other supporters of the women's movement, Hajn argues that there is a need for a new and more just sexual morality. He objects to the double standard of sexual morality in society in the article 'The Problem of

66 Ibid., p. 20.
67 Ibid., p. 21.
68 Hajn, 'Žena a veřejný život', ibid., p. 28.
69 Ibid., p. 30.
70 Hajn, 'Ochrana mateřství základem puerikultury', ibid., p. 58.
71 Hajn, 'Žena a veřejný život', pp. 33–34.
72 Ibid., p. 31.

Mothers and Illegitimate Children' (Problém matek a dětí nemanželských, 1908).[73] He objects to the fact that an unmarried mother and her child are rejected by society while the father of the illegitimate child is not criticized.[74] He notes the prejudices that exist against bastard children, and their lack of rights, for example, to their father's name or property.[75] He criticizes the Czechs for being 'behind' the Germans and Austrian-Germans in that they have not yet formed an organization for the protection of unmarried mothers and their children.[76] In 'Illegitimate Children' (Děti nemanželské, 1913), he notes that illegitimate children often become prostitutes and criminals because of the social prejudices they encounter.[77]

SPRING AWAKENING

In her essay 'Spring Awakening: Memories from My Childhood and Girlhood Years' (Procitnutí jara. Vzpomínky z dětských a dívčích let, 1915), Anna Lauermannová-Mikschová (1852–1932), who used the masculine pseudonym Felix Tèver, reflects on her friendship with Marie Červinková-Riegrová (1854–1895). Riegrová was the daughter of one of the most important Czech politicians of the late 19th century, František Ladislav Rieger (1818–1903). Although a number of Czech women authors were publishing at that time, Lauermannová's career was still rather unusual. Riegrová's devotion to charitable causes was more typical of educated, socially engaged women of her generation.[78] (See also Tèver's por-

---

73 Hajn, 'Problém matek a dětí nemanželských', ibid., p. 75.
74 Ibid., p. 75.
75 Ibid., pp. 76-77.
76 Ibid., p. 79.
77 Hajn, 'Děti nemanželské', ibid., p. 80.
78 In 'Ženino právo na svobodnou volbu povolání' (written 1897), Nováková laments the fact that exceptionally talented women, like Marie Červinková-

trait of the widow bored to tears with charitable activity in 'Solitude' [Samota], the concluding story of *Duše nezakotvené*, 1908.) Lauermannová's recollection supports a number of the points made by Nováková in her review of *The Kreutzer Sonata*. The description of her first introduction to the topic of sex reveals the extent to which girl were 'sheltered':

> Some red-headed friend at the girls' secondary school rid us of our ignorance of the things of this sinful world, ignorance of sexual relations. The shock was cruel. What had once been only dimly sensed and anxiously driven out of the mind began to take on a bizarrely definite form. At that time, when the world appeared to us in an anxious, murky scarlet light, like a gloomy landscape under heavy clouds before a storm, Marie and I came closer together for the first time; in our friendship, we shared the same new thoughts and the same new questions. Together we experienced that painful struggle between inquisitiveness and shame – a typical struggle for the years of maturing. A terrible revolution took place within us; our azure conception of the world was shocked to the foundations.
>
> We used to sit across from one another in Marie's room, at the desk covered with ink spots, and we whispered to one another like two people condemned to death awaiting their execution.[79]

Lauermannová describes the 'problem' of sex as one of the 'most difficult problems of culture – the problem of harmonizing the laws of nature with the ethical and aesthetic

Riegrová, still devote themselves to household chores. Nováková, 'Ženino právo na svobodnou volbu povolání', *Ze ženského hnutí,* pp. 194–195.
79 Anna Lauermannová-Mikschová, 'Procitnutí jara. Vzpomínky z dětských a dívčích let', *Lidé minulých dob,* Prague, 1941, pp. 15–16. This essay was first published in *Osvěta* in 1915.

needs of the human soul'.[80] Lauermannová states that this problem 'more cruelly distressed woman, with her spiritual nature, than it did man'.[81] Lauermannová here expresses a common stereotype of the period: the idea that woman had weaker sexual desires than man and thus was a more spiritual being.[82] This conception reversed the perception of woman as closer to nature, and thus more animal, than man.

As young girls Lauermannová and Riegrová, in their admiration for the legendary Czech maidens who had waged war against men, founded an association called 'Děvín', which included the most 'enlightened' of their girlfriends.[83] Contrary to Lauermannová's wishes, 'enmity towards all men' was not the founding principle of the association. Instead, the aims of the association were: 'education, the support of orphaned girls and raising the consciousness of the female sex "in general"'.[84] The association was eventually dissolved, due to lack of interest on the part of most of the members.

Lauermannová writes that in her conversations with Marie she came to a kind of understanding of woman's fate: 'In the chain of our knowledge, many links were missing that could only be provided by experience, but one thing was clear to us: the inferior position of woman in society, limited to the household, to love and the raising of children.'[85]

Lauermannová also writes about their experiences at balls, at which young women were introduced to soci-

80 Ibid., p. 17.
81 Ibid.
82 See: Nancy F. Cott, 'Passionlessness: An Interpretation of Victorian Sexual Ideology, 1790–1850', *Signs. Journal of Women in Culture and Society,* vol. 4, 1978, no. 2, pp. 219–236.
83 Děvín was, according to legend, the name of the castle built by the maidens who waged war against men.
84 Lauermannová-Mikschová, 'Procitnutí jara. Vzpomínky z dětských a dívčích let, p. 17.
85 Ibid.

ety and eligible bachelors in particular. She notes: 'They weren't any more worthwhile in those days than they are now; they were thoroughly disappointing [...]. But at that time balls were a more serious matter for young girls; they were a kind of higher learning for life, lasting two or at most three years and ending either in a doctorate in marriage, or in the failure of falling into the eternal shadow of spinsterhood.'[86]

CZECH WOMEN WRITERS

All of the writers included in the present volume were recognized in their own day. A number of other writers might have been included, for example, Felix Téver or Božena Viková-Kunětická. The stories presented here constitute a cross-section of the literary styles of the period. Tilschová's 'A Sad Time' is written in a Naturalist style; it also recalls the crimes and mental disorders described by Krafft-Ebing (1840–1902) in his influential *Psychopathia Sexualis* (1886). Jesenská's 'A World Apart' presents themes and motifs that appealed to the Decadents: the outsider, 'abnormal' sexuality, and the association of sex and death. In the character of Teresa Elinson, the narrator portrays a female Dandy. (One thinks, for example, of Teresa's appreciation for beauty, her cultivation not only of artistic talents but also of her own personality, manners and gestures, and her disdain for the world.) Both the satirical tone and structure of Malířová's 'The Sylph', written as a series of diary entries, recall Neruda's short story 'Figures' (Figurky, in *Tales of the Lesser Town* [Povídky malostranské, 1878]) and Šimáček's *From the Notebooks of the Student of Philosophy Filip Kořínek* (Ze zápisků phil. stud. Filipa Kořínka

---

86   Ibid., p. 22. On the theme of balls, see the short story by Viková-Kunětická. 'Kulhavá', *Čtyři povídky*. Prague, 1890, pp. 77–101.

[1893–1897]). Svobodová's ironical 'A Great Passion', with its rural setting and folklore motifs, reminds one of the writings of Erben (1811–1870), Němcová and Světlá. In its attention to dialect and folk customs, Preissová's short story may be read as a celebration of national folk culture. Indeed, this was one of the justifications for the first staging of the dramatization of the short story in the 1889–1890 season. On another level, the short story constitutes a strong criticism of the rigidity and prejudices of the rural society depicted. (The same is also true of Preissová's play *Její pastorkyňa* [published 1891, translated as *Jenůfa*], set to music by Leoš Janáček.) Benešová's 'Friends', in its presentation of the child's point of view, prefigures her more profound psychological study *Don Pablo, don Pedro and Věra Lukášová* (Don Pablo, don Pedro a V. L., 1936). 'Friends' is rather unusual for the period in its implicit criticism of anti-Semitism; at the time it was written, negative references to the Jews were still the norm in Czech literature.[87]

Not all the stories included here touch on the woman question. The stories by Benešová and Majerová do not treat issues specifically related to women. Likewise, there appears to be more literary convention than psychological realism in the presentation of lesbian passion in Jesenská's 'A World Apart'. The other short stories do touch on the woman question, but not in a didactic manner. Here one finds themes which were common in non-fiction as well: infidelity, the double standard of sexual behavior,

87 As it developed in the 19th century, Czech nationalism was linked with anti-Semitism. This was mostly because Czechs identified Jews with the German minority in the Bohemian Lands. The two key works on the subject are: Gary B. Cohen, *The Politics of Ethnic Survival: Germans in Prague 1861-1914,* Princeton, 1981; and Hillel J. Kieval, *The Making of Czech Jewry: National Conflict and Jewish Society in Bohemia, 1870-1918,* New York and Oxford, 1988. See also the short article by Robert B. Pynsent. 'Český ženský antisemitismus v první polovici dvacátého století', Dobrová Moldanová, ed., *Žena – jazyk – literatura,* Ústí nad Labem, 1998, pp. 102-107.

social prejudices against illegitimate children, woman's inferior social status and financial dependence on man and the degradation inherent in the institution of marriage. The stories do not celebrate women or condemn men; indeed, Malířová's 'The Sylph' presents a portrait of the sort of socially conditioned frivolity in women that Buzková condemned. The female protagonists of Preissová's 'Eva' and Svobodová's 'A Great Passion' are not simply the victims of their irresponsible lovers. The short stories are not complaints or calls for change; rather, they are attempts to portray the dilemmas, states of mind and fears of a variety of characters. In this sense, perhaps, some of them provide access to 'woman's mind', but they do not exhibit the 'sensitive vibrations' of that mind, despite the expectations of literary critics of the period.

FRIENDS

BOŽENA BENEŠOVÁ

Every day, Karlík Kučera used to play with his sister Minka and with little Došek, the neighbors' boy. They liked one another and they were happy all summer long.

Their kingdom was in the garden behind the Kučeras' courtyard – a strange, abandoned garden. Ever since Mr. Kučera had planted the nice big garden on the slope down to the stream, no one wanted or took care of the old one anymore. Year after year it grew wilder and wilder.

A few lindens and acacias arched over it in the damp twilight, the grass spread over all its paths, and the raspberries, once carefully planted along the fence, grew rampant like weeds. Nettles towered proudly in all the corners and in their shadow enormous burdocks opened their sticky leaves. Under the old hollow sycamore, the latticed arbor was falling to pieces and the bench inside it was so rotten it could hardly bear the weight of a grown man. The little fountain in the center of the main lawn had dried up long ago and now was nothing more than a cracked basin from which a rusty pipe protruded mournfully among rough, greenish stones.

But the children loved the shabby arbor, the black corners and the uncut lawn with its dilapidated fountain. They had unlimited right to everything there, and that was most beautiful of all. Mrs. Kučerová knew they couldn't hurt themselves there and she left them alone.

As soon as Karlík came home from school in the afternoon, he whistled at the window and the neighbors' boy Došek was in the garden even before the Kučera children could run down from the first floor. And when the garden door swung shut behind them, all three felt that it was nice to be together and that happy times would follow. Every day they investigated all the hiding places; they knew every nest, they knew every slat of wood in the decrepit arbor and all the stones in the old water-reservoir.

Of the three of them, Došek was happiest in the garden, although his laughter was never loud. His black eyes were shy and pensive, even when something pleased him, and his speech was somewhat halting; each word seemed to hesitate on his thick red lips.

'Oh my, oh my!' he often called out, because this was his favorite expression. For him it substituted for the many expressions other children used to show joy or sadness. If he was dejected, he sighed the words almost dismally, and shrank back into himself. But if he was happy he hummed the words like a tune, shutting his dark eyes, and the striking red of his lips shone for a moment in a blissful smile. And he often sang his favorite words in the Kučeras' garden because there he was most happy.

Došek was already waiting at home by the window a long time before Karlík gave the signal. If he had only had a little more courage, Došek surely would have waited in the Kučeras' courtyard, so as to be even closer to the garden when he heard the familiar whistling. But he was afraid of Mr. and Mrs. Kučera, and even of the maid, and he always pictured how he would jump if one of them suddenly asked: 'And what are you doing here in our courtyard, Jew-boy?' He never considered that they might ask something else; this simple question was horrible enough for him on its own. He only went to the garden, and even then only when he was invited. But once invited, his mother couldn't have kept him at home for anything in the world. And then he was no longer afraid to enter the courtyard. If anyone had asked him what he was doing there, he would have answered: 'Karlík called me, Karlík!' and he would have run boldly on because Karlík was his friend and his master and his shield.

Karlík could tell him anything and Došek would believe it. He could invent any kind of game, and Došek would agree to it without hesitation. And all sorts of tales were told in the hidden garden; one could play such wonderful games there with everything...

In May they had their favorite candle races which Došek was so bad at, but which he loved anyway.

In spring so many dandelions bloomed in the garden that the whole lawn was in flames.

'Look, the yellow ones beat the green ones,' Karlík would say. 'But they've only won for now. You'll see, soon yellow will fall back again.'

And he was right, as always. The blazing yellow heads quickly aged and before a week had passed, the lawn was flooded in gray fluff. The children welcomed the fluff as the most beautiful of toys and the candle races began.

First, everyone pulled up two fluffy candle-dandelions. They weren't supposed to choose them, but instead rely only on their eyes to find two good ones among the thousands that stood there. Then they held one in each hand and they lined up at the fence. Karlík counted to three and the race began. Whoever reached the arbor first, won. But only if the dandelions were still covered in fluff. If the dandelion heads were ruffled or totally bald at the finish, then the runner would lose just as surely as if he had got there last. The game was fun because there were a lot of possibilities and they didn't know how they would do or how they might spoil their chances. Karlík usually got to the finish first, but both his candles went out with the rapid movement. Minka got there second with one burning light and Došek on his short legs usually got there last, but he still held a burning white flame on the end of each stem. If Karlík hadn't been so clever, they wouldn't even have known who had really won. But Karlík knew right away what to do.

The wolves' den decided the question. Whoever jumped the furthest over the dried-out water-reservoir would win and command respect. And Karlík was always best at jumping. Minka barely managed to jump to the other edge, but Došek always got stuck in the den. He was the wolf. And because he really was clumsy, it always took a few minutes before he could get out of the trap. And more than once Minka gave him a hand and helped him out of the reservoir, while Karlík ran around the edge and laughed loudly at how they both worked so hard before the wolf was free again.

Of course when he saw Karlík laugh Došek laughed as well and looked as if he got some unknown kind of pleasure from falling into the wolves' den and getting stuck there. He didn't complain, even if he had scraped his palms against the rough stones so much that they bled.

Minka wiped his palms with a white handkerchief and Karlík explained to him that no boy cried because of a little pain.

'I'm not crying, I'm not crying,' Došek assured him vehemently, 'I'll jump again right away. Do you want me to be the wolf one more time, Karlík?'

Karlík nodded with approval, and sometimes even praised Došek. He didn't like friends who didn't listen to him and more than once he spoke about how he had argued with someone or other because he had not done what Karlík had commanded, or had doubted what Karlík had said. At such moments he looked severe and his blue eyes flashed. And Došek, who was only a year younger but smaller by a head, looked up to those bright, indignant eyes and could not understand at all how anyone could defy them. He did everything that Karlík wanted him to and believed everything that Karlík thought worth telling him.

Minka was strict and honest, and so sometimes she was exasperated by Došek's trusting nature.

'He thinks he can lie to us,' she would say to Došek in a low, solemn voice, 'and that we'll accept it all. Because he goes to school already and we haven't started yet. But we'll go there too someday. And soon, very soon, Došek, right after the holidays.'

'Oh my, oh my!' Došek answered each time and sighed deeply. He knew that he would go to school, but he could not understand why Minka said it so gaily.

'Are you afraid?' she would ask him in surprise. 'I can hardly wait. Mother says that school is wonderful when the children are well-behaved. And what does your mother say?'

'She says that I shouldn't get upset when the boys make fun of me,' Došek answered, blushing.

Now they often played 'school' as well. They had their classroom in the arbor, Karlík was the teacher and Minka and Došek sat very quietly on the sagging bench and stretched their hands out motionless in front of them on the blackened table. Karlík was very strict; right away he rapped Došek across the knuckles and stood Minka in the corner. And they got in trouble if they didn't keep solemn faces when they were being punished. Minka would have to kneel immediately by the table, because in the arbor there was no room anywhere else, and in a flash Došek would get such a lashing that the switch would leave a mark on his hands.

'You're only trying to scare us,' Minka would then become incensed, 'I know it's not as bad in school as naughty boys like to say.'

'Do you think it's some kind of game there?' Karlík replied, offended. 'All you have to do there is move and you're punished like you never could have believed before. Once one of the boys had dirty hands and the teacher ordered another boy to wash them. The second one took a brush and scrubbed and scrubbed until the blood flowed. I saw the blood flow with my own eyes...'

Tiny, cowering Došek quickly looked at his hands and froze. He shut his sorrowful black eyes and wished ardently that the 'school' game would end, that awful game which would soon be for real. He'd rather be the wolf a hundred times over, he'd rather scrape his palms a hundred times over against the stones in the wolves' den until they bled, than let them be scrubbed by a brush in school. These days he was really happy to be the wolf. He felt almost dignified when he could show Karlík that he wouldn't cry because of a few scratches, and he so much liked the moment when Minka took out her white handkerchief and carefully wiped both his hands, that he would have happily fallen into the den over and over again.

The school game was abandoned because Došek begged so much, wearing his most humble face, but they played wolf even when all the candles had gone out, even when the grass was so high that one could hardly run through it. Then the game was just called 'adventure in the jungle' and it ended each time in the wolves' den.

Summer started to burn over the abandoned garden and when the down on the lindens had disappeared and the raspberries had ripened, Karlík's holidays began.

He was even happier and more energetic than usual and now he liked to talk about his report card. Both Minka and Došek knew that he had received nothing but As and they listened to him with devotion because he called himself 'a pupil of the third year' and spoke scornfully about the second year which he had just finished. And they hadn't even started the first year!

'A report card makes me happy,' he once told them in the arbor when they were all too tired to run, 'because my parents are pleased while other parents are furious. The Šámals' Pepík, the one who always wanted to order me about, got three Bs, even though his father is the mayor. When he left school he was as pale as chalk and he surely caught it at home. But my father gave me a crown and said that I could even be a minister, if I kept studying like that.[1] As if I cared about being a minister...'

'What's a minister?' Došek asked hesitantly.

'Somebody who advises the emperor,' Karlík answered nonchalantly. 'But I'll be the kind of lord who has his own ministers. I'll have a castle like the local prince and I'll give everyone orders. I decided a long time ago I would be terribly rich and always give money away. Everyone all over the world will praise me. But in my kingdom only children will give orders; fathers and mothers will listen. People will begin school at the age of thirty, that's what I'll decree.'

'But by that time you'll be big too,' Minka objected.

Karlík quickly recovered. He hated it when someone criticized the things he made up. He really didn't know why he lied so much. He always began with something that seemed completely true to him and possible, and suddenly he was full of strange thoughts and before he knew it he was saying them out loud. It was beautiful. All he did was imagine and his lips formed the words right away. But someone always interrupted his account and it seemed to Karlík that that person had let a black curtain fall right before his eyes.

When Karlík fell silent and sulked, Došek started up, 'When I'm big, I'll go all over the world with my father and I'll wear a long coat just like him. And I'll have money too, money in all my pockets. When father comes back home from his trips, his whole coat rings. He shakes money out on the table and counts. There's always so much money, oh my, oh my!'

'Really?' Minka asked.

Karlík was silent; he only measured Došek from head to toe with a glance and smiled indulgently.

1 'Crown' meaning a coin.

But Došek's sad, dark eyes flashed and his feeble, dirty fingers moved inadvertently, like his father's did when he was counting money.

'But I won't give anyone anything,' he went on eagerly, stuttering a little as he always did when he spoke quickly, 'only to you, Karlík, and you, Minka. When you need money you can come to me and I really will give it to you.'

Minka said thoughtfully:

'That's good, Došek, I'll certainly come to you. Because when I'm big I'll have a lot of little children and they always need something. Then it's a terrible bother trying to find money. I think I should marry a shopkeeper and then everything would already be in the house. I know the daughters of a shopkeeper from Middle Street and they told me that they don't even need to go to market...'

All three fell silent and they thought for a moment about the future. It was so strange, so very strange, that they would someday all be big.

'But I'll always live next door,' Došek thought to himself, 'and I'll always come here to the garden whenever I come back from the outside world.'

The money, the long coat, the wonderful game of wolf and eternal friendship with Karlík and Minka blended together for him in one pleasing fantasy. He smiled happily.

The holidays were sunny, and every new day was hotter and more beautiful than the last.

So many times the Angelus rang, and Došek lingered on in the Kučeras' garden and asked Karlík if they really did have to go home already, when after all it was still light out and they were having so much fun.

But in August, the sunlight dwindled and the days began to race by. One had to think about school again and Došek grew sad. One day Minka, looking very important and wise, asked him:

'Došek, do you know how to write an "i"? I can do it already. Yesterday mama taught me how. It's not hard. You do it with two lines, a little bow at the bottom and a dot on top.'

She knelt on the path and traced a real 'i'.

Došek knelt beside her; he tested and scrawled and dug into the path, but he couldn't make an 'i'. He tried very hard, but the little bow at the bottom was too much for him.

'All the boys will laugh at me and the teacher too,' he cried after a while, his eyes full of tears. 'Oh my, oh my...'

'No, they won't,' Minka comforted him. 'You don't have to know how to write on the first day, don't worry. On the first day the teacher will only ask silly little things. He's sure to ask you what your name is and you know that, don't you, Došek?'

'Oh yes, I know that,' Došek brightened up.

Došek's attempts to write did not much interest Karlík, but his name did very much.

He stood in front of the kneeling students and pretended to be the teacher.

'So, what's your name, you there, the black-haired boy on the first bench?' he asked condescendingly.

Došek immediately stood and straightened up the way he should.

'Mardocheus Kupfergrün,' he answered slowly and emphatically.

The Kučera children exchanged glances. They had known for a long time that Došek had an odd name, but they always forgot it, and when they heard it again they were astonished.

'I wonder if the teacher will remember it,' Minka said with concern. 'That's a really difficult name you've got. And you'd have to sign yourself just like that, Došek. Almost everyone has a different name at school than he does at home. I'll sign my name as Vilemína Kučerová and you as Mar... Mar...

'Mardocheus Kupfergrün,' Došek finished it for her, but more quietly now. And all of a sudden he blushed from his neck all the way to his hair, as sometimes happened, and cringing, he fixed his eyes on Karlík.

Karlík understood that an explanation was expected of him and immediately assumed a knowledgeable expression.

'When you're a Jew you have to have a strange name, that's all there is to it,' he instructed Došek. 'Germans only have strange last names, but Jews have strange first and last names – that's the difference between them.'

Došek dropped his gaze and moved up close to his friend.

'And when someone is Jewish, does he have to say so at school?' he asked quietly. For many, many days he'd been mulling over this question, but hadn't ever got up enough courage to ask it.

Karlík grew even more serious.

'Of course,' he explained. 'After all, you'd be committing a terrible sin if you went with the other boys to religious instruction or if you made the sign of the cross before the lesson. That would be a tremendous sin, wouldn't it?'

'I don't know,' Došek answered, and he really didn't know. At that moment he was indifferent to all sins and interested only in Karlík's face.

'Why are you looking at me like that?' Karlík asked, even more condescendingly than a moment before. 'Do you think it matters to me if you're a Jew? It doesn't even cross my mind, my dear fellow!'

'We're your friends,' Minka affirmed.

'And anyway you're a totally different kind of Jew from the others in the town. You don't speak German at home and you aren't rich,' Karlík added quickly, to justify his tolerance somehow.

Everything from Karlík's lips sounded like praise to Došek and he was thrilled by the thought that he was different from other Jewish children. And that's the way it really was.

A number of Jewish families lived in town. They were all rich and dressed their children in splendid clothes. Only at the Kupfergrüns' was there no hint of ostentation or luxury. They rented an ordinary cottage and old Kupfergrün went about in a long-tailed coat with a basket on his back on his long journeys into the world.

He hardly returned home once a month to see if the children were healthy and to bring his wife some money. But it was never as much money as it seemed to Došek's eyes; at least his mother often sighed over it and told the neighbors that she wouldn't even have enough to dress the children if she didn't look to it herself. She was frugal and in addition to her housework she ran her own second-hand clothes business. Many times one couldn't get as far as the sitting room in the Kupfergrüns' house because of all the coats and trousers piled up in the little hall. And Došek and his three younger brothers always went about in very odd attire.

'When mama doesn't sell something, we get new clothes,' Došek would boast to Minka.

And the day after the conversation about strange names he announced joyfully:

'Mama's going to sew me a new sailor suit for school. She already has a beautiful coat ready that a gentleman used to wear at the train station. It has silver buttons on it with initials. And I'll have a collar on the coat too, just like Karlík has on his Sunday suit. Oh my, oh my...'

'And I,' Minka confided to him, 'I will get brown clothes with frills, clothes for the fall, and also brown shoes. And a hat with forget-me-nots and a bag made from leather. We'll go to school together, Došek. The girls' school is right across from the boys', so all three of us will go the same way.'

Došek smiled with his wide and very red lips. He could vividly imagine how he would go, dressed in the new sailor suit, with the Kučera children, and all of a sudden he was happy. He wasn't even afraid of school anymore when he realized that he and Karlík and Minka would take the same route to school together.

'I'll wait for you every day at our gate,' he offered, glowing, his feet pattering for joy. 'And if you don't see me right away, whistle and I'll run up behind you, just as if we were going to the garden.'

'But no later than a quarter to eight, not a minute later!' Minka commanded. 'I can't run over the square like when we have races here, understand?'

The realization that Minka could do a lot of things that Vilemína was not permitted to do flashed through her pretty red head. She already identified completely with that serious, almost mature, girl who would go to school in a week with fashionable new clothes and a leather satchel.

The last few days she did not even go to the garden anymore. She stayed at home with the seamstress and watched the progress of her new outfit.

'Vilemína Kučerová, schoolgirl of the first year,' she repeated in her head countless times. And when this quiet assertion was not enough for her, she ran out onto the porch, where no one could hear her, and said her name very loudly. And each time she bowed as if she were introducing herself to the bushy oleander which stood there.

Then on that great day, the first day of school, she woke up by herself when it was still dark, and when her mother went in to the children's room Minka was already standing by the window, fully dressed, the hat with forget-me-nots on her head and satchel in her hand.

This eagerness pleased her mother, who kissed Minka and told her she was very pretty – a real schoolgirl of the first year. And Minka felt the same way big girls do when they go to their first ball.

Even Karlík was solemn. He tried in vain to convince Minka that he didn't care at all what he looked like. She noticed all the same that he had dressed as if he were going to church and that he even squinted into the mirror to see how his dark-blue suit, with its wide collar, his soft hat and short socks suited him. But when he finally put his satchel on his back, he grew very serious and stood up straight and defiant like a brave soldier beside his delicate, glowing sister.

'Come on,' he said to her, roughly but kindly, 'I'll take you there.' And hand in hand they left the house.

It was a pleasure to look at them and see how graceful they were and how everything looked good on them, and their mother had no doubt that they were the most beautiful of all the children who would sit down on the school benches that day.

The square was full of bustle. There were more boys and girls there than big people on a market day and they were all well dressed. They smiled at one another rather formally and awkwardly.

'That big boy in the black hat is Pepík Šámal.' Karlík pointed him out to Minka. 'The one who wanted to order me about and then got three Bs. He's going into the fourth year, but he'll probably still want to be friends with me. Oh, I don't know, I don't know... one day I'll tell him what I really think of him...'

Minka did not notice how agitated her brother was when he talked and she did not ask him what he really thought about Pepík Šámal. She looked off into the distance at the groups of girls and it seemed to her that with each glance she was speaking to them about something joyful and important. Right by the fountain two girls stood, no bigger than herself and just as prettily dressed. They held each other by the hand and seemed to be waiting for someone. It was the shopkeeper's daughters from Middle Street. Minka knew them well. She'd gone on walks with them more than once, and exchanged old dolls for new marbles more than once. They had never, however, become proper friends; at first they'd been too shy to talk, and then they didn't know what to say. But today all of a sudden across the distance separating the Kučeras' house from the middle of the square, Minka felt that the girls were waiting for her, that they wanted to go with her and that they were looking forward to seeing her. She smiled vaguely in that direction and looked forward to seeing them too. She sensed her entire future life in that smile and without having to reflect she knew that this life would be companionable and important, as befitted schoolgirls with nice clothes, carrying satchels in their hands and many good intentions in their heads. She would have run to them immediately if Karlík had not held on to her. He stole a glance at Pepík Šámal and wondered whether he should go up to him or not.

'He has a real bicycle,' he said to his distracted sister, 'but he doesn't lend it to anyone. I wouldn't ask for it, really; it's only proper that he offer it himself, after all. But he doesn't even know what's proper, so it's a difficult matter...'

He uttered the words 'difficult matter' slowly and with relish, and was satisfied with himself, as he always was when he used words that he'd overheard from grown-ups. He did not doubt that Pepík would be impressed if he heard how well Karlík expressed himself. And even though Pepík couldn't have heard him at all, Karlík looked over at him as if waiting for an acknowledgement. And look, Pepík stood, a little defiant, a little hesitant, just like Karlík, and clearly he was having similar thoughts. Why, it even seemed to Karlík that Pepík was nodding at him. Maybe the new black hat had only slipped a little, maybe he really had nodded – Karlík just couldn't tell. These gestures almost made him uneasy.

He took a step forward and immediately fell back again, but from then on he didn't let Pepík out of his sight.

He decided finally that he would pass close by and if Pepík gave him a friendly, very friendly, smile, he would say to him: 'Hi, Pepík!', which would almost be the same as saying: 'I'd like to talk to you'. But if Pepík didn't look friendly enough, he would say only 'Good day', the coldest greeting, and would immediately turn to Minka so that Pepík wouldn't think Karlík was waiting for his reply.

'Come on,' he said to his sister, this time in a commanding tone, and both walked on in a state of agitation.

But hardly had they moved when they heard a piercing cry behind them.

'Karlík, Karlík, I'm here, wait for me, won't you? I was only waiting for you to whistle, oh my, oh my!' They looked around.

Došek was running as if he had to reach them from a great distance, although there weren't twenty paces between them. He was all on fire and laboring from the running. He held his slate so tightly that his fist turned red; his mouth was half-open and his cap fell back on his neck. Došek really was ridiculous. Karlík assessed Došek's new suit with one glance, and although he had other things on his mind, he couldn't hold back his laughter. Došek did have a wide white collar on his coat, but it didn't lie flat. It stood up behind his head like a piece of white cardboard and Došek's dark face looked almost black by contrast. The little sailor suit shone with big silver buttons, two rows of which were sewn on the coat, and more buttons decorated the trousers. Karlík recognized Došek's cap and thought he had seen it not long ago on the head of a train-station porter.

'My word, he's dressed up,' was all he said, but he pulled such a funny face at the same time that Minka started to laugh loudly. But right away she looked at the fountain again.

'I waited for you for a long time, oh my, oh my, I waited for a long time in our hall,' Došek told them, and as always when he wanted to speak quickly his tongue stumbled over his lips and he couldn't get a proper word out. But his eyes shone with happiness and friendship and he took Karlík by the hand and squeezed between him and Minka.

And at that moment the Kučera children saw something they had not seen before. It was as if they were setting eyes on their friend for the first time, the way they scrutinized him. And they saw that Došek was a homely and ridiculous boy who didn't belong with them at all; someone so different that they couldn't even associate with him. The lively square was not the quiet, hidden garden, and it seemed to Karlík and Minka that there had never been as much light as was glittering here today. And all of it would fall on them and all eyes would see Došek just as they had seen him now. The girls at the fountain stared in this direction and no longer smiled, but poked each other with their elbows, or so Minka thought. Karlík suddenly saw clearly that Pepík Šámal was grinning. A moment ago he hadn't been able to tell if Pepík had nodded or not, but now he was sure that Pepík was grinning.

Minka and Karlík blushed with embarrassed discomfort.

'Go by yourself,' Minka said to Došek and jumped away from him.

Došek's black eyes opened wide in bewilderment and he held on to Karlík all the more firmly. Now he gripped Karlík's hand more tenaciously than the slate.

But Karlík took him by the shoulder, which he pressed mercilessly with a well-practiced movement, and Došek's fist let go instantly.

'I won't walk on the street with a Jew-boy,' he told him quietly and contemptuously.

'Oh my, oh my!' Došek groaned from the pain in his shoulder and in his heart and for a long time he could not understand what had actually happened.

Minka and Karlík quickly walked on, but Došek didn't move a step. He only saw that Karlík had gone up to some big boy in a black hat, that he was speaking with him and did not turn around, not even once.

'Minka!' he called again with one last hope. But not even Minka turned her head to look at him. Two very pretty girls now walked towards her, took her by the arm and headed on to school.

The church bell rang a quarter to the hour and Došek was still standing there. A horror worse than he'd ever imagined descended on him, and a fear that made him cringe so that he was the smallest of all the children around. He did not even dare take a step forward and did not know himself how it happened that all of a sudden he was sitting in the hall at home, on a heap of old clothes, and crying tears as big as the buttons on his new suit.

Mrs. Kupfergrün, eternally breathless and overworked, came out of the sitting room holding her youngest son in her arms, and gazed for a moment silently at Došek's pain.

'They laughed at you on the very first day?' she asked, and her thick red lips, like Došek's own, trembled.

Without waiting for Došek's reply, she set the youngest boy down in the bright rags, took Došek by the hand and led him to school. All the way, she nagged him for not letting her take him there first thing in the morning, for insisting that he was going with little Karlík and Minka. And as always when she scolded and got angry, she spoke German. Došek didn't understand a tenth part of it, but his anxiety increased even more on account of the strange voice his mother had every time she spoke that language.

It was a journey he would not forget for the rest of his life, and his simple reason slowly and sadly grasped something complex, against which his warm heart rebelled.

He cried the whole time. When he finally sat in his classroom with the other boys, his eyelids were red and swollen, and so many thoughts went through his head and so much grief through his heart that he didn't take in a word the teacher said.

Došek did not remember anything from his first day at school, even though he sat totally motionless; even though he stuck his hands out on the desk automatically, just as he had on the blackened little table in the arbor. He did not, however, see the teacher in front of him, he did not even see Karlík playing at being the strict but condescending teacher. He saw only the Karlík who had pressed his shoulder until it hurt terribly. He saw both of his old friends – how they ran away from him.

No one spoke to him at school; no one asked him anything, not even what his name was. And suddenly there was a bustle; Došek heard that it was over for the day and he went out of the classroom with the other boys. Their loud, prolonged wave carried him all the way to the square, which was now as busy as it had been in the morning. But Došek didn't look at anyone and ran as fast as his legs would go to the street where the Kučeras' house stood next to his family's cottage.

Quietly, he slipped behind the gate and waited. And again there were children everywhere because school never lasts long on the first day, and he saw all the solemn boys and all the girls dressed up for the day, just as he had an hour before.

He saw Minka between the shopkeeper's girls, strutting, dignified in her brown shoes, speaking in a friendly manner with her new companions as if she had played school and races with them all summer, as if she had wiped their bleeding fingers with a white handkerchief.

And a moment later he saw Karlík as well. He was walking again with that big boy, and was so absorbed in conversation that he gesticulated with his finger and placed it on his temple, as he used to do when he was speaking very emphatically. Their conversation sounded more and more lively and when they reached the corner, Došek could already hear everything they said.

'What bothers me most about you is that you play with little kids,' the big boy reproached Karlík. 'I'd be ashamed. This year you should go to the playing fields with me. It's a lot of fun there, boys from the council school come too, and before you know it, you can play soccer. And then you're just like them. But you prefer little Minka and that dirty Jewish brat...'

Karlík broke into laughter.

He laughed from embarrassment. At that moment he was deeply ashamed of all the games he had ever thought up in the garden. Why, he was even ashamed that Minka was still young and had only started going to school today. But he was most ashamed of Došek. Face to face with big Pepík Šámal, who had honored him today by not wanting to boss him around, Karlík could no longer understand how he could have played with a foolish little stuttering Jew-boy.

'Maybe I'll come right over to the playing field this afternoon,' he promised Pepík with excessive eagerness, 'Minka can go with the girls. And there was nothing at all with that Jew-boy. It's a difficult matter when someone is always at your heels. But today I really told him what I thought. I won't walk around with him and he'll never be allowed over to our house again.'

'My dear fellow,' Pepík answered condescendingly, 'you don't know the ways of the world very well. Every Jew is shameless. He'll come to your house a thousand times more.'

Karlík tossed his head.

'Not once, I can guarantee you that!' he cried, so that Pepík would finally understand the full measure of his dignity. 'All he'd have to do is grab the door handle and he'd be out in an instant, that Mar... Mar... Mar...'. And he began to laugh in loud bursts so that Pepík wouldn't notice that Karlík couldn't remember the whole name. He was still laughing when he disappeared through the front door of the house.

Došek didn't listen any longer. He lay again on the pile of old clothes and he didn't cry anymore; he just groaned.

His mother found him there after a while and was surprised by the way he looked.

'Did something else happen to you?' she asked, dejected.

Došek thought about his precious garden and didn't answer.

'Get up, so you don't wrinkle your new suit,' she ordered him, 'stop crying and answer me!' Došek obediently sat up, but he continued to wail. He couldn't help it. He thought he would suffocate if he didn't groan.

His mother sat down next to him, wrapped her arm around his neck and asked him again why he was crying. It had been a long time since she had treated him so tenderly and looked at him with such emotion and concern.

'I'm crying because I'll never, never be the wolf again,' Došek finally gasped. 'Oh my, oh my!'

His mother grew very worried and put her hand to her little boy's head to see if he didn't have a fever, his answer seemed so strange to her. And she couldn't get another word out of him. So she led him anxiously into the sitting room, put him to bed and wrapped a cold compress around his head.

Došek lay down without resisting; he stayed completely still and stopped crying. He closed his eyes and for the first time in his life he thought very hard. He lay for a long time, but when his mother thought that he was sleeping deeply, he straightened up unexpectedly and tore the compress from his head.

'You see, now I'm just like the other Jewish children,' he told his mother, and didn't stutter even once. 'I had nice clothes today, you spoke German with me, and the Kučeras stopped being my friends. Oh my, oh my!'

This time he did not sing or moan his favorite words, but uttered them in a totally changed, quiet and serious voice.

A WORLD APART
RŮŽENA JESENSKÁ

It grew dark and a mist spread over the countryside like a curtain. We were at the Bohemian border. Customs control, shouting, the din of the station, and finally the train moved on with a monotonous drone.

'It was right here that I met Teresa Elinson,' Marta said, in the corner of the cozy compartment.

I replied: 'Who is Teresa Elinson? I don't remember you ever mentioning her.'

'No, never. It was a kind of adventure. That time too the train hurtled into the dark, where red sparks flew and lights flashed, scattering in the mist...

At that time I was travelling from Nuremberg and Miss Teresa Elinson boarded here. She entered the compartment, tall and straight, greeted me, took off her hat, sat down opposite and fixed her penetrating dark eyes on me. I continued to look outside, but felt her gaze. At that time I was in low spirits and decided I would not be drawn into conversation with a strange woman who was clearly waiting for the slightest opportunity to chat... I looked obstinately out the window. But the woman suddenly spoke with a vehemence and ardor that surprised me and completely confounded my intentions. With curt words she began to praise me, her enthusiasm culminated in the wish to paint me, and she added in a trembling voice: "You are close to my soul. I say that without any explanation, in total certainty! "

I responded with a few embarrassed, vague words that were lost in the clatter of the train.'

Marta fell silent, she shut her eyes as if absorbed in a faded image from the past.

Finally she spoke, continuing in her train of thought: 'She was a strange woman, but perhaps, after all, strange only from my point of view. I was totally incapable of getting close to her soul.'

After a long pause I asked: 'Didn't you get to know each other better?'

'Yes. Right away in the train we spoke a great deal. And in Prague we parted with the promise that I would visit Teresa Elinson in her isolated manor. The manor has a beautiful name. It's called – A World Apart.'

I was glad that Marta had been drawn into telling a story. There's nothing more pleasant on a lengthy journey.

'And soon after that you visited Miss Elinson?' I asked.

Marta sat up, wrapped herself tighter in her plaid, bent forward so that her pale face gleamed like a pearl in the twilight.

'It's almost private here so it will be easy to remember that secluded place. All right then. Yes, about a week after we met, Teresa came to Prague for me. There was pathos in every sentence she uttered and in the simplest movements, as if she had practiced and perfected them beforehand; but in strange contrast to this she had almost imperious manners at the same time, something hard, which one could see in her appearance as well. Clearly she deliberately refined the features of her character so as to make them more captivating.

When urging me to visit she said: "But come for a long stay; forever if you like."

I laughed at that.

She nodded: "There only the moon may enter, and the stars, the sun, the quiet clouds and birds."

It was a quiet winter day full of sunlight. We traveled three hours by train. Miss Elinson's attentions were limitless, sometimes culminating in outbursts of happy warmth, to which I responded dejectedly with questions: Do you paint landscapes? Do you cultivate flowers? Do you go on long walks? And I silently reproached myself for being such an unsociable creature.

From the station where we got off the train, we walked for about a quarter of an hour on a path through a field to a road, along which stretched the spruce hedge of a park. We went through a little gate. The tree-lined avenue and translucent paths glittered with gold flecks, and the low Empire-style manor appeared in the bright light of a white afternoon.

Miss Elinson's domestic staff was discreet: an old, sullen gardener and a few female servants, one of whom, an old woman, looked like a skeleton. Her face had no muscles, only yellowish bones, and something like darkness trembled in her eye sockets. The woman attracted my attention, so that I stopped and looked at her.

"One gets used to her, that's my Nany; she's very helpful to me, she keeps the chambers in excellent order," said Miss Elinson, leading me to the room prepared for me. It was full of shades of yellow, which I love very much. I must have mentioned this to Miss Elinson when we became acquainted. Above the bed hung an engraving by Correggio, "Leda and the Swan". On a little black marble table under a Venetian mirror stood an old, turquoise-blue faenza vase with a bouquet of blossoming *Helleborus*. From the window could be seen the distant shining surface of the frozen pond like an enormous pearl with lustrous curves.

After lunch, Teresa Elinson showed me the entire manor – the private chambers with many precious books and works of art – and then we set off into the park. There I recovered slowly from the dejection into which I fall so easily when under the obligation to make polite conversation. Such charming perspectives opened onto the countryside, and then more turns in the paths, with simple wooden benches and arbors creating the intimate scenery for the romances which had surely taken place here.

The birds flew down to rest on our hands and circled above our heads, calling. I grew happy along with them and was pleased by this winter visit. The air practically sparkled, the snow glittered and the sun permeated everything, just as blood runs through the body.

"I want you to be happy here," Teresa said, a tone of happy warmth in her voice, "do whatever you like, come to me when you want to, read, play, go for walks in the park, write poetry, compose symphonies, paint Madonnas, note the course of the stars, philosophize about the purpose of a life without purpose – just don't get bored. Tell me and we'll go wherever you like: to the glaciers in the high mountains or to the blue sea between the cypresses and palms."

"You're spinning fairy tales," I laughed.

"No, you will not leave me from now on," she said in a deep voice, as if pleading and commanding at the same time. She pressed my hand firmly and kissed me on the lips.

"How could that be?" I said timidly.

Teresa sighed thoughtfully: "It's beautiful to live in a world apart."

We returned to the manor. Teresa opened the piano cover. For a moment she looked at me excitedly, then she began to play Beethoven's "Farewell" sonata. Her performance surprised me, not only the maturity of her technique, but also the profundity of her expression. She performed the "Return", in particular, with a strange power of joy. When she had finished, she turned around: she noticed the effect her playing had had on me.

"You hardly speak at all," she said, "but that is beautiful. The return..." she closed her eyes, "because of you, life is returning to me again, you don't have any idea that it's because of you." And she said very quietly: "Will you like me?"

At that moment I heard clearly the tones that had just fallen silent, as if they still echoed, trembling, in the chamber. An irrepressible anxiety seized my throat. Teresa's eyes were fixed on me in strange expectation; I sensed that her question was not motivated by the simple kindness of a woman who thought I was nice and longed for my friendship. Something deeper sounded in that tone, like a lifelong goal.

"I'm not fully aware of the connotations of that word," I said, with a forced smile, "it's so difficult to fathom, much less predetermine, emotions."

"No, don't speak, don't speak..." Pained and impatient, she stopped me and grew very pale.

I stood up so as to interrupt the awkward silence. Teresa sat at the piano like a statue.

"Will you show me your studio?" I asked.

"My work will disappoint you," she waved her hand, "art, that is my empty dream. Only I, Marta, would never disappoint you. We hardly know each other, but I feel you could be as close to me as Berta was. Oh, you will understand me, you don't yet realize that we met so we could belong to one another forever. How happy our life will be, Marta..."

"Who was Berta?" I asked uneasily.

"I'll tell you about her tomorrow. Today I want only the present, in a mood of expectation. I have your hand in mine." Nany entered and called us to dinner.

"One gets used to her," Teresa again gestured with her head, as she had when we first arrived at the manor.

After dinner I expressed the wish to go to my room. Teresa reluctantly let me go and said goodbye, kissing me passionately.

I was relieved to find myself alone. Soon I put out the light, sat by the window and stared out at the white moonlit night. In the room above mine, in Teresa's bedroom, steps could be heard, muffled by the carpet. They began to move monotonously and incessantly from wall to wall; like the pacing of a person who repels pain or worry through repeated movement, Teresa walked around her chamber.

I listened in suspense. The steps continued, accompanied by a sort of smothered crying. What did it all mean?

Agitated, I stood up. The first thought that occurred to me was to run upstairs, ask her what had happened, calm her weeping... But I turned hesitantly to the window. If she were suffering from some violent fit of grief, there would be no way to hold it back. The pacing finally stopped, but the protracted sobbing could still sometimes be heard... Disturbed, I looked out into the illuminated park. Teresa fell silent.

It was now completely silent everywhere... And then a tall figure loomed on the path below, wrapped in a cloak... Teresa.

She disappeared behind the white branches of the bushes...

In the morning at breakfast she gave me a bouquet of roses.

"Now? In the winter? How is it possible?" I looked at her searchingly, but could not find the slightest trace of crying in her eyes.

"Everything is possible," she answered cheerfully.

I calmed down again and, carrying books from the library to my room, said to myself that I would sensibly and comfortably spend a month here; each day we would go out on longer walks, and I would cure Teresa's sentimentality. All morning I succeeded in carrying out my intention. Then from midday on we sat in the blue room. Teresa again grew somewhat gloomy and held my hand in hers feverishly. Finally she spoke, as if continuing aloud in her recollection:

"Berta was gentle, sensitive; her appearance was so spiritual. You have her eyes. You look very much like her." She opened up a locket with Berta's portrait, hanging on a chain around her neck.

I smiled: "Then I certainly don't know myself."

Teresa grew talkative:

"Ah, likeness, for me that is something else than what you imagine. You have a soul like hers, a kind of radiance invisible to other people. Berta lived here with me for six years. Apart from me she had no one in the world. She was always near me. She helped me in the studio, she arranged the library, the scores, she tended my orchids in the greenhouse, all her work was concentrated on me. She was so devoted! If only you could have heard her sing! She had a rather frail, but moving voice. The beauty of her song was in the performance. She was quiet, humble and full of charm."

"She died here?" I asked.

And Teresa went on:

"Yes, for two years now she has rested in a tomb in the park. How terrible those two years have been. But life is returning to me through you. I have placed so much hope in you."

I did not dare to speak.

Teresa continued:

"I would like my home to be your home, I would like our thoughts to merge, our pleasures to be shared. To have your heart, your trust, so that you will not long for the world."

"And have you never loved anyone?" I asked finally, very timidly.

"Didn't I just confide to you that I loved Berta?" she wondered.

"Yes," I concurred even more shyly, "but a man..."

Teresa's eyes widened in surprise. She stood up and walked to and fro with long steps, as if rocking on waves. Then she stopped in front of me and said quietly: "No, Marta, never. That is totally foreign to me and incomprehensible." And after a short silence she added:

"There's so much beauty in you!"

We went out into the park.

"Let's go to Berta," she said. And several times on the way she repeated: "It will be night, and the moon will hide behind a white cloud."

Two beautiful plane trees formed the entrance to a small area, bordered by spruce trees. In the middle stood a small Gothic tomb. Cypresses overshadowed the entrance. The white path to the fields rising beyond the park clearly shone up to the place where a red lamp burned, hanging from a silver chain.

"Our future home," Teresa said when we went in.

Muffled, regular strokes sounded in the great silence, as if a heart were beating underground.

"What's that?" I asked. "Where do those sounds come from?"

The cross on the white altar, the stained glass windows, the prie-dieu, all this appeared ordinary, without mystery, and yet an anxiety seized me when Teresa, instead of answering, drew me to the right to a set of stairs and pointed down.

I followed her... A metal coffin stood there, with a small lamp flickering above it. On the wall hung a great clock, the ticking of which carried through the tomb like the pounding of a heart.

"Every night I come here to wind it," said Teresa, "and I stay with her. Time passes..."

She bent over the coffin. She lifted the lid... She really did lift the heavy metal lid. Under a second glass cover, the dead woman lay in a green silk robe, her face yellow, her head leaning somewhat to the left, with an expression of peace on the closed eyes, on the lips pressed together, on the crossed arms, on the smooth high forehead.

For a long time we stood without a word and left without a word. We made our way through the park to the manor. The sun set, shining crimson like the lamps in the tomb. The long reflections trembled over the frozen pond.

The cries of birds sounded in the crowns of the trees and, in the distance, the drawn-out whistling of the train...

The evening had a strange atmosphere. In the manor too, in the twilight of the chambers, it was as if someone had walked about and left behind the scent of grief and the expectation of return.

Teresa said: "We will have dinner in the studio, in remembrance of those evenings which have passed and will return..."

Thus I saw her work-room. The embers in the stove shone, an intoxicating aroma rose to the magnificent high ceiling, flooded by the crimson light of a chandelier with a red silk shade. Spots of light trembled over the little pearl-inlaid tables and heavy Japanese textiles. The park appeared there through the glass wall in blue twilight, very close, present.

In a corner by an Empire-style couch stood a table set for dinner, on which branches of pale blossoming lilacs wilted in an old porcelain vase.

I began to examine Teresa's paintings. Aside from a few motifs from the park, the same female figure was repeated on the canvases, sometimes half-hidden by a veil, sometimes naked, in strange, undulating movements and spasms. There was something alive in those lines and expressive poses, but at the same time there was also an asymmetry in the choice of technique, much that was daring, but also jarring.

Teresa pointed to a blank prepared canvas: "It's waiting for you."

And she added a moment later: "*J'aime de vos longs yeux la lumière verdâtre!*"

I can see her, how she stared for a long time into my eyes.

"I cannot take Berta's place," I said, firmly.

She waved her hand dismissively. She led me to the couch. We had dinner. Teresa poured some strong wine and became unusually elated.

She tried to prove to me that only I could bring her happiness, great happiness in life, that she had sensed it unmistakably right away that time in the train and that she believed in me.

After dinner I rose and asked Teresa to excuse me if I left early for my own room.

"Look how the night is drawing near," she pointed to the park, "and you want to flee from it."

"Oh, don't leave now," she begged me, "come, please, allow me to make a sketch... Art will bring you closer to me, make you more familiar... Will you allow me?"

"Tomorrow, all right? Today I so much need to be alone," I said, agitated, but determined. She drew me to her and arm in arm we walked downstairs. A moment later, Teresa came into my room, carrying a rare old pendant made from chrysolite and large, dark-gray pearls. She spoke in flustered, disjointed sentences, fixing the pendant around my neck... She said good night and then, mysteriously, "How many more times will I go to Berta in the night?"

A moment later her steps sounded above me as they had the night before. I took off the pendant and looked at the green precious stones, the gray pearls, and inhaled the strange scent of the old gold which had probably adorned Berta, and before her some long, long forgotten beloved woman...

I walked to the window. A white glow trembled in the crowns of the trees, penetrated along the paths of the park and made a mirror of the surface of the pond, in which the sky with all its lights looked down upon itself.

And as I stared into the white night, I saw Teresa again: she disappeared on the bend of a path leading to a group of birch trees. I knew that she was going to Berta...

An inexplicable anxiety overwhelmed me. I rang for the servant. Only when I heard her steps in the corridor did I think of what I would say to her, why I had called her.

A girl as pale as parchment, with quiet, sad eyes, entered.

"Why do you look so unhappy?" I asked her clumsily.

"My Lady is mistaken," was the servant's restrained response.

"I would like some tea," I said hurriedly.

The girl soon brought the tea. She bowed and left.

I roamed around the room, glancing out the window every few minutes.

Finally I locked the door, put out the light and lay down… I fell asleep. Some time later I was awakened, as if by a confused heavy dream or some kind of rustling. It was as if someone were breathing behind the door. I listened. Someone really was breathing close by the door. My face felt hot and my hands were like ice. The embers still glowed in the hearth. The white night looked quietly through the uncovered windows.

"Marta, Marta," a muffled voice whispered suddenly behind the door.

I held my breath. My heart beat loudly.

Was it Teresa? What did she want from me? Why was she calling me now like a lost soul, like the spirit of the deceased Berta?

A terrible anxiety gripped me. What kind of scene would follow if I turned the key?

"Marta, Marta," the words could be heard behind the door in pauses, words that were pained and plaintive and culminated in a horrible groaning.

I heard the pounding of my heart. I was afraid to move lest I betray that I was awake.

"Marta, Marta," the words trembled behind the door more insistently, like an incantation.

With my hand I suppressed the pounding of my heart and felt as if I would suffocate. No, no, I won't move, I won't open the door, I said to myself with all the vehemence of determination and horror.

I could not associate this pleading, humble voice with that almost imperious figure, with the face and its firm features. Finally, Teresa knocked on the door – quietly but clearly.

At that moment Teresa's possible entry into the room struck me as terrible, inscrutable – as if some ghastly element would penetrate the air I breathed, would lie on my breast and smother me, smother me to death.

I lay motionless in terrible anxiety... Each recurrent cry suffocated me.

Teresa finally fell silent. The steps moved indecisively, slowly, away from the door, but nonetheless they moved away. Then they sounded up above and disappeared. A prolonged sobbing trembled in the midnight quiet.

I sat up cautiously in bed, rose and lit a candle.

Suddenly, I realized that it was impossible for me to live here, to spend one more day, or even one more night, here. I had to leave, to do something to rid myself of this horror. I will go, I will go, I repeated to myself feverishly. There, beyond the motionless trees with their miniature branches, etched into the great brightness of the azure, beyond that small spruce gate the world was full of storms, disappointments and cares, but I longed thirstily for its waves, for its rapacious power, for its freedom.

Fear of delay shook me.

Quickly and quietly I dressed.

On a piece of paper I wrote in pencil: "Forgive me, Teresa, I must leave immediately with the first light, before you get up. Forgive me. I cannot stay here." I placed the paper under the chrysolite and pearl pendant.

I saw from the window how the moon, grown pale, was slowly departing, how the stars were disappearing, and the blue as well, until a greenish, horizontal strip of light appeared beyond the tangle of branches. The air turned gray, then pearl-colored, as if teary-eyed, panting, more tired than the night before.

Quietly opening the door, I went out, down the stairs and found myself in the park. I trembled as if I were fleeing from prison, as if danger lurked in every window.

I quickened my steps and shook with the cold. Another moment and I was beyond the wall of thick bushes, and still further along the beech paths, and still further in the spruce wood – and still further on the long path by the hedge. The door, however, was shut. I looked around. Twilight still lay on the earth. Now they were all sleeping. Teresa was probably also sleeping. With an effort, I managed to break a spruce branch in the hedge and drag myself through the gap.

The sky arched over me, low, submerged in morning fog. There wasn't a living soul about.

I felt a freedom both within and without myself. I was only oppressed by the knowledge that I was leaving this way, that Teresa would be so disappointed. But there was no guilt, every hour I stayed on at the manor would only have been a burden.

The fields far and wide received the new daybreak. The horizon grew light.

I arrived in time for the train.'

Marta fell silent.

'And you never met Miss Elinson again?' I asked Marta. 'You don't know how your departure affected her?'

'I haven't spoken to her since then. She sent my luggage to Prague without a word of greeting. Several years later I saw her, but she didn't notice me. It was on Rigi, in the Alps. She was sitting in the grass beside a pretty young girl, they were holding hands and looking down into the green lake.'

For a little while longer we spoke about Teresa Elinson and fell to talking about the strange loves that grip the human heart.

MY FRIEND, MY BROTHER

MARIE MAJEROVÁ

The ship had been at sea all year long; it had sailed along the shores of Asia, here brushing past a city, there staying awhile in a foreign port. It had steered and tested what it was capable of on the wide sea, carrying on like a young swimmer let out for the first time from the pool to the river.

And now it was returning to Trieste.

It dropped anchor into the depths a good way off from port, and planted itself firmly, settling in a silken nest of waves, a metal mother hen, sheltering under its wings a hundred restless chicks. In truth, the crew, catching sight of the sun-bleached houses of Trieste, was possessed by a fever of discovery; nonetheless, routine was not disturbed, and service ran on smoothly like a ship engine. Fear of being punished and denied leave onto solid earth, which, after such a long separation, was as beloved to them as their own native land, restrained their rebellious tongues and tamed the impatience of their agitated limbs.

It was a new, three-masted ship with a narrow deck and wide, vaulted sides; the metal plates, clasping the ship in a gray-blue shell, were scrubbed clean, and even the chimney shone with a fresh coat of paint, and taut flags fluttered every now and then when the wind hit them.

The clear, azure Adriatic Sea tossed little waves, laughably small beside the great sides of the ship; the light breaking on their crests cast a flickering gold net on the dark surface of the iron plates. The simple letters of the inscription appeared fleetingly in this light network. The name of the ship was the SMS *Erzherzog Ferdinand Max*.[1]

---

1 Erzherzog: Archduke. The name suggests a member of the Habsburg family, the rulers of the Austro-Hungarian Empire, and may refer to the Archduke Ferdinand Maximilian Joseph (1832–1867), who became Emperor of Mexico. He served as a rear admiral in the Austrian navy.

Finally the men were off-duty, and a motorized dinghy, allotted for the transport of the crew, carried the first officers to firm ground. All who were not working bent over the deck's rail and followed the dinghy with their eyes as it rocked almost imperceptibly on the water and cut mercilessly forward, spoiling the transparent and flickering game of the waves... They saw the officers in white uniforms gesticulate excitedly. Although the officers controlled themselves with all their might in front of the stoker, they could not hide their nervous agitation: here an arm in a white sleeve swung up like a rocket, there a cigarette, hardly lit, hissed as it was thrown into the water. The oil-smeared engineer stuck his sweaty head out to gulp some air.

But the dinghy shrank and disappeared, the officers merged into a white blotch and all that remained in sight was a cigarette bobbing on the waves like a white bubble.

The big trade ships, steamers and barges admitted the dinghy amongst themselves; and the eyes of the sailors rose again to the town and its faded orange roofs, more precious and beautiful to them than all the green shores of Asia.

The dinghy soon returned and unloaded all the eagerly waiting privates in small groups. Many had a leave of several weeks, others rushed to celebrate a vacation of a single day.

They stepped out on firm land and soon, with noisy abandon, they filled the cafés and bars, scattered over the narrow streets of the old city, where the oil under frying fish emitted a pungent smell and the scantily clad beauties of Trieste waited for them in the windows. In the evening, when the taverns no longer satisfied their overflowing hearts, they took to the sidewalks, and their liberated throats sang a hymn, welling up from unconscious melancholy, a hymn to solid earth, white cliffs, the gentle shoulders of the vine and the green of thick turf.

Each one sang of the beauty of his land; there were boys from sad Tyrol: their convulsive voices became tangled in shrill knots, jumping about like a herd in the mountains. The lanky Italians with olive complexions hummed sweet love songs, their sly eyes darting cunning glances. Awkward Slav boys walked hand in hand, and snatches of sad tunes escaped from their lips, tunes harsh in their despair and moving in their languor.

When they searched in vain in the steep little streets for the soothing peace of home, when wine sparked in their heads the wild fires of frenzied instincts, they scented freedom under the straining bond of solidarity, like stallions when the reins are slackened. The crew had lived in brotherly love in the middle of the vast waters, cramped together on the frail island of the ship, but now on firm land they recalled all those forgotten passions they had left behind – and they fought – Italian against German, German against Slav.[2]

In the night they raged like beasts; they fought in clusters on the corners of streets and drew wide, concealed knives. They fought like blood enemies, as if they didn't all have on their caps the single, unifying motto:

Ferdinand Max.

The harbor guards moved out of their way.

Voborník did not wait for evening.

He jumped smartly onto the pier, stamped his feet and straightened his uniform.

Stepping forward with a broad stride, he did not look back at the sea, but mumbled only:

'My friend, my brother!'

And the curse accompanying these words resembled an oath that never, never again would he return to the sea, not for the love of God…

He felt the pavement under his feet, hard as steel.

2   The fights that break out among the members of the ship's crew recall the nationality conflicts that plagued the Austro-Hungarian Empire at the turn of the century.

Kindly steel! I rely on your sure support, crust of the earth!

He looked only at the ground, a little ashamed that he swayed his hips so much, and his feet dropped to the pavement from an unaccustomed height.

He didn't look around at the sea or the city.

Trieste was – foreign. From the ship he had gazed at the brick crest of the roofs and clearly felt its strangeness. It was a totally different Trieste from the year before, when he and his friend Jirka had blustered into town.

Voborník had gone to school with Jirka, the schoolmaster's son, a straight-A student and a teacher's pet.

That time they had stood there on the pier and the sun had set in blood. Voborník had said: I don't know why, but the red sun makes me sad. It looks as if it were soaked in our blood.

Jirka, the schoolmaster's son, had laughed.

Voborník himself was from a poor brickmaker's family, a barefooted boy spattered with yellow clay, smelling of mud. As foolish as a fly, and yet Jirka found a friend in him because Voborník knew how to admire and love. Pampered Jirka needed love and admiration.

And how Voborník loved him! When he laughed at the red sun and ran to the end of the pier as if to challenge it, Voborník's soul trembled in his body, and he rushed to hold Jirka back; just a little bit further and both would have fallen into the sea.

Even as a schoolboy, Jirka had known about everything, understood everything. He knew about the land of the Indians and he knew where sugar cane grew, which the brickmaker's son imagined as gigantic sticks of colored sugar. Jirka would sit over an old atlas with outdated maps, and colorful words would flow from his lips. The words adorned the maps with a curious nature, or brought savage people to life with gold in their ears, or even better, illustrious Brahmins with white silk on their wise heads and lotus blossoms in their laps.

Voborník would hang on his words.

And when he had finished, the brickmaker's boy grew sad and everything went out before his eyes. 'I'll never see that, Jirka!'

Jirka did not respond, but assumed an air of mystery. And then, when they came to Trieste, Jirka's only answer to all of Voborník's sighs was this: a wide sweep of his frail hand, a little too daring, as if throwing a gauntlet down at the world.

Voborník used to be the guardian of the weaker boy, whom not even the authority of his schoolmaster father could shield from the attacks of local ruffians. Jirka repaid his protection with tyranny. And in spite of that, the broad-shouldered Voborník would fight until blood was drawn for Jirka; and for Jirka, even when they had grown up, the brickmaker's boy would have followed him into a burning building! And if into the fire, how could he not follow Jirka onto the sea!

The schoolmaster's son, whose longing for foreign lands expanded with the widening horizon of his knowledge, found the only way to tame his hunger: soldiering on the sea. Both were enlisted and assigned to the same ship. The schoolmaster's wife cried and the old brickmaker waved his hand:

'The devil take you, boy! Toil in the brickyard, toil at sea. It's all the same.'

And with this they sent them off.

At the port, the *Erzherzog Ferdinand Max* was waiting for them. How Jirka rushed to it! He practically kissed the deck and threw his cap high into the blue air:

'Hurray! Hurraay!'

He had such a feeble little voice. He couldn't even shout out the muffled drone of the engine.

The schoolmaster's wife was right to cry! And the threat the sun made that time was serious too!

Jirka and Voborník sailed around Greece, they danced on the small, green waves of the Mediterranean Sea and in health traded them for the dark-blue, heavy waves of the Red Sea. As for toil, there was more than enough, and soon Jirka had hands as heavy as those of the brickmaker Voborník. There were bitter moments when work and fatigue hung round their necks with a leaden embrace. But there were also happy moments of leave, and these made them forget the hardship. Enraptured by the fairy-tale mysteries of cities in the East, Jirka yearned with childlike eagerness for India, the land of Brahmins, lotuses and sacred rivers. The green shores with the mystery of divine groves emerged from the mists in the pure dawn, only to disappear again, swallowed by the steam of the evening.

Voborník did not move from Jirka's side. The latter's physical frailty awakened in Voborník the gentleness of the strong towards the weak. He felt the need to care for and protect someone; this spring of tenderness, welling up from his shy heart, sought a plant which it might surround, satiate, soak. The old attachment from their boyhood years changed as they matured. The adolescent friendship, which was romantically loyal and had driven Voborník to enlist with Jirka, grew on Voborník's side into a powerful paternal feeling; at that time, the brickmaker's son took the work from Jirka's hands, fought with him over the right to clean his boots, wash and repair his linen and his clothing. Jirka resisted, and the childish flush on his face, his thin, white arms and aching hands, awakened in Voborník the devout wonder of the Christian who contemplates the wounds of Christ.

Voborník was as tender as a lover towards Jirka. He embraced him in the evenings when the other sailors lolled about on the ropes, and in the mornings he woke him with a kiss which Jirka, embarrassed, tried to laugh off with a joke.

Mute and deaf, Voborník avoided the other sailors: foreign languages found no path to his brain. The Germans, Italians and Croatians laughed and sneered at him, but with a spiteful, cowardly caution because they feared his strong fists. His superiors looked down on him and shunned him as they would a strange dog, which was not dangerous so long as no one touched its master. And the more he turned away from all those on board the ship, the more tightly he clung to Jirka.

After sailing a long way, the ship moored in Bombay. But neither Jirka nor Voborník was given leave to go ashore. Although he longed for Indian soil, Jirka bore the loss of Bombay easily, in his free time examining with indifference the pompous English hotels on the waterfront through his binoculars.

Finally the *Ferdinand Max* left Bombay and sailed along the shores of India proper. Jirka grew more uneasy the further they sailed. He told the frightened Voborník stories about wise people with almond eyes who saw the sun, moon and heavens as gods and worshipped the flowers and fruits of the earth. When Madras appeared on the coast, he stared at it in ecstasy, and when it disappeared into the abundant green tropical vegetation, he recalled, more for himself than for his friend, the palm leaves on which the thoughts of Indian wise men were written, and the solemn processions striding over scattered rice.

The evening before the *Ferdinand Max* was supposed to moor in Calcutta, Jirka begged for an entire day's leave. He confided this happily to Voborník, and in his excitement did not notice that his friend was startled and followed him everywhere with fearful eyes.

Voborník did not dare to intervene, but when, the next day, all dressed up and cheerful, Jirka prepared to climb down into the dinghy, he asked him falteringly:

'Jirka, aren't you afraid?'

'Of what? Silly! It's safer there than among the Italians! Indians – they're a cultured people.'

The two friends had never been separated like this before. At any other time, Jirka might have given up his holiday, but India enticed him too strongly.

The son of the evangelical schoolmaster had inherited the family's persistent attraction to religious meditation. While his grandfather and father had been satisfied with the Holy Word, religious songs and psalms, Jirka, in restless longing, had turned to the religions of the Indians, Chinese and Turks; he snatched up the details in esoteric articles and stuffed himself with mysterious names; the Bhagavata Purana, the book of the Brahmins, bewitched him with promises of lotuses, gold temples and sacred rivers.[3]

Seeing how happy Jirka was as he stepped down into the dinghy, Voborník was a little jealous of the mysterious country that so lured his friend. With clenched heart, he watched the dinghy disappear in the distant harbor.

When evening fell, the day suddenly grew dark without transition; the ship fired a shot and the soldiers returned to the deck. Voborník stood, pale, by the railing, and in a trembling voice he asked those who had just arrived about Jirka. They looked at him in surprise and did not answer; in his agitation he had forgotten that they couldn't understand him.

Finally Jirka's rosy face appeared on the gangway. Voborník immediately cheered up, and the painful dejection fell away from him so completely that he dug out his long untouched harmonica, sang and played one tune after another, as Jirka commanded.

3   The Bhagavata Purana is the most celebrated text of a variety of Hindu sacred works in Sanskrit known as the Puranas, and the one held sacred by the Bhagavata sect.

And he demanded many of them because he was happy and satisfied.

In the morning, the ship lifted anchor and sailed away from Calcutta.

Voborník worked at the anchor. He rose early and, busy with work, had no time to think about Jirka. Only when the ship had moved and the miraculous city became a small point on the great sea did he search for Jirka among the deck-hands scrubbing the floor. But Jirka wasn't there. Voborník went down to the cabin. He found Jirka in bed with a fever. He was thirsty and complained of pains in his head.

Frightened, Voborník searched for a doctor. The doctor shrugged his shoulders and said:

'The young man had too much to drink in Calcutta?... When he gets a good rest he'll feel better.'

Jirka really did fall asleep soon after that and was still sleeping in the evening. Voborník brought him supper and tried to wake him. He did not come to. In the morning, his temperature rose; at Voborník's insistence, the doctor descended irritably to the cabin. He examined Jirka, who was in a delirious stupor; all of a sudden the doctor grew thoughtful, drove everyone out of the cabin, and when he finally emerged himself, gave orders for a strict disinfection.

Voborník ran about in a panic and forced his way through to Jirka; finally the doctor, on learning that he was Jirka's fellow countryman and friend, permitted him to tend the sick man.

The ship tacked across the waters of the Bengal Sea, and on its sides it rocked the young life as it was draining away.

Jirka died on the ninth day, in spite of Voborník's cursing and anguished cry, which faded out over the endless sea:

'My friend, my brother!'

They buried him at the bottom of the sea with military honors and at the next port, sent a written notice to schoolmaster Kupka in Košíře saying that his son the sailor had died of yellow fever on board the *Ferdinand Max*.

From the time of Jirka's illness on, Voborník hated the sea.

When they drove him from the cabin of the dying man, he stood alone on the deck and stared at the sea. It uncoiled, expanded, swelled like a vast blue cloak of bright silk, shimmering to a white light. Suffocating rushes of powerless rage rose in his throat; and when he threw Jirka's body, stinking of phenol, into the water, his hatred intensified to such an extent that he had to shut his eyes. He was afraid he could not bear to see how the blue hostile element swallowed the prey it had lured from so far away...

He hung about all alone on the ship, angry at the whole world. Time had once passed as sweetly as a light breeze with Jirka's storytelling, his frequent excited moods, enthusiastic outbursts over the beauty of the sky or the earth. Now time horrified Voborník like a single, dense, heavy matter gripping his body tenaciously, like a shroud on a living person.

Now he was all alone between the sky and the sea.

He hated the sea, the wide open sky, everything that reminded him of that terrible time of the endless blue cloak. If it had been possible to run away from the ship, Voborník certainly would have done it. Life now was abhorrent to him and unbearable, work uselessly tiring, every step purposeless; the sense of life escaped him entirely. He held on carelessly to the thread of daily habits; he ate, he slept, he toiled away, and he did not even get annoyed when they forbade him to leave the ship. Secretly he slipped money to his shipmates; in exchange, they brought him alcohol because they were afraid to anger him.

He got drunk on the sly and neglected his duties. Only on the return trip did he rouse himself from his stupor; the dim image of home sparked a faint taste for life in him.

Jirka's death seemed like a heavy dream, and a quiet hope grew in him that home might replace his loyal friend.

He had that kind of devoted character. To cling to someone, surround him with tender thoughts like spreading roots, to place his heart at his feet – Vobornik needed that. And when Jirka, his jewel and his god, disappeared, Vobornik felt alone in the world.

His spirit, suddenly free, released, flitted and tossed about, like a helpless strand of gossamer tugged by the wind. Perhaps the wind would drive it on to a goal, perhaps not; but in the end all would be in vain, even the goal.

He remembered the train station; it was nearby.

He headed there directly.

But the train for home was departing in the afternoon. He was annoyed by this because he had pictured himself immediately sitting down in a train and being home in one jump. Listless and disappointed, he slumped down onto a bench in the waiting room.

He lit a cigar, smoked it, wrote his father and brother-in-law a message in pencil on a colorful postcard, showing the white Miramare Castle against a blue sky, examined all the posters, and not knowing where to rest his eyes, put his head in his hands.

Several hours later the station porter, assuming that Vobornik was asleep, shook him by the shoulder and asked him rather rudely where he was headed.

His unfamiliar cinnamon-colored uniform drew glances from the station attendants who did not know about the arrival of his ship and attracted a few peddlers who did know about it.

A young girl, selling postcards, approached him.

Without looking up, he turned her away unkindly.

She grew curious about this gloomy, but not ugly, sailor with a muscular physique, sat down beside him and offered herself in a soft, lisping Italian.

She had a pocket full of mussels which she cracked open and ate live; she smelled of the sea, and Voborník moved away from her in irritation without a word.

Astounded, she stopped swallowing the little morsels. Her curiosity was so great that she followed him out onto the platform and waved her kerchief when the train departed...

His father was waiting for him at the station. They kissed each other with emotion.

'Well, you're a proper fellow, aren't you? They straightened your back up there!'

'What about you, papa?' Voborník suddenly cheered up, touched by the sound of the native dialect he had not heard for so long. 'Your tooth fell out, the front tooth at that, and you're going gray behind the ears...,' he noted the most striking changes.

'Ha! Ha!' his father brushed him off, 'that's nothing. I'm an old greenhorn, my boy... and the tooth, that one fell out so I could get a better grip on my pipe!'

They teased one another as they walked home, like two old friends. Voborník had grown up without a mother, and the friendship with Jirka had awakened the feeling of tenderness in him for the first time. He treated his father like an equal, especially in the period before he enlisted, when he was already working with his father in the same brickyard.

'I came out for your sake,' the old man said, brushing the dust off his black formal jacket with his rough hand. 'Václav is working until five, and Mařena is lying in bed. They've got a little squirt, with big eyes and a big mouth. You'll see them this evening.'

They talked cheerfully and easily about Voborník's siblings, news in the town and changes at the brickyard. It seemed to them that the year hadn't even been that long; and truly, little had happened in the time Voborník had been away.

They walked as far as the schoolmaster's house.

'Look,' said the old man, 'I forgot to tell the teacher you were coming.' Not seeing the sudden scowl on his son's face, the old brickmaker ran up to the ground-floor window, cluttered with fuchsias laden with a heavy harvest of pink blossoms, and banged on the frame.

'Papa!' the sailor shouted, 'don't you remember?'

But it was too late. The dry face of schoolmaster Kupka appeared in the window.

'Oh Lord!' the shrill voice of a woman, hidden behind him, blurted out, 'Voborník's here and... and...'

At that moment, the yellow face disappeared, the fuchsia curtain closed and the fall of a body and the thud of a chair knocked over could be heard.

That was Jirka's mother who'd had such a shock.

'There you go, papa, I shouted at you... but it...' the son reproached his father. 'After all, you know all about it... and it...' The words floundered somewhere and got in a tangle. His clenched throat could not be persuaded to speak properly.

The old man stood there dumbfounded, and obeying the emphatic gestures of the yellow face, which had pushed apart the fuchsias once again, he left with his son, grumbling:

'But I meant well... I did...'

In the sitting room, beer was going flat in the stone pitcher set on the table.

The old man went into the room first, saying: 'Welcome home'. Removing the worn book that covered the pitcher, he poured out two glasses and said a little ceremoniously:

'So... drink up!'

'To your health!' Voborník rattled off.

'To yours.'

They sat down at the table across from one another, and soon it became apparent that they had nothing to talk about. They had already covered the main events on the way, and when the old man asked about his son's voyage, he was told:

'We were in Trieste and Calcutta. Jirka died there. He could tell you stories, papa, until your head would start to spin. He ran about like a squirrel!'

'And what about you, you?' his father insisted.

'Me?... I don't like being at sea, papa. I would rather stay in the brickyard.'

'That wouldn't be wise,' his father hinted, and the conversation between father and son came to an end.

Voborník unbuttoned his cinnamon-colored jacket and placed his cap on the table by the pitcher.

His stiff, shining hair bristled above his ruddy forehead.

The old fellow quietly enunciated the motto on the cap:

'Erz – her – zog... Fer – di...'

The young man rose and circled the sitting room in six strides. The stove at which he had dreamed as a boy of far-away lands now seemed small and shabby. The pictures on the walls had turned yellow; during that one year everything had somehow grown old and wasted, like his father.

In the afternoon they went to Mařena's for coffee. She was lying under a striped feather duvet, beside the red little face of a sleeping child. She felt embarrassed in front of her brother and hid her head in the bedding.

'Don't be shy, silly,' Voborník said and kissed her moist lips.

A schoolgirl, the neighbor's daughter, prepared a big pot of coffee, which she poured into the hand-painted mugs on the table.

She slipped away unobtrusively to spread the news; soon curiosity seekers leered in the windows, and the more daring among them even crowded in the door along with the family acquaintances.

They waited a while so that they could drink the coffee with Voborník's brother-in-law: the day before a holiday the brickyard operated only until five. Václav, Voborník's older brother, dashed in the door just after him, already washed and dressed in his Sunday clothes.

Both of them greeted Voborník noisily and smacked brotherly, somewhat formal, kisses on both his cheeks.

'So what do you think of her?' the young father turned towards the bed and pointed happily at his first child.

'She hasn't been christened yet because we wanted to name her after you... little Francka, Fanča, Fanynka... Would you be her godfather, Franta?... It's such a coincidence, after all!' He turned suddenly towards Voborník.

Surprised by this unexpected attack, Voborník did not know what to answer. He sensed, however, that he should not offend his brother-in-law by refusing him.

So he nodded and the brother-in-law gleefully rubbed his hands together, as if he had brought off something really special.

'Help yourself to what we have,' he said, sitting Voborník down in front of the coffee and pushing over as close as possible to him a very yellow, sliced cake.

Questions again showered down on Voborník.

'Tell me,' the brother-in-law spoke with his mouth full, dipping cake in his coffee with relish, 'is it true about sea-sickness? Does everyone get it, every single person? And is it bad? What about sailors who are always on water? Do they get used to it?' he asked eagerly.

Voborník answered reluctantly.

The brother-in-law, who was in a fine mood, did not notice and threw out all kinds of foolish questions, adding frivolous comments, and finally, rather amazed that he didn't yet know, he asked Voborník insistently:

'And how about you? How did you like the sea?'

Voborník had been expecting this question for a long time, and he trembled as if suddenly chilled when he heard it. His low forehead wrinkled angrily, and he blurted out:

'Don't go on all the time about the damned sea! I think I'll never lay eyes on it again!'

They were all startled, and the father peered anxiously into his son's face. It was stuffy in the sitting room, and suddenly quiet.

To avoid disturbing the woman lying in bed with the child, and also to celebrate the sailor's triumphant return, they went out to the pub.

In the bustling streets all sorts of people turned to look at them. Václav and the brother-in-law stuck close to Voborník; their pride in him was so obvious that it roused the soldier's vanity and the elegance of his uniform went to his head.

He was in a mood to swagger.

He thrust out his chest and, from the way he looked about, it was clear he knew how his youthful body, with its supple muscles, filled his uniform. The girls even turned their heads to catch another glimpse of him. They had never before seen a soldier like that in Košíře! That was a uniform for you, with earthy colors and a very light weapon, sparkling like a jewel, more for decoration than for murder. The cap sat smartly above the bronzed forehead and aquiline nose.

And what a cap! A falcon in flight, a flag in the wind; gold letters blazed on the rim:

Ferdinand Max!

He walked on and did not turn his head. Who would turn and look around in Košíře!

We were in Trieste, my darling, we kissed handsome Italian girls; their skin was fragrant, like oranges, and they wore yellow scarves in their black braids! What do you local beauties, with your hair ironed in curls over your foreheads, you beauties from the brickyard, what do you know about the wide world?!

We saw Japanese girls with slanting, treacherous eyes, blackened teeth and painted nails; and they all liked our uniforms. The little Siamese girls even draped themselves on our uniforms!

And yet, you local girls should be glad you don't know about the sea. About endless pain, corroding all of life, a pain that unfolds like a psalm, and its refrain is a lamentation of a lonely soul...

Girls, dear local girls, don't set your heart on seeing the sea, don't long for it, don't ask me about the sea.

And so Voborník's mood collapsed before they arrived at the pub. The happiness waiting for him at the train station with his father had scattered under the schoolmaster's window. The piercing memory of Jirka had worn out his heart; the calm at home only reminded him that he would have to return to the ship, that the ship would sail out to sea, and Voborník, like a criminal who returns to the scene of the murder, would find himself in Calcutta again, would lift the anchor with a heavy winch, and, like a stunned beast, would stand and watch for a long while how the blue cloak coiled and uncoiled with the movements of a silver shimmering snake.

And then the terrible moment would come when loneliness would murder him. Then the sea, the sea would have his corpse just as it now has yours, my friend, my brother...

The men sat down at a table and ordered beer.

Voborník drank the first glass in one gulp.

They laughed at him.

'Tastes good, doesn't it? Beer, beer, a little foaming glass of beer. Ha, ha!'

He swung his legs.

'Sure, it's good,' he said curtly.

And again they drank, almost silently, letting a word drop now and then.

'Come on, František, you're not saying anything!' Václav spoke up after a while.

'What's to tell!' Voborník put him off.

The rainbow colors of foreign lands blended into a gray, dull, tired stain; there was nothing to remember and inside only the gnawing of an incurable grief.

They sat and drank long into the night.

Once in a while, the publican wound up the barrel organ, and Voborník's brother-in-law threw him a few kreutzers;[4] curious old women drifted in out of the evening with pitchers for beer. They peered over from the beer counter and, seeing so many male customers, disappeared.

'Is this your boy?' the brickmakers asked, sitting down to throw back a shot of liquor, and old Voborník proudly nodded until his pipe shook.

Later in the night, both the male and female visitors trickled out; the father dozed and banged his head on the table.

Waking suddenly from a particularly hard bump to his head, he said sleepily:

'We could turn in.'

'I see you're nodding off,' said Voborník.

'I'll go too,' said the brother-in-law, and joined the old man. He had long been waiting for the signal but didn't want to start talking about going home himself for fear they would make fun of him as a married man; and yet he was concerned about his young wife.

When they went outside, the spring air, cold and fresh, hit them in the face. Still steaming hot, they shivered on feeling the cold, and buttoned up their coats as they walked. They

4 The kreutzer was a small coin formerly current in parts of Germany and Austria.

said a brief goodbye in front of the brother-in-law's house. The old man was in a hurry to get to bed. He was not in the habit of roving from pub to pub.

Václav, however, winked at his brother and said, when the father opened the low gate:

'We won't go in just yet. We'll walk off some of this beer.'

'Go on, go on,' the tired old man quickly replied, 'just don't wander about 'til morning. And don't get up to anything!' he added, banging the door shut.

'And… where do you want to go?' Voborník asked his brother.

'Do you have money?' Václav said, instead of an answer.

'Well – the money's there,' Voborník said hesitantly.

'So come on!'

The streets were deep and sounded hollow in the desolation of the night. The beer took its toll on Voborník's mind; it seemed to him that a piece of his skull had come off and fallen, as if from a broken vessel, and now his exposed brain quivered in the cold breeze, as sudden as the touch of a knife.

'My head hurts,' Voborník complained.

'We'll drive away the pain, František, we'll drive it away.'

He took him by the arm.

They stopped at a wine bar, then went to a café. Václav acted mysterious. He had a place in mind. It wasn't far off. Voborník hung his head feebly.

Pretty girls, that's right, Czech girls. Girls from the country, real fillies. Shall we go there then? Forward march!

Voborník did not resist. His head was heavy, an unbearable burden, swinging from shoulder to shoulder. The beer, to which he was unaccustomed, poured lassitude into his limbs, and sluggishness into his movements; it also brought a delicious relief, equilibrium and calm into his rankling thoughts.

Forward march!

His ridiculously heavy and disobedient legs slipped on command, and this made Voborník laugh – a quiet, inward rather than outward, laugh. He didn't care where his brother dragged him, he had only the pleasant awareness that someone was looking after him, supporting him with a shoulder, persuading him in a friendly manner.

'Just come on, you old fool,' Václav held forth, cheerfully drunk, 'I know what it's like when a man comes back to his country. I was only in Vienna, but even I had to run away!'

His prattling died out in the long, narrow passage, against the low vault of which the syllables echoed. An old woman stationed in the passage encouraged them on with flattering words like a clucking hen; she didn't make much of an effort, however, as there was no reason to doubt the intentions of customers who knew where they were going.

The narrow steps led to a porch that opened onto the river. The lights from the bridge trembled in the water; the sky was very black. On the porch, a little window blinded by a curtain shone with a red light. Someone's hand quickly dropped the curtain at the sound of their steps.

'Aha!' Václav sneered. 'The mermaid's looking at the water.'

A gas flame, turned down low, burned in the room; there were two girls there and a stout woman beaming with promising smiles who greeted both brothers warmly. Business was not good, and newcomers were doubly welcome.

A tall blonde with an ample figure rested her head on her hand, but remained lying on the couch, clearly out of laziness. A thin girl with a dark complexion who was leaning against the window waited until the men had entered the circle of light under the gas flame. Hardly had she seen Voborník's uniform, when she stiffened, dashed over and raised the gas flame all of a sudden, so that it blazed and blinded the young men for a moment.

The sleepy boredom in the room dispersed under the shock of light. The madam, rich in conversation, twittered sweetly and asked what the gentlemen would like.

'Make us some coffee,' Václav commanded, blinking significantly in the direction of the couch.

'Some for me too,' the blonde drawled and threw her feet off the couch, as if she wanted to stand. But sluggishness overcame her, and not finding enough energy to get up or to pull her legs back on the couch, she slid slowly down towards the floor under her own weight.

His head bowed, still sunk in quiet, blissful musing, Voborník did not seem to notice that he had come into a parlor; he stood there as if he wanted to leave and was only waiting for his brother, who kept lingering.

Václav took this behavior for shyness and said:

'Take your things off, František, make yourself at home, at home. You're not in a foreign land... you're with your own!'

And his words were drenched in the cheery senseless laughter of drunks.

The madam brought a coffee grinder back from the kitchen, sat down on a stool and, assessing the situation, commented: 'Anděla,[5] pay more attention to the gentlemen!'

'Am I supposed to be a hostess?' the pretty blonde hissed proudly, hanging off the sofa. 'Let the mermaid entertain them!'

But hardly had she said this when her balance, long tottering, collapsed entirely, and Anděla fell to the floor. Her soft body spread over the floor like dough.

They all burst out laughing. Václav did so noisily, grateful for the opportunity to snigger unconstrained. Voborník uttered a short laugh, as if he had just noticed Anděla and

5 Anděla is the Czech version of Angela. The name suggests the Czech word for 'angel' – anděl.

was distracted by her from his thoughts. Slim Vlasta giggled mischievously, and the enormous bosom of the madam shook with laughter over the coffee grinder.[6]

Anděla liked to exaggerate her laziness, so she remained spread out on the carpet. Examining Voborník from below, she asked:

'You're a soldier?'

'A soldier,' said Voborník, looking down on her indulgently.

'He's a seafaring cavalier,' Václav crowed. His laughter was deliberately prolonged and degenerated into a kind of idiotic cackling.

The coffee was served and soon drunk.

Voborník did not reply to Václav's silly words or the fawning exclamations of Anděla; he did not hear them.

The modest bourgeois luxury of the carefully furnished parlor evoked for him the image of a dear, loving home to which he was returning after long trials, a wounded, slowly recovering soldier. His wound was there, he could feel it, but the pain had gone. The sharp, corrosive, feverish pain had gone. A breeze touched his wounds with loving fingers, gently and devoutly, as it would the wounds of a saint. The breeze had already wiped from his mind the cause of the deadly wound; you don't know anymore: was it a dagger, a gun, a grenade, or a blade? The cause seems immaterial; it disappears in the dense, blue haze covering everything, everything that was.

Voborník did not listen to the chatter; he did not understand a word that passed between Anděla and Václav. He sensed only that they were speaking a kind of tender, long familiar language, the same language a very dear person had spoken many years ago. And so to him their senseless

---

6   Vlasta was the name of the leader of the Amazon maidens who, according to Czech legend, once waged war against men.

talk sounded like the rustle of the stream in his native village where in his youth he had tended goslings and to which he was returning, a thirsty traveler, after a long voyage abroad. The stream is not yet in sight, but here is the cluster of birch trees, and beyond the bend in the path, the silver willow which, like a young girl washing her hands, dips its thin branches into the stream.

It's very, very blissful here. The sun splashes through the branches of the birches; there, behind the thickest trunk, someone is hiding, fixing curious eyes on the wanderer; the wind combs the overhanging tresses of the weeping willow, and behind them the curious eyes of the persistent, unknown observer appear again. They are even on the burdock leaves, and they tremble on the branches of the poplar.

'Are you asleep?' said a husky voice above Voborník. It was the voice of his brother Václav.

'He's sleeping all right,' came the comment from under the table.

Voborník waved his hand. Everything disappeared. The convalescent in him wept over the lost peace.

Would the wound, just healed, flame up again?

He waved his hand once more, but the fixed, insistent eyes did not go away. He looked up: just opposite him Vlasta leaned across the table, with her chin in her hands; she had been watching him all evening with eager, green eyes.

Vaclav noticed his brother's gesture and turned on the girl:

'And what about you! Eat him up with your witch eyes!'

And Vlasta flung her young body across the table, clasped Voborník's head between her strong arms and whispered passionately in his ear, pressing the nape of his neck with her long fingers:

'Come with me, sailor!'

On hearing the command, but also the plea, in her voice, Voborník shuddered and stood up.

He wanted peace and rest so much that instinctively he would have done anything to find them again. 'Goodbye!' Anděla shouted as they left.

They found themselves alone in a dark little room. Vlasta felt about for matches, and the yellow flame of the candle lit up a divan and, behind it, a mat covered with postcards.

Voborník shifted hesitantly from one foot to the other, and as soon as the light spread he sat down in a dark corner on a tabouret.

But even here he did not feel at ease.

'You know what?' he said to the girl. 'Let's go to sleep.'

She agreed and began to undress.

At first Voborník only glanced at her, then he looked with interest.

She had a supple, slim body, which was also strong and mature. That was evident only now when she took off the first layer of clothing.

Her green eyes turned black in the light of the candle. In the shadow, they flashed at Voborník like the eyes of a beast of prey.

'Put out the light,' he commanded, somewhat disturbed.

They lay on the narrow bed and did not touch one another. An invisible barrier restrained them, a kind of inexplicable anxiety, a defensive instinct, a retreat before an attack.

They were silent.

And the silence was such that they could hear the rustling of their blood, its rapid pounding at the temples, and wild circulation through the body.

At first, Voborník really did shut his eyes so that he could doze. He was weak from lack of sleep and from alcohol, but the presence of a woman excited him; his restless blood would not let him drift off.

Finally he sat up on the bed and turned to the girl.

She was very quiet and held her breath, but her eyes burned in the dark.

She waited for a movement from Voborník, and suddenly, throwing off the bedcover, she whispered insistently: 'Sailor, I'm beautiful!'

A white blotch shone in the darkness of the room. He embraced her. And the rushing of his blood weighed down his arms.

As soon as she was certain of victory, she slipped out of his embrace and, grasping both of his broad hands, begged in a strangely softened, almost weeping, voice:

'Tell me what the sea looks like!'

'What?' Voborník shouted in alarm.

'Tell me about the sea! About the sea! I've longed for it since I was a child. This terrible longing has led me all the way here. Once they promised that they would show me the world, that they would give me the sea, if I would only listen. I listened. They took me to a foreign city, among the Germans. I insisted they show me the sea. But there was no sea in the city, or beyond the city; only the sad, wide river with its black banks. I used to cry, and one night I ran away from them. They didn't keep their promise, so why should I listen?'

Voborník looked into the darkness and his heavy head slowly comprehended the girl's plaintive words.

'I ran away, but what good did freedom do me? I wasn't used to work or caring for myself, and the sea lured me again. I left my hometown for Prague, and again I sold myself for the promise of the sea. Tell me, what is the sea like? What colors does it have when it burns in the morning and in the evening? Is it strong enough to charm a person? Talk, tell me, answer!'

Voborník looked at the white blotch; as his eyes grew used to the dark, the blotch assumed the features of a person. Those white hands tore the bandages from the convalescent and made the blood flow from wounds that had hardly healed. A smarting pain flared up.

'Shut up,' he said, irritated, 'I didn't come here to –'

She didn't let him finish.

'I know why you came. I'll do anything you want, but first tell me, tell me something about the sea! Who can I ask, if not you, who have just come from the sea and carry its scent and taste on your body?'

'Shut up,' Voborník threatened again and shook off her hands.

She staggered, but talked on all the more insistently:

'Since childhood... this longing has hounded me. I'm obsessed with the sea, the devil's invention. Tell me, is it great, magnificent... is it beautiful?'

Voborník got dressed without a word.

Anguish and panic jumbled her words:

'Tell me at least... was it worth the loss of my virtue?'

'Leave me alone,' he cut her off and got ready to leave.

But she stood in front of the door, a white blotch in the dark little room, and stopped him from going.

'I won't let you out until you answer,' she said menacingly.

Voborník was tired of quarrelling.

Several times he crossed the dark sitting room, knocking over objects which lay in the way.

She waited, thinking he would at least say something. Quietly she pleaded:

'Who was I supposed to ask, who? No one would answer my questions. They had not come to me for that, they said, just like you. I know that. But I decided that a soldier would come, a sailor, and I would not let that one go. Your brother promised he would bring you here. He said you had traveled far in the world, you had sailed over the sea all the way to India, I know...'

'Shut up...' hissed Voborník. All the pain suddenly rushed back inside him, an incomprehensible, deadly grief fell on him, a pressure that turned him to ice.

My friend, my brother!

The blue cloak fluttered over his head, enormous waves welled up, unbearably blue, they neared his head, crashed against it, broke in a silver, foamy spray, and under their weight Voborník fell somewhere into the depths. He struggled with his arms and legs. Long, white tentacles coiled around him, restraining his movements. In the most savage fear, he drew his hidden weapon, a wide knife, and thrust it at the murderous, white monster.

There was a short, sharp cry, but at that moment Voborník overcame the hostile element, broke open the door and fled across the porch, through the passage and into the silent streets.

He ran to a park and finding an empty bench in a little birch grove, he sank down upon it and fell asleep almost at once...

The gray dawn timidly poked into the dark room of the mermaid, and then a golden ray of sunlight struck the wall, illuminating a yellowish mat, plastered with postcards, and on each of them blazed a piece of the garish blue sea... In the wide, slanting strip of sunshine which lay across the room there appeared the dark body of a girl thrown back on the floor, with a thin, red trail of dried blood on her throat, and just by the window, where it had fallen, was the smart cap with the gold motto:

Ferdinand Max.

THE SYLPH[1]

HELENA MALÍŘOVÁ

12 January

What do you say to that, my young man? I'm thinking of starting a 'new life'. That means: farewell, poor sweet little fool. That means: farewell, freedom and adventure; it's time to lead a sensible life.

The good sense of twenty-three years… yes, twenty-three years. God knows I have no intention of flirting. God knows I have the best will in the world to be straightforward, strong, wise and not to flirt. Likewise, it is probably known to God that I haven't the slightest talent for this; that I'm a mad weakling and a flirt; that there is no simplicity, beautiful, precious simplicity, in my thoughts, my deeds, my heart. Now, for example, when I want to write simply and succinctly – merely to give an account – when I'm all alone and addressing no one but myself, I'm constantly asking myself: do I really feel things the way I write them down here? Is this me? Don't I have a secret purpose? Don't I want to seem other than what I am?

I'm not speaking to myself, I'm not writing for myself! The world is meant to hear me, everyone in the world is meant to hear me and pay attention to me. That's what I long for, and yet I know that no one could be bothered.

Today in Café Slavia Jetmar said I was… but the devil take me.[2] God, if only I could find someone more interesting than me!

1 The name the narrator gives to his sweetheart, 'routička', is a diminutive for routa, or rue (German Raute), a small, hardy, evergreen aromatic shrub which has been grown in herb gardens as a medicinal plant; its flowers are greenish-yellow. But it also refers to Rautendelein, a character from Gerhart Hauptmann's *The Sunken Bell* (Die versunkene Glocke, 1896), which was well known at the time. I have translated Routička as 'Sylph', a word which has more connotations for the English reader.
2 Slavia is a well-known café in Prague.

Jetmar? Yes, Jetmar. I'm afraid of that man. But I like him. I like him very much. Often I'm lonely and awkward in his company, but I like to sit with him anyway in the shabby, noisy beer halls; I like to suffer with him through the joyless, but still sweet, drinking bouts.

He's a melancholy, unhappy person and immensely dear to me. The others – Reichert, Váňa, Šedivý – compared to him they're children, hollow and simplistic.

I won't even talk about the others. That petty, pathetic Janatka, who's so satisfied with himself, so enamoured of himself. I don't know how some people can be so self-satisfied and not notice their own shallowness and redundancy in this world. Actually, I'm very much like him, that's why I hate the fellow so much; but at least I can observe and despise my own self-love, while he does not, cannot, observe a thing! Satisfied, terribly satisfied, and even amazed by the miracle of his own self!

Is it like that everywhere in the world? Or only here in Bohemia?

Such pettiness and complacency, and such short tempers too. Heaven forbid one should say something unpleasant to these people. That's why it's so banal and boring in this country.

Three o'clock. Time to go to the café. It's sheer tedium, but what can I do? I'll start the new life tomorrow. Anyway, I still have to get hold of one more lecture and then, oh, new life! Oh, first state examination! Then, I'll relish you!

18 January

There, I've already covered several pages of my diary and so far I haven't mentioned... a woman. I'm proud of myself. A novel without love. No one would read it, which is, come to think of it, an advantage. What a comfort it is to know that no one will look into my soul and conscience, no one will profane...

A novel without love. Without a woman. Ah, how easy it is to breathe, how refreshing after the loathsomeness of fine literature, crammed with love and women. Apparently Klárka will go to the law students' ball tomorrow; that's what she told Šedivý, who understood her meaning and conscientiously passed the message on!... Well, let her go. What a dissembler. She's not even pretty, really. If she didn't use powder and fix herself up in such a crafty way, who would give her a second look? What a wretched life, if she would only return those verses which I, ass that I am, wrote for her. I could hit myself. Such a stupid goose and so wily at the same time.

A novel without love, that is the only possible novel of the future. Oh, Romeo, wherefore art thou Romeo! Oh, Staněk, wherefore art thou Staněk!

20 January

I didn't go because she was there: no, I know for certain that's not why I went. Because all I wanted was to say something rude to her. To laugh at her. Kick her. The little witch, the way she fawned on me. And cried. They're monsters, they can even cry if they have to, and if they know it becomes them. How deep and beautiful her eyes were when they shed such passionate tears...

No, Mademoiselle. Adieu! My love belongs to the first state examination and my novel – is a novel without love. Si, si. Sing your Grieg to Mr. Janatka and company – my heart is too fastidious; it can't bear to hear any old girl from the street, like you, singing Grieg.[3]

I'm very happy like this – without love. Today I will cram all day long. I'm already looking forward to it. Really, I feel ten feet tall. Reichert, that decent fellow, is so small;

3   Edvard Hagerup Grieg (1843–1907) was a composer who founded the Norwegian nationalist school of music.

yesterday some lass was driving him crazy; an interesting creature, apparently – all three were raving – but I think she'll be nothing special. What 'interesting creature'? A woman! A twenty-year-old girl!

Yes, if there were interesting creatures...

30 January

The law of succession...

My head aches. I studied all week long. I didn't even go to Slavia.

The interesting creature is truly inter... That is to say... amusing. She's the daughter of a clerk, from a rather mysterious family; I hear that the mother had a murky past, but she raises her daughter very strictly; yes, that's the way it goes. But she shouldn't even let her dance rounds at the balls; what good is she if she sits by the wall in her black silk dress, her white gloves with the first button undone and thick bracelets, when her little daughter is gallivanting about with bohemians who have borrowed tails and set themselves the task of spoiling the innocent patrician fools with modern poetry? How foolish and powerless even the most astute mothers are!

Let dear Milenka have some fun,[4] let her enjoy her youth a little, not as much as mama did, but a little bit, in an innocent, decent and permissible manner; yes, in a permissible manner, at Žofín Island, in the best society.[5] My dear Madam, when we borrow tails and clean shirts, no one can tell us apart from decent people, from good families. You say that it doesn't mean a thing if your little daughter dances with fellows like us? If she has a bit of fun with such chaps? That she won't marry any of them? Not that! But who knows if later she will want to accept the 'good match' you arrange

4 Milena's name suggests the Czech word for 'lover' or 'mistress' – milenka.
5 Žofín Island – in German 'Sofien Insel' – is located in the Vltava river in Prague.

for her! Of course she will want to; she will learn some sense, surely. But what if it's not too late already? What if she manages to fly away after all from under your protective wings, oh esteemed mother hen, even if only for a moment – and what if she loses, even innocently, her reputation?

Beware, beware, esteemed mother hen! My friend Reichert is a philosopher and a poet. Friends Šedivý and Váňa are anarchists. They only borrowed the tails! They share a topcoat and dinners at the refectory. And your little chick is terribly amused by all this. Apparently it's 'something totally different'. Your little chick is a kind of sentimental, modern chicken, a more profound chicken. I'm very worried that she might stray away from your brooding-basket and away from the good grain. Those wings of yours, hmm, those wings of yours...

We're cheerful fellows, talkative and charming. We have cultivated and profound natures. We love the great Russians, great Germans, great men of all nations. That impresses Mademoiselle Milena.

Mademoiselle Milena goes to cookery school, but it will be the end of her. She's skipping school. She had her very first rendezvous. With friend Reichert. Friend Reichert is radiant and speaks of a rare, splendid female soul.

He speaks of a delightful little girl, a child with enormous, heavenly eyes. Those eyes, he says, warm a person's heart so very very much! Those eyes say so much!

Woman has a soul! That's the latest discovery of the old fool, the philosopher Reichert.

5 February

Have no fear, Mademoiselle, the Madam won't notice a thing. I'll ask you to come to the party with me; my friends and I will reserve all the dances until midnight – don't give them to anyone else. The hall will be packed; in that tumult, in the spirit of the masquerade chaos and lost among all those masks, you can easily slip away from your mother's vigilant gaze for an hour. She'll think you're in the gallery; in short, she can't keep her eye on us all the time. We'll lead you out of the hall; outside we'll get into a carriage and five minutes later we'll be in our garret. We'll make some tea, smoke cigarettes, and then we'll return to the hall again, as if nothing had happened. You'll wear a mask and throw a cloak over your shoulders; no one will recognize you. It will be a pleasant little adventure. Life is so marvellous! Youth is fleeting; in a year's time your mother will marry you off to some respectable gentleman who earns two thousand a year, or even more...

She smiled and trembled with longing... but her eager eyes filled with tears at Reichert's last words. Then she laughed again, a loud, gleeful laugh...

Yes, she will dare to do it! She dares do something outrageous, come what may. Life, life... Will the rest of you be happy too? Because she cannot be happy on her own; she must cheer others up as well.

Yes, she will dare to do it! She will sin terribly; she will sin against propriety in an outrageous manner. She will carry off an outrageous piece of mischief. And yet, it's completely harmless. It will be such an innocent adventure... much more innocent than the tricks of well-brought-up girls, trying to lure a man...

It came off. Reichert got his grant and spent it all on this brilliant plan. He arranged costumes – dominoes – for all of us; he arranged for the carriage, for everything.[6]

Milena wore a marvelous, exotic costume made from cloth that was fresh, silky, quietly fluttering; a cloth that was golden, bedewed with silver, softly clinging, most ex-

6 A 'domino' is a loose cloak with a mask for the upper part of the face, worn at masquerades.

traordinary... She looked a little bit like a sylph. Her arms were bare; she wore only golden straps over her pretty, rosy shoulders, only golden straps... And she was strewn with flowers. Streams of tendrilous blossoms covered her loose hair, the color of pale gold; hair and flowers tumbled down over her breast; hair and flowers tumbled down over her dress. On her feet she wore sandals. She was childlike, she was lovely, dressed as a nymph, or A Sylph, A Dream, A Poem – even though she's hardly lovely otherwise.

We vanished from the hall – it was easy – we vanished. We left behind the fantastic whirl and motion, the lights, the music, the magnificent, flaunting parade... The Sylph (or Dream? Happiness? Youth?) wrapped her golden, silken, blossoming and bedewed beauty in a great, gray, hooded cloak; she was snuffed out under that cloak; only her eyes burned in the shadow... and she slipped into the carriage with Reichert and Váňa. Šedivý and I followed behind them on foot.

When we arrived at Reichert's – the samovar was already humming, smoke was twirling from cigarettes, the stove was crackling, the boys were chattering and she sat there with them, a Sylph once again, Youth, Delight...

The hour flew by like five minutes. The Sylph began to grow uneasy.

'It's so beautiful here, a thousand times more beautiful and free than it is back there,' she said with a regretful sigh, 'but I'm afraid and I can't be happy here anymore... Oh, why didn't I grow up with you, in freedom, in the sunlight of a free life?... I think that one day I'll run away from home.'

'Where to?'

'To you! "To the Human World!"' A Sylph... A fairy tale. She stood up and looked about sadly. 'Here it's so... gentle.'

Childish tears glistened in her eyes. Her shoulders hunched up and she stroked her cheeks with both hands...

'I love to spoil myself... I love to be alive in the world. But not there...'

While she spoke she looked at me.

'Come, let's go now! Goodbye!'

We returned to the hall. No one noticed a thing. It was a daring stunt, only now do I see that; but at that moment, everything was possible. Obstacles were easily overcome. It's true, all one has to do is want a thing.

A novel without love. Yes, because flirting is not love. Jetmar would laugh at me, of course. But Jetmar is a rather spiteful fellow. It's a good thing he's still at his father's. If only he would stay away for a while longer. It's silly, but sometimes I fear him – as the devil fears the cross.

22 February

Two letters lie in front of me. One from Jetmar and one from her, from Milena.

Jetmar writes:

Dear Staněk,

I must admit that you confuse me. Perhaps you overestimate me. I definitely am not the mature character you take me for. It's just that I've lived more intensively than the rest of you; I've lived through more, I've risked more. I understand people, that's the main thing. I see through them sooner and more thoroughly than you and the others do.

Your letter is somehow insincere. For God's sake, what has happened? Actually, I know what's happened. Why don't you speak openly? Why don't you say honestly: I'm in love, I'm infatuated, once again, as usual? Why these false, coy phrases, this brilliantly masked sentimentality – I don't know why!

Are you afraid of me? Are you trying to prepare me for something? Do you want to disarm me in advance? I find it rather painful. What do I care about your affairs, after all? You really are afraid of me. You dread my return to Prague. You wretched boy, I'm coming back soon. I'll be there in a week's time, or fourteen days at the latest.

I find no peace here. I don't even feel at home. Father is glad that I've come; he'd like to keep me here a while. But I find it painful. The poor old man believes in my future; he believes that I'll finish my studies. But that won't happen. I find no rest here. I so much looked forward to coming home, like a child. Prague seemed detestable to me; I trembled with love for the village where I was born. But the village where I was born disappointed me, and now Prague calls once more!

I'm coming back. But don't be afraid of me, or you'll be disappointed someday... someday when the giant appears rather small to you.

I wish you happiness and all the best! She's an angel, that is understood. You believe in her, you believe, you believe! Reichert, Váňa et al. – oh, that was nothing, nothing at all. She never loved anyone. She loves only you and you alone – in short, she's an angel! All the best, my dear fellow, all the best! You believe – and therefore you will be saved. She has sweet, innocent eyes. She says that she loves you, ergo it must be true. Until we meet again! Your J.

Milena writes:

My dear, sweet, handsome boy, I am yours and I'm so terribly happy – you probably can't imagine how happy. Isn't it so – you simply can't imagine it? You have no idea how desolate my past has been, how horrid all the years of my childhood and adolescence were.

True, I come from a good family. My father was a minor official, but mama had money, I'm told, and so we always lived well. The tidy, little country town where I spent my first years lies in a pretty, green dell; it has a white main square with alleys lined with chestnut trees; the forest is only ten minutes *away; oh, how I love the forest... But I wasn't happy there; for me, something was always missing. When I began to mature, papa applied for a transfer to Prague. Mama wanted him to, for my sake, she said, so that I might be introduced to society and, more importantly, get married. She had some powerful relative, and because of his influence papa was able to transfer to Prague. Once in the city, mama started to take me around to the dances and concerts...*

I always found it so dreadful, but what was I supposed to do? And anyway, I was sad at home as well. That engineer you heard about, that was nothing, my dear. He was such a fop, terribly stupid and conceited and not very handsome either. Of course, mama wanted me to marry him. She invited him to our home and made a fuss over him; they all kept pressing me, but I didn't want him. Maybe he didn't want me either because all of a sudden he stopped coming to visit, and now they say he's getting married. He's going to marry a very rich woman. I'm not a bit sorry. I don't want to marry. In those days I used to think that I had to marry; that I would consent to anyone, just so long as I could get away from home, away from the boredom; but now I don't want to marry anymore. I never liked anyone, remember that. And I won't like anyone else but you, do you hear? You are the first and the only one, you, no one but you, Vincík Staněk, a student who will never amount to anything. I'm absolutely mad about you. I don't know how to say it as nicely as you do. I don't know how to write as nicely as you do. I'm a silly, ordinary girl. Why do you like me? What do you see in me? I'm not even pretty. They say I have beautiful hair. But who cares about hair? Vincík, Vincík, I love you madly, I repeat this once again and would love to repeat it forever. What did all the others matter, those I knew before I met you? What are all the rest compared with you! Reichert is perhaps tolerable; he's amusing, and, I think, even rather profound – though I don't understand that sort of thing. You see, I'm empty-headed, Vincík. But you must still like me! I'll come to your room again as usual – I don't even care if my parents find out; I'm strong and ready for anything. Vincík, please, you must like me as much as I like you. Yours, eternally yours, Milena.

These two letters lie in front of me on the table. I practically know them by heart already. I feel odd; I'm very annoyed and irritated. Why? I like her; I can hardly wait for her to get here. But that letter from Jetmar shouldn't have arrived at the same time as hers...

Jetmar is beastly. I'm furious with him. He spoils everything with his cynicism, and poisons every joy.

23 February, afternoon

She has left, hurt and offended. My lovely fairy tale, my good, my golden heart... Why did I act so strangely? Why did I hurt her? After all, I believe her. I don't know why, but I believe her, I can't help but believe her. But that letter, that damned letter of Jetmar's...

In short, it spoiled my mood. I had to keep thinking of that letter, and whenever I did, I felt a pang...

I can't control myself. If I'm not completely at ease, then I'm peevish and inconsiderate. I love complete happiness, a bright, joyful frame of mind. The slightest stain on this can provoke me. When she arrived today, all dressed in blue, with a creamy fur wrapped around her neck, an enormous velvet hat, scented with violets, her cheeks pink and icy from the frost – my heart was in pain... for her sake and for mine. We might have shared a beautiful time together, we might have, we might have, my heart moaned... if it hadn't been for that letter, that damned letter, so terribly clear, assured, persuasive. That Jetmar, what penetrating insight he has, what a persuasive tone... Yes, that tone of his... Milena was uneasy; she looked into my eyes anxiously and asked me too many times if I liked her. Then she talked once again

(102)

about that engineer and about Reichert. God knows I would never have asked her about them. Why did she have to mention them? And Jetmar's letter was lying on the table...

Once she even picked it up. I tore it from her hand. She was startled but she didn't say anything. I asked her what would have happened if that engineer hadn't had second thoughts. She burst into tears. I saw her – not through my own eyes... but through the eyes of Jetmar. Jetmar was in the room, he spoke with poor Milena, he was unsparing with her and with himself...

Now I'm alone, I'm sniveling and getting ready to write her a humble supplication, a groveling apology...

Jetmar is not in the countryside; Jetmar is already here.

I must make sure he never meets Milena. He wouldn't spare her with his venomous remarks. He is rather shy when speaking with women, but he can't help making venomous remarks anyway. She is so kind, so sensitive... it would hurt her. And offend her.

At night

I burned Jetmar's letter. I feel somewhat better for it. And even if he's right, even if he is – I'm happy, and all the rest is meaningless. I don't want to know anything. I am happy. She is my delight and my happiness. A person wants to be happy – must be happy. All the rest, I insist, is meaningless. I want to be happy – and whoever makes me happy deserves my gratitude. Milena has brought me great happiness and does not deserve to be hurt by me. How could I hurt her? Why would I hurt her, when I'm so happy? Let her be whatever she likes, let her even be the sort of girl that Jetmar takes her for, let her lie to me, what does it matter? All the while I feel so blissful.

That Jetmar is a strange one. He really is an idiot. He has never known love; he has never known happiness; he doesn't know how to enjoy life; he has never been young.

He's a pessimist who imagines he has swallowed up all the wisdom in the world. He's hard-hearted because he's dissatisfied. What does he know about life? A strange fellow like him.

Actually I feel sorry for him.

2 March

Infinite, perfect happiness. Every day is different; every day brings some new wonder, adventure, excitement. I can't study. I'll go home for Easter – I'll catch up on everything – but right now I can't. Every day Milena is more beautiful, more lovely and astonishing. Every day I come to know a different woman.

She visits me, even though in doing so she runs the risk that her parents will find out about it. In the beginning she even had to endure my landlady's suspicious glances. Now that has changed. She has won over the strict lady of the house; they've become friends and now the old woman would go to hell and back for her.

She refers to her only as 'our little miss', and her face lights up when she talks about her or when Milena comes for a visit.

Milena has an unusual gift: she can find the right tone when speaking to anyone; effortlessly, she can put herself in that person's position, condition and age. With my landlady she talks in a jovial, respectable, neighborly tone; she has a broad understanding of the present bad times; she fervently shares all her interests, joys and worries. Why, her butcher is just the same – selling meat that's nothing but bone; it's appalling, what a butcher like that thinks he...

Everyone likes her. Must like her. She's not even pretty, but everyone looks at her with pleasure. She spreads warmth, radiance and joy all around her. Her dress is charming. She loves bright, vivid colors, big hats with fluttering trim, white gloves, costly, little lace scarves, and costly, subtle perfumes. She brings light and fragrance to my nasty, dark den, covered in dust and clutter... I never smoke at home anymore so that the scent of her violets lingers in the air...

I think that... even Jetmar would have to like her. That is, if he can like a woman – or anyone at all. At the very least, he would have to tolerate her. To acknowledge that she's very different from the others; that she's clever, talented, sensitive and kind-hearted. He would have to be amazed.

I'd like to see his surprise. At other times I'm terribly afraid of the two of them meeting. Whenever I think of it I freeze up. He'll be savage, he'll make some venomous remark... he'll spoil my wonderful bliss and poison my joy... Of course, I'll never stop liking Milena, I'll never suspect her again, but... in short, I won't be quite as happy anymore.

13 March

Upon my soul, now anything is possible. That is, Jetmar is seriously thinking about completing his studies. What got into him all of a sudden? Why, not long ago he wrote to me insisting that that would never happen. All of a sudden... He's an odd fellow. In the end, he'll finish law and maybe even complete a doctorate, while I... Oh, best not to think about it. Milena is seriously thinking about us getting married someday... well I do too, but I'm not doing anything about it, I'm not making any effort. She reassures me: 'There's still lots of time, we're young, and anyway you can get a job without a degree... my father didn't finish his studies either.'

She's unbelievably gullible and flighty. I like this; it's attractive, but where will it end? Where will it end? I would like her to be mine as soon as possible too... I'd like to provide her with all the comforts she is used to. She doesn't know how to work, can't deny herself anything, can't bear any sacrifice. She's a child of luxury...

The meeting with Jetmar came off surprisingly well. He hardly noticed her when I introduced her in the café, nor did he pay any attention to her later. Intentionally, I think. He hasn't said a thing so far. It's almost irritating.

16 March
Reichert and Váňa are up to something. Šedivý brought it to my attention, but I had already noticed them whispering suspiciously, as if they were planning an experiment. Reichert is furious, of course: he was thrown from the saddle. Váňa had his eye on her too, and so did Šedivý; but he's more aloof and anyway has plenty of other women.

For a long time I couldn't figure out what they were scheming. All those mysterious hints – as if they wanted to provoke Jetmar. As soon as he returned they tried to set up a meeting between him and Milena. I understand! Jetmar is supposed to be the instrument of their revenge. Jetmar is supposed to throw me from the saddle, just as I did Reichert. He's supposed to show me that anyone can have Milena. Well, all right. We'll see! They want to arrange a party and invite Milena and Jetmar. All it would take is one word from me and she wouldn't go; but I want her to go, to meet Jetmar and to show them all –

17 March
The party is the day after tomorrow! They're in a rush! I hear that Jetmar doesn't want to go. That would be silly. I must persuade him myself.

20 March
The law of succession, yes, the law of succession! Now I really will cram; now it really will be a novel without love.

Jetmar is right. Women are all the same; they're all fiends. All you have to do is point your finger and you can have any woman you want. Any woman at all.

The party was a success!

Milenka didn't want to go either. Ha, ha. No, no, she said, she didn't want to socialize. She'd rather be alone with me... But in the end she went. She sat down; tea with rum was served, rum with tea; people smoked... Jetmar was sitting across from her and for a long time was silent. He only drank and smoked and looked at her. She noticed this and was somehow uneasy. Then he stood up and sat down right next to her. She was sitting back a little from the table, caught up in conversation with Šedivý and Váňa. Jetmar sat down and joined their conversation. All of them grew excited and watched in suspense. Reichert grinned like a devil.

In short: Jetmar escorted her home (late in the evening – with me she never wanted to stay out that late), and she's meeting Jetmar again tomorrow.

'Yes, he knows how to handle a woman!' Reichert chuckled, 'My dear boy, he's had so many already! He could show you letters – and not from any old sort of woman either! They weren't your average sort of romance! You should have been careful around him, Vincík!'

But I am calm. Let her go to the devil, that kind of woman...

12 April

Run away somewhere. Start a new life somewhere else. Surrounded by different people. Everything here suffocates me.

Yesterday she came to my room. She is going out with Jetmar now; Jetmar is enchanted; he is gentle; he worships her passionately; but he is also cruel and torments her with his jealousy; he reproaches her for her past; he reproaches her for Reichert, Váňa, Šedivý, me... He loves her deeply... I can understand that. I used to suffer from similar, mild fits, but my happy nature triumphed and I was content with trust and calm, loving light and joy above all else.

She came to see me... I hardly recognized her. Thin, scruffy, careworn. She cried in despair and begged me to help her... She didn't bother a bit about whether or not I was suffering; she was not gentle with the fresh wounds. In wild distress she rambled on about him, only about him, saying that she loved him terribly and that he should never find out what happened between us... For the love of God, she begged me never to tell him that we had once been on familiar terms, that we had kissed, that we had wanted to marry... She would kill herself if he ever found out...

My heart quivered... Why, this is my Milena, my Milena! Why, this is my lovely, sweet fairy tale! My Sylph...

But she did not see the pain in my heart; she did not bother about its trembling. She was delirious with a terrifying passion for that strange, cruel, sad person... She would do anything for him...

Is she really so flighty? Can anyone have her? That's what he – Jetmar – says. He ridicules her. He is not happy with her love, as I once was. He takes no pride in winning such a common prize.

Maybe he is right...

I stagger, astonished and confused. I pity her and I pity Jetmar – but I'm also suffering. Sometimes I'm gripped by rage... the longing for her hasn't died yet –

How she loves him! How beautiful their relationship might be... How beautiful it already is!

Gradually my character retreats entirely from the stage. I am no longer interested in myself alone; I am no longer the first and sole being in the world. How ordinary I am, how petty my concerns and miseries are compared to theirs...

I would like to do something for them. I would like to trample on my bleeding heart, shout down its groaning and sacrifice it to them...

The longing has not died out, but it will die out, I know. It will recede before a more intense and reeling emotion. Their longing, their emotion.

Most of all I would like to run away, somewhere far away.

20 May

Greetings, oh nesting place of my birth! May you be blessed! For the peacefulness, the deliciously clean air, for the span of the horizon, the calm of quiet, merry woods... and for the blossoming orchards, the green fields...

I would like to stay right here for the rest of my life. Prague is far, far behind me, with all its charms, with its abominable cafés, scandals, women, literary polemics – oh, how disgusting all that was and how free I am now...

I'm not happy... but that's not even necessary.

In the morning I go out and the sweet-smelling crispness of May blows over me. I lie down in the woods – for a long time I search for the right place, I choose and try out the spots where I can doze most pleasantly and not think about anything. Finally, I find some corner or other where a blue glitter shimmers through the crowns of the trees. I lie down and stare up at the sky... Perhaps my heart does not even ache any longer.

A tiny, bustling life is all around me. The ants toil through the grass as if it were a virgin forest; the ground moves in places – that's the small forest mice and moles digging under the soil; dry leaves rustle... how mysterious and beautiful it all is...

Perhaps my heart... perhaps my heart does not ache any longer.

The last few days there – such a long way back in Prague – were painful and disturbing. My longing for her died out; my Ego, once so majestic and all-important, shrank humbly back and got out of the way. Jetmar can bring everything under control, can master and dominate everything.

He has broken up with Milena. He believes in it. After appalling and painful scenes, at which I was present, he said the most bitter truths to her face; he was merciless, implacable, artfully vicious. He is within his rights – why, he loves her. And in the end he is also right. She really is the 'lover of all' – the entire world.

She can be faithful for the first month or two – she was faithful to me – as long as no one else comes along likewise demanding total fidelity. If each of us could be satisfied with half, she would love us both. She's just a good-hearted soul. She can't refuse anyone anything.

But her childish and fearless devotion to him is strange. At the same time she is the one who's closest to him, the only one who knows him well.

Some consider him a cheerful fellow, a witty companion, because that's what he shows them. Others are afraid of him; they find his caustic frankness unpleasant; it disturbs their comfortable peace. No one really knows him. Only she is allowed to come close. He can be natural with her – and she is not afraid of him. Calmly, with complete trust, she curls up to him, and I know that she would accept even death from his hands without hesitation.

If he really does leave her, she won't survive the loss. I'm convinced, however, that he will return to her, despite everything I witnessed, despite his own iron-clad arguments.

In the evening that time in the café, a chill ran over me; horror overwhelmed me, horror at his calm, his heartless reason, his truth.

Cold and deliberate, with mathematical precision, he – such a callous lover – listed the reasons compelling him to act as he did.

First of all, she was and always would be a nothing, a nobody. She must marry. And soon. How could he, a creature so decrepit, he, who was so used to his beggar's freedom and joyless nights of boozing – how could he – no, really it was laughable! Was he supposed to trail about the streets with her for a few years, rob her of her reputation and only then perhaps leave her? It was all so clear.

Besides, he wasn't suited to that kind of relationship. Certainly not to marriage. Even if he finished his studies after all and was able to marry her... what kind of marriage would it be? Why, he was useless at everything.

I am another matter altogether, he claims. I should return to her. I am much better suited to her. His nature is too gloomy. He doesn't know how to enjoy life, youth, the delights of the moment, love.

He would be Milena's ruin. She wouldn't save him; she wouldn't be able to make him happy. Not even she could do that. There is no salvation for him any longer! In his life, everything had gone wrong from the start. He had had too much freedom and too soon the fate of the poor drove him out into the world, into the struggle. He was delicate, sensitive, and what he saw, what he encountered, wounded him and deprived him of strength and the ability to live.

He would be Milena's ruin, as he had been the ruin of every woman he had met. While he spoke he trembled nervously and pressed his temples, as if a series of melancholy, desperate scenes, like the one I was witnessing at that moment, were passing before his eyes; as if he were trying to drive away those scenes. As if the eyes of the pale, enraptured, hopeless female creatures who had succumbed to him were fixed on him – that's how he trembled.

At that moment I remembered the many verses by good friends and their stories – how many women they'd seduced, how many women they'd ruined. Oh, those verses and stories! I thought to myself: unwritten verses are the most beautiful and true. A man who has never written or told stories about the women he has ruined, but rather turns pale and quakes at the mere memory; a man who, for reasons of weariness or conscience, calmly steps out of the way of such good fortune – that man is a hero. A man who can arouse a genuine and lasting passion in such a frail girl as Milena, yes, that man is a hero.

I will never forget that evening or the rest of the night. Jetmar drank to excess and yet remained calm, even sober. He talked a great deal, that's true, he talked continuously; the hours passed and morning drew near; he continued to drink and hold forth, but reasonably and calmly, whereas I was already drunk, unable to speak, though I had consumed much less than he... At the very moment we were about to leave, I toppled to the ground...

The next day – I slept in late at Jetmar's – Milena came by. She had received a letter from him, a letter in which he said the same things I had heard the night before, only more bluntly. She came by; she fell on her knees and implored him in God's name; she writhed at his feet, writhed in despair, gripped by convulsions. I still turn pale when I remember that grim scene. How brutal lovers can be... He stood above her, motionless and pale, but without uttering a word, without trembling. Then he spoke:

'Go home. It's impossible.'

After a while, when her agony and weeping had reached a peak, he added, as if intoxicated by his own cruelty:

'Vincek will take pity on you. You'll get over it soon.'

She fell silent and stood up, staring in alarm. He watched her intently, but with ruthless calm. Her eyes roamed about her, confused; she saw something on the table and grabbed it: a knife, a large open pocketknife. We jumped over to tear it away from her but she cut her face inadvertently as she lifted her hand to prevent us from taking the knife.

Fresh blood spurted out; her hand fell and the knife dropped. She pressed her scarf to the wound and rushed out. Jetmar shouted:

'Go after her, please, don't leave her.'

I took her home; on the way she did not speak a word. The cut was slight. I returned to Jetmar's. He was lying on the bed, smoking. One could hardly breathe the air in his room. For a long time we were silent. I was incensed. Finally I began to rebuke him vehemently. He interrupted me:

'For a while she will cry and be in despair, but in a year's time she won't even remember – and she'll be beside herself with joy when her parents choose a groom for her. She will kiss him as passionately as she did me, as she did you; she will swear to him that she never loved anyone before she met him – and once again she'll believe it.'

Devastated, I fell silent. I stayed at Jetmar's that night too, and when I woke towards morning, I saw him sitting at the table. He had her picture in front of him, her letters, and he was crying bitterly.

I don't believe they have separated. I think they will be reconciled – they must be reconciled. They will never be happy together, but they cannot live apart from one another. Whatever sort of girl Milena is, he has had too great an influence on her, and she won't be able to forget him. And he found in her much more than a lover; she was also his best friend – whatever her flaws. She is a rare good-hearted soul. That's important. We should not make fun of good souls. They are precious in this sad world, and we need them.

Thus my thoughts run on, and peace and languor leave me in this most lovely forest twilight – in my thoughts I'm back in cursed Prague, in the whirl of life; I can't cut myself loose! I can't heal myself!

1 October
So summer has passed, beautiful, fiery, golden summer has passed... I'm in Prague once again; I stagger through the streets; I know that I have lost a great deal; there, in the tedium of the eternal sunlight and peaceful woods, I was

happy, healthy; here, turmoil and cares await me; but I am refreshed, and it seems to me that there is a moist, grateful, tender glitter in my eyes...

To the café! All my friends are here. Hello there! But not all of them are here. Where is Jetmar?

He has not yet returned. He's ill. He coughed up blood. He never was healthy and always lived in poverty...

Yes, he wrote me once in the summer, saying he was feeling poorly. I soon went out again to the street. It was almost evening; Petřín Hill was turning black against the scarlet sunset. I thought I might go home and write to Jetmar.

I saw Milena in front of the house. Quiet, beautiful, deathly sad... a Madonna... She still has a scar on her left cheek. A small, pink scar.

'What have you heard about Jetmar? Is it true he's ill?'

True...

'I write to him – he doesn't answer. It's over, long over, I know. But I can't accept it. I can't forget. Write to him yourself, he'll answer you – and then you can give me news...'

I have to sit for the state examination in fourteen days. God knows I'm indifferent to it all.

20 October

Jetmar's back, terribly wasted; he drags himself about like a shadow; he doesn't have an overcoat, doesn't eat dinner... I go walking with him. We talk about all sorts of things...

It is silly, comic and silly. Two people have sworn to themselves: we won't talk about her. Two people have taken a solemn oath: not one word about her. They don't think of anything – of anything else but her. A desperate craving burns in the eyes of one of them – a craving to hear some news, to hear even her name... The other would desperately like to talk. His longing was extinguished long ago, broken, shouted down. All summer he sought a substitute, all summer he sought and believed that he would find one, that he would forget... Now he is entirely theirs once again.

She knows that Jetmar is in Prague. She has already seen him. But she doesn't want to meet him. She is bitter. He doesn't love her, he never loved her. A lover could never write such a wise, noble letter. Lovers are never noble or conscientious. He liked her when he was cruel to her. But now it's all over. Well, she's not going to throw herself on him! Mr. Jetmar better not think that! And not one more word about him.

She will be happy, happy once again, as she used to be. She laughs loudly, yes, but her eyes glisten with pain.

A terrible comedy – I can't watch – my heart aches. In the end they will be reconciled, that is certain, so why all this heartrending distress and torment?

Funny how someone as clever as Jetmar can act like such a child...

27 October
So yesterday they made up. 'No, never! The end, impossible!' It went on and on like that on both sides. And all the while both hearts were yearning, seeking one another... But perhaps they didn't even realize that they thought of nothing else but how to meet again as soon as possible.

Yesterday he waited for her from the morning on, in the street where she lives, until finally she came out before noon.

Once again they are the happiest of lovers and can't keep their eyes off one another...

Until his misery erupts again, until mistrust rears up, until he begins to wonder how she passed her time in that lively spa town where she spent the holidays this year with her parents... It will be terrible! She doesn't think about it; she believes that everything has been resolved once and for all. Poor little lamb!

How will it all turn out? I can't imagine how it will end. Is this love or only the senseless torment of two sick, weak, passionate souls who had the misfortune to meet?

What about his good sense, the reasons he gave that night in the café, the letter he sent... He was telling the truth that night, after all, the iron-clad truth.

How will it all end? Once her parents find out... They believe she has listened to reason and left him. She's very careful now, but one day they'll hear about it all the same. Then, I think, she will be prepared to do anything. She might even run away from home. Certainly someday she'll run away from home...

19 November
Fate has intervened.

I stand before a mystery that I will never be able to solve. I ask questions, I call out – no one answers anymore. I analyze this peculiar case; I know that anything was possible – but what might have happened, that I will never learn.

Nothing would have surprised me. Anything was possible with my friend Jetmar and his good, childlike sweetheart – once upon a time my Sylph. Not even the wildest imagination could have overshot the mark in this instance.

Fate severed the thread. Oh wretched, ailing heart, now you will rest.

They covered up the pit, they covered up the hushed heart for which everything was a torment: youth, love, talent, happiness...

What will the Sylph do now? They have taken her off somewhere, so that she can forget... That is, if she doesn't die!

19 November, once again. A year has passed... exactly a year. Oh, my friend, you said it yourself – 'in a year's time,' you said.

This morning I went down to the embankment to take in the view of Prague after the first snowfall. I was feeling fine. I had a good chance to get a nice little job – I could still complete my studies if I wanted, but even if I didn't complete them – which was more likely – I wouldn't be lost. I was feeling fine. I had pictured a completely different career for myself, but so what? In the end a person doesn't need much to feel content...

I'm walking along, looking at the ground... And on seeing the footprints in the loose, fresh snow, I suddenly feel as if the past were stirring from that snow, yes, from that snow... I recognize some small footprints, I hear a familiar rhythm of steps, slowly I raise my eyes... I see the hem of a skirt winding like a snake over the footprints, over the rhythm of the steps – I raise my eyes still further...

'How do you do, Miss...'

'Oh, Mr. Staněk, hello!'

A childlike, rosy little face; large, lovely, innocent eyes; little teeth which flash in happy laughter... The scar on the left cheek has already vanished...

We exchange all the latest tidbits of news; she – is engaged. What do you say to that? Well, I'm surprised, that is... I'm not surprised, it's totally natural after all... Congratulations...

'At first I didn't want to, you know – but when mama tried so hard to persuade me, when I saw what joy I would bring...'

'Oh, so you sacrificed yourself...'

'Well, yes, almost, don't laugh; it's wonderful to make someone happy... To submit... And now we're shopping, we're preparing the trousseau, I'm learning how to cook...'

We chatted together for about half an hour, no longer. Then I said goodbye. But during that half-hour her shallow, simple exuberance somehow seemed to grow pale... As if she remembered something sad and beautiful, from long ago, as if she shuddered at the tawdriness of her present joy, at the wretched emptiness of her days... The poor good soul!

At first I was furious – a memory of the dead ached in my soul – but now, when I reflect on it more reasonably, I feel compassion for her and envy for him.

His life was bitter, but he lived it in his own way. He was no one's puppet; he was no wretched, ridiculous puppet, without will or character. But she, perhaps only because she was born a woman, was a slave, and always would be a slave.

Or was she better off? Was it her good fortune?

I don't know. But I'm still sorry for the poor good soul.

EVA

GABRIELA PREISSOVÁ

A Picture from Slovakia[1]

Finally both peasant women, Mrs. Mešjanová and Mrs. Kotlibová, finished their shopping at the fair and set out for Mrs. Mešjanová's cart, engaged in friendly conversation; they were ready to go back home to Mikulec. Mrs. Kotlibová, a sluggish, stout woman, carried in her arms a charming spinning-wheel for her daughter and a little sewing chest; it was all in the latest fashion, with a simple ridged pattern done on a lathe and sanded down to the yellow grain. In addition, she carried a full bag over her arm, and umpteen gingerbread rosaries for her godchildren and the tenant's children were strung around her neck. It was such a burden that she could hardly breathe. Although she considered herself better off than Mrs. Kotlibová, dry, lanky Mrs. Mešjanová was not ashamed to carry a canvas basket on her back, and so she walked along in greater comfort, with her hands free, and looked around on all sides in order not to miss anything.

Thus they arrived in front of Ehrenstein's tavern on the edge of town on the Skalica road; Mrs. Kotlibová was the first to climb up on the cart and settle both herself and her purchases comfortably. Meanwhile, Mrs. Mešjanová went into the tavern to pay the landlord for the pint of new wine she had ordered for the driver when they had first arrived. To warm herself for the return journey, she ordered a little tot of sweet spirits. It was the third one she had had in Skalica that day; people knew that, to her disgrace, she liked to tipple.

1 The short story was written two years before the drama bearing the same title (Gazdina roba).

Only then did she make her way to the cart, throw her basket into the straw and sit down beside her neighbor. 'Let's be going and God speed,' she ordered the driver.

'So the sun came out from the fog before All Saints' Day after all,' Mrs. Kotlibová, who was flushed and sweating, said loudly. 'I needn't have taken the fur coat. If I'd put a bodice on underneath, I'd take my coat off right now.'

'I feel best in my fur coat,' Mrs. Mešjanová said with satisfaction. 'Since the marriage of my eldest daughter I've had such chills that I wear a fur coat even in the summer.'

Mrs. Kotlibová bent over the bag placed at her feet next to the side of the cart and took out a bottle wrapped in a scarf.

'I didn't forget you,' she said, with an affectionate smile; 'I bought you a bottle of Kümmel in the shop further up. A body gets all shaken up on the road – here you are, have a drink.'

'God bless you, neighbor,' Mrs. Mešjanová thanked her for her thoughtfulness, and took a swig from the bottle – but ever so demurely.

'Go ahead and drink as much as you like... it's good for you,' Mrs. Kotlibová urged her again.

'Now it's your turn...'

'Oh, I wouldn't dare; the blood is rising to my head as it is – I'm so hot,' Mrs. Kotlibová excused herself. But in truth, every kind of spirit disgusted her because her deceased husband had committed so many sins on account of them. 'You just keep that bottle for yourself,' she urged her, "as it is we've still got the plum brandy from last year at home, in case anyone feels poorly.'

'I'll have one more sip, just to please you,' said Mrs. Mešjanová, 'and then I'll set this bottle down here among the shopping so that it doesn't fall over. Thank you kindly.'

'You're welcome,' said Mrs. Kotlibová, and her voice grew softer: 'Why, we've been friends for so long, and the Lord visited widowhood upon us both. Only your poor late husband left you your farmstead in good order. Dear God, what worries I had day and night before I could pay off those few acres of ours for the two girls. And for myself I plan to keep only that cottage across from the church; I'll rent half of it to a tenant and I'll live off that in my old age, together with the bit of land I'll keep. And I'm always telling the eldest one, Mariška: there's no other home I'd rather let you go to than those two big Mešjany farms – if only on account of that good neighbor of ours.'

'Yes, I know,' Mrs. Mešjanová nodded her head, smiling, 'and that's what I think too: Mariška would fit in nicely with us.'

'And she – I'd only say this to you – never talks of anyone else but Mánek. I know it would ease your mind; you've got your daughters married and for the boy – for him only a decent bride will do. What do you need worries and toil for? The same with me – we've already done our share. But,' she finished with a heavy sigh, 'Mánek is his own worst enemy, on account of that seamstress...'

'You don't think I want him to have her? Except as a joke.'

'Oh, I know. But he causes you and his sisters so much suffering and trouble. That stuttering Káča told us recently that she sees him going there night after night.'

Mrs. Mešjanová straightened up in a huff: 'That's her disgrace, not his. I'm not going to stand guard over the boy.'

'On top of it all she's a Lutheran, dear God,' Mrs. Kotlibová wistfully commiserated out loud with Mrs. Mešjanová's difficulties – but leaning over, she suddenly grew alert again: 'Look, look – it's her – over there!'

They were drawing up on two young people who were also making their way back from the fair on foot, walking along a path by the road following the woods. A country youth – or rather, an older man, because except for the feather in his hat he didn't look youthful and the poor fellow limped a little – that was Samko Jagoš, the furrier from Mi-kulec. Both of the women knew that, although a Lutheran, he was a decent and capable man. Not long before he had made such handsome fur coats for both of them that other Slovak women at the fair, strangers, had turned around to admire them. In addition, he was equally skilled at sewing trousers, bonnets, even slippers and regular shoes. He had inherited a little house from his parents; out of his savings he had already bought six half-acres and he also had a pret-ty tidy sum in florins from the goods he had sold people; if it weren't for that physical defect of his, every peasant girl would have her eye on him.

By his left side walked a tall, agile girl with a dark complexion, piercing black eyes and above them shining eyebrows that joined in the middle, making a rather star-tling, strange first impression. But all in all there was so much grace in the regular features and healthy color of her face, in the coral-red lips and white teeth, that everyone said she was pretty. She carried a bag filled with string, silk and wool for embroidery, and a roll of cloth under her arm. Her clothes were clean; the apron and white tulle scarf were remarkable for their embroidery; her bodice and skirt, for their design and elaborate edging; her high boots for their new shine. 'She's a good seamstress,' envious girls would say, 'and she keeps her best work for her-self.'

When the girl was pointed out to her, Mrs. Mešjanová's forehead wrinkled and her lips puckered. 'Stop, Jano!' she shouted to the driver, when they had driven past the pedes-trians, adding in a hushed voice to her neighbor: 'Wait and see what I tell that tart.'

And she got ready to climb down.

Mrs. Kotlibová did not hold her back. She suspected that Mrs. Mešjanová intended to humiliate Eva and she wished it upon the girl.

'Careful – be careful,' was all she said as Mrs. Mešjanová climbed down, holding her by the tail of her fur coat out of friendly consideration.

As soon as her neighbor reached the ground, Mrs. Kotlibová looked back so that she could watch what happened.

Sure enough, Mrs. Mešjanová rushed back about ten steps, then came to a stop, and seeing the two young people cross to the other side as if to avoid her, she also hurried across the road and came up practically face to face with Eva.

The furrier doffed his hat and Eva greeted her quietly and politely: 'Good evening.' At the same time, she bowed her head unusually low, and a visible shudder passed over her.

'Listen you shameless, meddlesome hussy,' Mrs. Mešjanová brought her up short, and in her agitation she tugged at her scarf with both hands, quivering with anger like a whip, 'it's no disgrace for our Mánek, but for you, you Lutheran tart, you blowzy hussy! How dare you entice a boy with two farms down to your beggary – you've got no God and no true faith!'

At that point, she stopped short. Lame Samko had reared up in front of her like an outlaw – he made as if to whack her over the head with his stick...

At that, Mrs. Kotlibová shrieked, 'Oh my Lord – calm down, Samko!' Climbing down quickly, she hurried over to separate them. The astonished driver also jumped down and ran over to defend his mistress.

Eva had turned as pale as a sheet; yet, on hearing Mrs. Mešjanová's insults, her look grew defiant. Her protector's hand dropped after Mrs. Kotlibová's shout, but he began to defend his companion with words:

'How dare you attack the girl? You should tell off Mánek instead – that would be more appropriate! And you reproach her for her faith? Do you think your God is better than ours because you kiss a stone or wooden statue? Come on, Eva, let the mad woman rant – why, she's probably drunk again!' he added, more gently, speaking to the girl.

And they walked on. At that moment Eva was not even aware that he was leading her by the hand...

Meanwhile, Mrs. Mešjanová had succumbed to tears of anger and fright. Mrs. Kotlibová consoled her by berating Eva and Samko, and solicitously accompanied her neighbor back to the cart. In her heart she was pleased by Mrs. Mešjanová's indignant fluster because she knew that Mánek would come in for it at home too – and it served him right. Why didn't he pay attention to Mariška, after all?

Samko headed straight for the woods with the girl; the path was not as good underfoot as the one by the road, but he wanted Eva to get away from the angry looks of the women who were driving off.

They walked on for a good while in silence, until suddenly, when they had come up to a barrier across a track cut into the woods, Eva stopped and held onto it; a look of pride changed her face and she said bitterly:

'They accuse me of shamelessness and enticing a man – and believe me, Samko, upon my soul, I avoided Mánek for a long time because he was my social superior. Maybe that family of his thinks my father and my aunt are trying to talk him into it – and meanwhile they torment me because of him.'

Eva's voice grew wistful, yet she did not break into tears. Samko fell to thinking, and as they walked on slowly he said awkwardly: 'Evuška – Mánek will never marry you...'

'That's what they all tell me,' Eva retorted sharply and lifted her head again obstinately, 'but I say that he would lead me to the altar in spite of all the world – only I wouldn't marry him.'

Samko looked at her in astonishment: 'So why do you talk to him and act like his lass in public, at every dance?'

'Because I feel like it,' she explained curtly, and then more kindly: 'It's hard to say...'

'You know, Evuška...,' Samko began again, humble and dejected, after a short silence, 'you're a strange girl – I don't understand you. But I do know this much for sure: you wouldn't want Mánek as a husband, on account of the difference in religion and the reproaches for your inferiority. But why do you worry yourself so needlessly? Me – don't be angry with me – I never stop thinking about you, and if it weren't for this defect of mine I would have fought Mánek for you a long time ago, even if it cost me my life.'

He fell silent, blushing all over; his tender gray eyes were clouded by a mist and something seemed to struggle in his throat as if his voice would fail him. As he walked, he poked holes in the ground with the metal tip of his stick, and studied this useless work attentively, without looking at Eva. She suddenly came to a stop.

'Samko,' she said, quietly but earnestly, dropping her eyes, 'you needn't be afraid – I will marry you. But what about your parents? Won't they hold it against you that I have nothing to bring to the household except the decent clothes I've managed to afford with my embroidery work?'

'Oh, Eva, my dear heart!' Samko laughed happily. 'How can you think of something so childish? On the contrary, they'll say to me: "Look at that, you got such a pretty and capable woman!" Until I die, I will cherish you and act accordingly, so that you wouldn't have had it any better with the Mešjanys! When will we have the wedding?'

'Maybe after Christmas – when I've finished the work I'm sewing at home for customers, as well as some bonnets for myself,' Eva decided, speaking in a firm voice. 'I have a fine sheet and feather bedding too – left to me by my mother...'

'If you had nothing,' Samko gestured casually, 'I would be even happier; that way you wouldn't think I cared about such trifles.'

'The farm went to my younger brother,' he continued almost peevishly, as they walked on, 'and on top of that the good Lord granted him health and better looks than me. He got a thousand florins as his wife's dowry – but I have to laugh at him when I compare my own good fortune to his!'

And now he really did laugh, happily and wistfully.

When Eva, overwhelmed by the extent of her promise, still did not feel like talking, Samko noticed a little snail on the path and picked it up.

'Look,' he said, showing Eva his palm, 'the Lord has granted existence to all sorts of things in the world. How lovely and ridiculous it is in its insignificance!' A moment later he noticed the yellow, fallen leaves on the path, swirling in the wind. He talked about how the geraniums, rosemary and marjoram in his windows were still as green as they had been in the spring. Then he started looking forward to renting a meadow in the spring, and if Eva wanted, he would buy her two cows so that she would have something to farm with.

Gradually it grew dark. They arrived home around seven o'clock, when the stars were already out, and the happy Samko accompanied Eva all the way to her cottage. He pressed her hand warmly, wishing her good night, and promised that he would come by the next afternoon...

When she went into the cottage, Eva greeted her father and her aunt and silently began to take off her good Sunday clothes. She changed into her everyday clothes, removed her boots and remained barefoot.

Meanwhile the aunt, an old woman already bent with age, examined the purchases in the bag and then brought dinner to the table: potato rolls with damson-cheese left over from lunch and re-heated in the oven.

'How was the fair?' her father asked.

'The same as it always is when the weather doesn't spoil it,' Eva answered briefly, sitting down to dinner without any appetite at all.

'You've come back in a testy mood!' her aunt commented.

'I'll tell you all about it,' Eva said, absorbed in thought, 'but later, when I feel like it... Please don't ask me questions now...'

The old folk were used to letting her have her way; their reproaches were sighs, and they used threats in melancholy prophecy. Eva was their main provider, since the old tailor couldn't manage much anymore. So they partook of dinner in silent expectation. Then the aunt, having cleared the table, began to cut up the skeins Eva had bought and to braid them into little coils for embroidery. The tailor lit his wooden pipe and, giving himself up to his beloved puffing of tobacco mixed with clover stems, he started to darn a child's blouse. Eva also fetched some work – worsted cloth for embroidered dress shirts – and she sat down at the table close to the lamp.

Then she looked about in a rather more lively manner at the old folk and said:

'Papa – today on the way back from Skalica I agreed to marry Samko the furrier; we'll be married after Christmas...'

'What did you say?!' her father shouted, and her aunt suddenly dropped the box of coils and balls of thread from her lap. 'Oh my – what was that?' she called out in turn.

'It's done,' Eva continued; their surprise brought a weak smile to her face. 'Tomorrow Samko will come to speak to you. You always prophesied that I would come to misfortune with Mánek: now you can be reassured; today I will send him away for good.' At that her lips contorted and trembled a little, but the old folk did not notice because she had bent closer over her work.

'Praise be to God,' her father said and taking his pipe from his mouth, he bowed twice. 'That is good news. How did you fix it, Evuška?'

'I can't help wondering if I'm dreaming,' her aunt said, childishly, 'for me it's a joy beyond belief.'

'You can believe it now,' Eva said, 'you well know I never say anything I don't mean. Like the others, you used to say that a young man who would inherit two farms hadn't been raised for me, but I'll show you that I don't care for him, even if he goes crazy. At least that family of his will find out who was enticing whom.'

'Those are golden words, Evuša, you've got good sense. And Samko is of our faith – so your union will be blessed.'

'He will cherish me,' the girl went on, grateful for her father's praise, but first she had to swallow a bitter memory she did not want to share. 'He told me that he didn't care if I was poor. When we get married, he'll buy me two cows; both of you will have enough help from us.'

'Thanks be to God,' her aunt sighed happily. 'You see, my dear heart, even if you had gone and married Mánek, I wouldn't be as pleased as I am now. It's true that he has two farms and a handsome face, and neither of you is to blame for that church of his, as you sometimes used to say. But truly, he's not a good man. He doesn't have Samko's heart, nor did anything good ever come from him. I remember how as a little boy Mánek once arranged a procession of birds and dragged them over the outskirts of the village. He tied them together in pairs on a string, always a goose with a hen, ducks with chicks, and those poor goslings at the end. He and his gleeful friends thought it was so funny the way the fowl limped after him with their legs bound together. I was just walking by and I said to myself that even if his mind matured, a good man would never grow out of a heart like that. Otherwise would he have talked so often here about his own mother with such disrespect?

And he was so rude about his sisters too: bony hags, witless, foul-tempered, and whatever else tripped off his tongue.'

'He's not so bad or so coarse,' Eva said, staring at the flame of the oil lamp, which was as good as new. 'It's just that he doesn't let people see the good that's in him.' And the sweet gaze and words of love she knew so well flashed before her dazzled eyes. What could anyone else know about his kindness!...

'Whatever he's like – let the woman he gets find out...' her father said.

Eva looked at the clock and put down her sewing.

'I'm so tired today from the walk,' she excused herself. 'I'll go to bed early. Anyway, after eight Mánek will come for the last time to the window, or to the hall. In the meantime I'll watch for him in the twilight and figure out what to say to him. Good night, papa.'

'Good night!' her father alone replied, for the aunt slept in the same room as the girl.

Eva went out through the dark hall to the outer door. At the doorstep, she looked around. As yet, no one was around. The autumn evening was warm, even though there was a slight wind, rustling the withered climbers and runner beans on the low fence, as well as the thyme and the sunflowers in the little garden in front of the cottage. To the left, beneath the window of Eva's room, lay an overturned trough against which Mánek used to rest his knees, for when he stood up, the window at which Eva's head appeared was too low. Now bareheaded Eva sat down on the trough and folded her hands in her lap. A shiver passed over her because of the heaviness in her head; she stamped her bare feet and looked up at the starry sky.

As she did, something seemed to lift her up and transplant her to an unfamiliar plot of earth; she did not see the fence, or even the familiar cottage across the way. She remembered the song of her melancholy friend Zuzka Líčeníková, who had recently returned from service in Moravia. It welled up in Eva's breast too, so that she crooned it quietly:

'There's a weight,
a weight on my heart
as if it were bound
by a ribbon...

A ribbon
I can undo but
you, my lass
I cannot forget.'

Yet she was at home in her garden after all – Mánek was hurrying this way. Eva stood up and took a few steps back towards the front door. 'Hello...' she said shyly, not at all as she had intended to address the young man. He grabbed both her hands and said breathlessly:

'I've been running and I'm as mad as a devil. You have to bring me to my senses or else I'll get shamelessly drunk tonight and smash something.'

'Why?' Eva asked, suspecting something, and slipped out of his grip.

Mánek did not even notice because of the important explanation he wanted to give. Leaning against the doorpost, he pushed his cap down over his eyebrows and began with frank urgency: 'What I've had to endure today because of you! Mama came back from the fair ranting and raving and started going on about you, and my sister Beta, who had run over to our place, joined in too. She said that I would have to stop seeing you and pay attention to freckle-faced Maryša Kotlibová instead. But I said: "What's that?! Anything else?" Well, she said that she would dispose of my inheritance, the thousand florins my father left me, and would make both farms over to my brothers-in-law. I really let her have it then. She can go ahead and do it! We've got plenty of money to make a start together; we'll rebuild your cottage and I'll be happy to go work in the fields. Then let my family be ashamed of me.'

'Nothing of the sort will happen to you,' Eva retorted, gathering all her strength to speak in a cold, preaching voice. 'I will never marry you; after Christmas Samko the furrier and I are getting married – I've already given him my word.'

'You must be joking!' said Mánek. 'Don't say such things; it sends a shiver down my spine.'

'It's not a joke – I'm speaking the honest truth, I swear to God! Go on home, Mánek, tell your mother you're sorry and stay on good terms with your family. Even Maryša Kotlibová – or another woman, as long as she's rich and Catholic – be happy with her, as I will be with Samko. Your mother cursed me, calling me a blowzy hussy and saying that I was godless. For a long time I've known that I would never marry you, but now I swear on my soul that the heavens will fall before I go to the altar with you. Tell everyone that I wouldn't allow it, and if you still care for me a little, stay away from me...'

Towards the end her voice began to fail her. She turned away quickly in front of the stupefied Mánek and, running into the hall, she locked both halves of the door.

Dumbfounded and lifeless, the youth stood there on the spot for a long while. It seemed to him as if he had grown numb from the inside. Finally his head began to ache and his eyes moistened.

It occurred to him that he didn't deserve such cruelty from Eva. Even when he was in a bad mood he didn't distress her with hard words. He still did not believe what she had said.

He reeled into the garden and sat down, cowed, on the trough, with his head hanging.

After about two hours, when the whole village had already grown quiet and the sky had grown lighter, he stood up with difficulty, moved over to the window and tapped on the glass pane.

Nothing moved inside the room. The youth tapped once again, more vehemently, and called out: 'Evuša – Eva!' His voice was tinged with anguish. At that moment a woman's dejected voice called out inside the room: 'Take care of yourself, Mánek – and may God look after you!'

The youth forced himself to stand up by the cottage, and when this farewell had sunk in, he broke into a wild run.

Four years passed and those who earlier had met in bitterness and passion on the paths of Mikulec found themselves together at one table at a wedding feast.

The Mikulec village magistrate was hosting the wedding of his only daughter, and for the sake of her constant love and a good livelihood, he was giving her, a Catholic girl, away to a Lutheran farmer from another village. Thus two kinds of wedding ceremonies and festivities were being celebrated at once, and the magistrate's family had cordially invited almost the entire village, except the poorest cottagers and farm laborers. Out of neighborly good will, all of those invited came; and to the delight of the hosts, both of the officiating clergymen had honored the celebrations with their presence – the elderly Lutheran parson and the young, gracious priest from the Catholic parish. They sat next to one another in harmony at the head of the endless table, engaged in brilliant conversation. The serious parson voiced the wistfulness, and the young priest the hope, of certain ideals, but when their eyes met those of the other guests, they encouraged them to go and enjoy themselves. The young people did not need to be encouraged. They were gathered all the way from the corner where the groom had humbly withdrawn with the radiant young girl, still wearing her wreath, to the further end by the door, and their ardent faces would have liked best to run away from the plates and goblets to the musicians in the room opposite.

'Well, I'll be damned, the Gypsies are going to play,' the youth sitting furthest away said excitedly, 'it's going to be some dance!' And he whispered this to one of the bridesmaids, hardly able to keep himself from letting out a whoop.

Now they were already playing. Who would be first to rise from the table?... It should have been the newlyweds, but they, grown serious, waited for the others to drag them there; one of the groomsmen clapped his hands in vain to the music as he capered about. At that moment the bridesmaid to whom the youth had whispered stood up as if she were only going to brush something from her skirt – but all the single men and women stood up at once as well and dragged the newlywed couple along with them; they all rushed out in a flurry across the hall to the room opposite.

The door stood wide open; from the table one could see how the skirts and high boots were already flying...

Even after the young people had left, things livened up in the dining-room as well, stirred by the sound of the Gypsy music. A beribboned old groomsman, having ushered the young people out, returned to the room flashing his fine teeth; he went up to one older woman, of whom it was said she would dance with the devil himself. And indeed, she did not turn him down...

Young Mešjany, now married, followed their example and led out his wife Maryša, dressed in her new silk skirt, to dance. Marriage had hardly changed either of them; Mánek demonstrated to those present how much he loved his wife; he led her from the room with an arm wound gallantly around her waist – yet he could not completely conceal a certain awkwardness. His mother and Mrs. Kotlibová, who were sitting next to each other, smiled after them; and when they had gone through the door, Mrs. Mešjanová's gaze slid across to the furrier and his wife by the window. With gentle malice, she poked her neighbor with her elbow and whispered something to her. She, in turn, curled her lips contemptuously at Eva, Jagoš's wife, who was staring over at them at that moment. With visible indignation, Eva tossed her head and her eyes flashed like two coals. In the meantime, the young cartwright Mucha was negotiating with her husband: 'Will you kindly permit me, Samko, to take a few turns with your wife. My Borka has already grown too dignified, she doesn't want to move from the bench...'

'Eva can go, if she wants,' Samko said good-naturedly.

The tall woman stood up obligingly and without a smile left the room with the cartwright. Meanwhile, Mánek was returning with Maryša, and they met in the hall... At that moment Eva gave Mánek such a strange look that he started and Maryša felt a stab in her heart. If they had been at home or somewhere on their own, she would have scolded her husband for letting himself be unsettled by a glance – but what could she do here at the feast?

Mánek led her to a spot beside the cheerful teacher and his wife, but after drinking a little wine, he left again in a hurry, rather uneasily. Where to? Maryša inclined her head. 'Just as I thought, back to the dance, perhaps to her...' A moment later, the cartwright Mucha returned – alone... As soon as the cartwright had stopped dancing with Eva, Mešjany grabbed her. The Gypsies had just finished playing a rather long song, but like a madman, Mánek, without letting go of Eva, took a handful of coins from his pocket and threw them to the musicians, calling out: 'Play!'

Obediently, they launched into a csardas mazurka. Mánek clasped Eva close to him and they began to dance. Once they had been graceful dancing partners, but now their feet did not move nimbly over the floor. Mánek felt the beating of Eva's heart and he lost the tune of the mazurka in a wild medley of emotions, delight and pain. And Eva slipped from his arms – suddenly they were standing in the corner by the stove, while the others reveled noisily in the dance. Just then the groom let out a whoop next to them; unrestrained gaiety was swirling by, but to them it seemed like some oppressive dream.

Finally Mánek said in an uncertain voice: 'How are you, Evuša?' – and every vein in his face tingled in agitation. While Eva was thinking up an indifferent reply, her eyes flickered over to the door and once again they flashed like two coals. Maryša was standing there at the side of Mrs. Mešjanová, and then they headed rather angrily towards Eva and Mánek.

'I can't say anything now,' Eva mumbled hurriedly, 'if you want, come tomorrow at nine o'clock in the evening to the path on your corn field.'

Now it was Mánek who did not answer – the women were already standing in front of them.

'Is it proper for you to leave your wife sitting while you catch hold of this woman?' Mrs. Mešjanová asked in a subdued tone, but with a contemptuous emphasis on the last word. 'You should be ashamed of yourself!'

Eva's words alone resounded in Mánek's head and chest. Confused, without uttering a single word of protest, he returned to the dining-room with his family, and Eva stayed where she was, alone.

After a moment she collected herself and without looking around at anyone else, she went to sit down by her husband. Samko was also anxious; he was ready to go home, for he missed their little daughter Katečka.

'Then let's go...' Eva agreed – and so the Jagošes were the first to leave the celebration, saying their thanks and accepting a gift from the mother of the bride.

The next evening, Mánek walked about on the path in the field with a beating heart for half an hour, but Eva still had not come.

It was a warm night after Whitsun, but so dark that it was most likely about to rain.

When he had left his house, Mánek had been pleased it was so dark, but now it distressed him; he imagined that Eva, expecting rain, would not come, or that she had come by another route and they had missed each other in the dark. Or was it all a plan to hurt him? Suddenly he sensed, with his heart rather than with his eyes or ears, that she was nearby; and indeed, a moment later she came hurrying up with a spinning-wheel in her arms, which she set down on the ground.

'You came after all,' Mánek addressed her softly. 'I'd started to think that what you said yesterday was meant to make me suffer.'

'Well, it was foolish of me,' Eva complained dejectedly. 'What's the point?'

'And I was so pleased in my heart,' the young farmer replied. 'Believe me, Evuša, I'm often in a bad way. It would have been better perhaps if I had taken my life that time when you sent me away – taken my life, as I had wanted to do. Only the mortal sin which would have fallen on my soul kept me from doing so. What do I have from life now? I have the two children, but they too are unable to please me. I get along with Maryša all right, but only for appearances' sake – my heart cannot grow fond of her. Don't be angry with me for such harsh words, but all of this is on your conscience.'

His voice became tearful – and he even began to cry.

Eva was touched to the depths of her soul. Yesterday and a thousand times before she had felt that she was unhappy, that she would have to carry Mánek in her thoughts until her death. His lovely black eyes were with her day and night, while she was working and in her thoughts, and in her sleep she heard his voice. It was a hard life, as if under the curse of a love violently crushed ... And that family of his and Maryša still persecuted her, instead of recognizing that she had put them to shame.

'I had to do it because of that persecution,' she lamented in turn, without her old pride – 'and so that everyone would know I hadn't enticed you – whenever he thought of you, my poor dead father would always sigh, and he and my aunt prophesied all the worst for me. Now my aunt is always saying when she's at our home: "You've provided well for yourself, so you must be happy," – but no one knows the truth. Samko is a good man, but I can't get used to him; he still repels me... On top of it all he went on at me today, scolding me as he would a foolish child for going to dance with you yesterday without his permission. He forbade me to speak to you ever again. At that I said to him: Don't press me! If I feel like it, I'll go after him right now!'

'You would have me even now?' Mánek asked in a trembling voice.

'Why, if you were a Lutheran, maybe I'd get a divorce and marry you. They would give me custody of the little girl, just like they did the notary's wife in Hrozenkov, the one who got married again and her former husband remarried too... Samko would truly be happier with another woman. Oh, dear God!'

'Evuša,' a feverish thought occurred to Mánek – 'let's not allow others to trouble us! If you did not give free reign to your heart when you were single, do it now – oh, I know that you love only me, as I do you! In my church, it's not possible for me to get a divorce, but I could convert to your faith, and then it could be done. Once I heard in the pub that a painter from Vienna did that, and the daughter of a grand gentleman, a general, married him. In the meantime, come with me anyway – what do we care what people say? This year I have a farming contract in Austria; I've promised to take two hundred people there for seasonal work on a great estate; I'll manage them there from Trinity Sunday until the beet is harvested. We'll stay there for five months and it will earn me at least eight hundred florins. My wife won't come with me: someone has to stay here to mind the place. I wanted to take the sexton's widow with me to do the woman's work – but why couldn't I present you there instead as the mistress of the farm and my wife? For the duration of those five months we would be two happy people, and in the meantime I would take steps with some lawyer or other for us to be able to marry. In the meantime, your aunt could look after your daughter.'

'And what about your children – your wife, your family?' Eva objected gloomily.

'But you would be making the same sacrifice. And Maryša – you know they forced me on her; and she knew that too – so why did she marry me? I would see to the children; I'm not made of stone, so I couldn't turn away from the poor things. That notary couple from Hrozenkov had children too and yet they even managed to settle things well with them; they are held in respect.'

A long, painful silence set in. Finally Mánek spoke up: 'Why did you bring that spinning-wheel?'

'I couldn't get away from home except by saying that I was going to a spinning party somewhere,' Eva replied. 'They thought it was rather strange.'

'So, my dear heart, what answer will you give me?' Mánek whispered, and seizing her in his arms, he covered her cheeks with passionate kisses. Eva finally freed herself and began to run away from him ...

'Wait!' Mánek called in a hushed voice. 'The spinning-wheel!'

She came back and, taking the spinning-wheel he was holding out to her, made to run away again without a word.

'You're in such a hurry,' Mánek reproached her, 'and you don't say a thing about what we should do.'

'I have the little girl here,' she whispered in a trembling voice, 'I can't do it because of her... But come here again a week from today.'

'A week from now I'll be in Austria; I'm leaving on Sunday, Trinity Sunday. But I'll be coming home every weekend; we could see each other here. Perhaps you could come tomorrow – or the day after tomorrow?'

'The day after tomorrow then... But don't leave with me now – someone might recognize us after all. Go another way, or at a distance behind me.'

'I'll follow at a distance,' Mánek promised obediently, and thus they parted.

On the outskirts of the village, a figure flashed suddenly on the path in front of Eva, and in horror she recognized Samko. What was he doing here? She pulled her scarf over her face and quickened her pace, turning her head away.

'Evuša, Evuša!' she heard a cry behind her, but she did not listen and ran on. Of course, with his affliction he could not keep up with her. 'What made him think of spying?' she wondered. She had never felt as much fear as she did now. Would he meet Mánek? Where would she tell him she had been?

It turned out badly. Samko had easily recognized his wife and not far behind her he also met Mánek. He returned home with a sure suspicion, in a miserable state; for the first time he lost control and beat Eva desperately; she did not defend herself at all... Perhaps that was the main reason why Eva, having sent a message to Mánek through Zuzka Líčeníková, disappeared from home on the morning of the next day...

A short time later, she found herself on an Austrian estate on the Danube as the mistress of the farm. The farm was vast, but the lodgings for the two hundred workers were very humble. There was nothing but a large, emptied stable with a porch, the former farmhands' sleeping quarters used as a kitchen, and finally two small rooms for the contracted farm manager in the loft right under the roof. Mánek had taken care not to bring a single soul from his home county who might have known about his circumstances to work there, except for Zuzka Líčeníková, with her mother and child; Eva herself had spoken up for them. They had not said a thing – but God knows how it happened: all the workers found out just the same that the mistress of the farm was not Mánek's real wife, that she had run away from her husband, and amongst themselves they called her 'the boss's mistress'.

But it soon spread around Mikulec too. At first there came a wailing letter from Mánek's wife; soon after that, old Mrs. Mešjanová arrived, but Mánek cleared Eva out of sight and in private he denied everything to his mother, taking refuge in the lie that Eva was an ordinary worker under him, of whom he otherwise took no notice.

Instead of going home each week, as he had at first intended, he went once every two weeks and only stayed a few hours each time.

In the beginning, of course, he had intended to divorce Maryša and convert to another faith – but when he secretly turned to a lawyer for advice, the latter dissuaded him so vehemently that Mánek, more passionate than resolute, lost all hope that it could turn out well and all desire to undertake anything. At home, in front of his wife and family, he wore the mask of innocence. And no word at all came from Samko. When people said something about Eva now and then, he immediately put an end to it by walking away from them without answering. Not even the aunt, who looked after Katečka like a mother, dared utter a single word about Eva...

Meanwhile a strange relationship was developing between Mánek and Eva while they were working in Austria. Both of them were busy all day long. In addition to his managerial fee – two florins for each member of his labor force – the contracted farm manager made considerable earnings by providing board for the whole group. He himself distributed the measured amount of food and wages from the estate owner; he supervised the fields and allocated piece-work. Eva, meanwhile, took care of the meals. She had several of the most capable women at her disposal – cooks who baked bread and prepared breakfast, lunch and dinner. Of course, as mistress of the farm, she gave all the orders and did so with a kind of affected pride, all the more severely and ostentatiously after Zuzka Líčeníková confided to her, swearing on her soul that neither she nor her mother had said a thing, and yet all the women and even the men knew that she had run away from her husband and amongst themselves they called her 'the boss's mistress'.

'Don't they reproach Mánek for anything?' Eva asked Zuzka, pained by the awkwardness of it.

'Not him,' Zuzka replied honestly.

Eva seemed lively and valiant, but in the evening, in Mánek's company, she would change. Her appearance grew somewhat melancholy and there was no trace of her former obstinacy...

'What are you so busy making?' Mánek asked her once, sitting down to dinner with her and noticing that not even in the evening did she set aside her elaborate embroidery. It kept her occupied until late at night and, when Mánek left to go back home, all Sunday long as well.

'I embroider all sorts of things this way,' she replied, with a wistful smile. 'It's my former trade after all... I suspect that hardly anyone will have a camisole embroidered like this,' – with obvious pleasure she showed him the work she had begun – 'with an openwork pattern along the length and each flower different from the next.'

He smiled at that and stroked her hair, which was ruffled in waves and braided into a circle of little plaits. He had always liked her hair and her eyes best of all – they were so unusual, unique...

She looked at him keenly and then she took him by the hand, stroking the calluses on it.

'How do things look for us?' she asked for the first time since she had been living with him. 'Will it still be possible to arrange our marriage this year?'

'Well, I suspect that – it's unlikely to work,' Mánek replied slowly, blushing and avoiding her gaze. 'I spoke about it with the lawyer and I didn't even want to tell you because it might have bothered you. He explained to me that it could take years and even then apparently it wouldn't have any validity for Catholics – he said people would point their fingers at us... He advised that we give it up... I also think it would be better for our children if we simply belonged to one another the way we are, in the sight of God. If you don't intend to return to Mikulec, they won't learn anything shameful about you there... We could live here together every year as long as the season lasts; I could always arrange work here or somewhere else, even at a loss to myself, and during the other months of the year I could drive down to see you and pay your living costs – wherever you wanted to settle. What do you think?'

'Nothing...' Eva replied, after a moment, when she raised her head from her sewing and stared into the flame of the lamp, just as she had that time when she was still single, when her aunt had mentioned that childish prank of Mánek's...

'She's a strange woman,' the young farmer thought to himself. 'But that's why I love her so much.'

The season drew to a close and ended with a lively social evening. As a parting gift from the estate the workers received several barrels of wine and plenty of white bread; they collected money amongst themselves for soup, meat and ham-and-pasta bake – each person gave twelve kreutzers – and kindly Mánek added something on top of that so that they would come back when he needed them next year.

They were Slovaks – poor upland farmers and rag-gatherers from the most poverty-stricken frontier areas of Moravia and Hungary.

They had good music that day too – how could there be a party without music? Why, they had brought it with them! At the insistence of all present, Žiga, the head musician, jumped up after the meal and took a battered violin down from a nail on a beam. He was joined by a fair-haired youth named Joška, the son of a shepherd, with his pipe, and the veteran Petráň with his nephew, both of whom had violins – there were enough musicians.

'So – what will it be?' Petráň asked tersely, casting a merry winking glance at his younger companion Žiga, whom he acknowledged without envy as the better musician.

Žiga in turn looked enquiringly at Mánek, who was there among them, along with the farmer's mistress, Eva.

'Play whatever you like,' said Mánek; he was in a good mood because Eva had silently consented to everything he had proposed.

Žiga thought it over for a moment.

'Play the one about the lily,' Kristina Rubačová called out shyly from her bench. She was a plump girl with a rather pretty face, whom Žiga liked to oblige best of all.

'A recruiting song!' called out the men, who had in the meantime gathered together in a group.

But this time Žiga paid no heed to Kristina or to the men, and on his own he began to play a long-drawn-out hay-harvesting song. He played one line by himself before the others caught on; the other three joined in with the right harmony at the second line; and at the third all the young men and women sang along with them:

> 'Dry yourself, where you got wet
> and leave my cheeks alone,
> they're sore enough
> from your pinches.
>
> See my skirt of Arras wool,
> see...'

As they sang the next words 'how I look', they were startled suddenly and stopped short. Out of the blue, three figures appeared at the door of the barn.

'It's the baron,' Petráň whispered and climbed down at once from the wooden partition which had remained there, after all the equipment for the cattle had been cleared away, as a kind of memorial inviting a sad comparison. Žiga was the last to lower his violin, and the crowd, together with the musicians, began to retreat towards the back wall.

Some offered greetings, others just gaped, curiously and stupidly, at the newcomers. Only Mánek stepped forward politely to meet them; he doffed his hat and greeted them in the broken German he had picked up while still a boy, when his own father – now deceased – had managed workers in similar circumstances in Austria.

'Good evening!' the baron thanked him indulgently. A tiny woman clung to his arm – she was undoubtedly his wife. The steward had led them in; this year they had come for the first time to have a look about since they were staying in Vienna.

'We were just passing by,' the baron continued, enunciating each word separately and nice and loud – with the good intention of making himself understood by the Slovak – 'and we heard that you were having a fine time.'

'Tell them to sing something for us,' the baroness said to the steward. 'I'm fascinated by the study of such simple folk and their ways. Do tell me, what nationality are they?'

'Slovaks, if you please,' the steward answered with his head bowed. 'Mostly from Upper Hungary.'

'Do they speak Hungarian?' the lady asked, looking about through her monocle.

'No, if you please. They have a Slavic language, similar to Czech.'

Meanwhile Mánek, who more or less understood this exchange, stood respectfully in front of them. Slowly Eva came up beside him. The steward turned to the crowd, calling out:

'Their lordships would like you to sing a song for them.'

'A folksong,' the baroness added.

Mánek repeated it after the steward, in Slovak.

'Perhaps we can play "My Love Is Knocking at the Door",' the high-spirited Žiga suggested, regaining his presence of mind, and he began to arrange his musicians and the singers as well.

'Take care and don't shout much, let's do it nicely! Boreš, don't you sing, you've got a bleating voice, and you, Junáč, don't sing either, you growl too much. Girls, don't take it too high! All right?'

They started a little uncertainly, but then gained in strength as they sang the plaintive melody characteristic of Slovak songs:

'My love is knocking at the door
and my heart is aching.
I must not go and open it
or even speak to him.'

'Go open the door, daughter,
and welcome him graciously,

open the door to the hall
and welcome him warmly.'

With her left hand she opened the door
and with her right she welcomed him:
'Welcome, my dear, be welcome here,
what news do you bring us?'

'My dear, I'll tell you the truth,
I came for rosemary;
a bouquet of rosemary
to comfort my heart.'

'Where would I, in sadness, get it?
I haven't even cut it yet,
for you, my lad
I have only this blue violet.

You used to come here
and wake me from my dreams,
but now you don't come by anymore,
are you so afraid of my mother, my father?'

'I'm not afraid of your mother, your father,
but I don't love you anymore,
you should have been true,
and you wouldn't have lost me!'

'But I was true to you
I remained all alone,
alone, alone, all alone
like a turtle-dove in a field.

The dove in the field
summons its mate

and I, in sadness, cannot
summon my love.'[2]

While they were singing, the baroness noticed Eva's charming dress, in particular her apron.

'Did you embroider it yourself?' she asked her.

'Yes,' Mánek answered for her.

'Perhaps you could sell me that apron,' the baroness suggested.

'Sell it? What a thought – give her the apron, Evuša,' Mánek said to her.

Eva obediently ran over to Zuzka Líčeníková, and borrowing a shabby apron from her, she carried her own, wrapped up, to the noble lady.

As she handed it to her, Mánek added: 'Accept it as a gift; she won't sell it.'

'Give me my purse,' the baroness whispered to her husband, and when he handed it to her, she took out a banknote. 'Take it,' she urged Eva.

Eva obeyed, and as she turned to look at Mánek, the baron smiled at her affably.

'Is this your wife?' he asked the farmer.

Eva intuitively understood this question and, holding her breath, she fixed her eyes on Mánek's lips. He blushed a little, shook his head weakly and replied quietly in German: 'No.'

The steward explained something quietly to the baroness, and she measured Eva with a look in which contempt and compassion were mixed.

After that Eva slipped away unnoticed.

2 Rosemary is an emblem of remembrance. In ancient times, to wear rosemary signified a wedding. In the language of flowers, it means 'fidelity in love'. The blue violet is an emblem of faithful love. See: *Brewers Dictionary of Phrase and Fable,* revised by Ivor H. Evans, Cassell, London, 1970, pp. 935, 1130.

The baroness, who was used to judging folksongs by comparing them to Styrian and Tyrolean tunes, told herself that this song was monotonously plaintive and melancholy – did these people, the women in particular, want to burst into tears when they sang those exaggerated, trembling tones? It was a pity she couldn't understand the words.

Nonetheless, she praised the song and, giving Eva's apron to the steward to carry, she and her husband departed.

About a quarter of an hour later, Eva returned, carrying two bundles. Her eyes sought Mánek and Zuzka Líčeníková.

Mánek was smoking and chatting with Petráň, who was telling him about his military service. Zuzka was sewing something on a basket in the corner and talking with an old woman she knew from Piešťany.

Eva leaned against the ladder that led up to the loft and, without even wanting to, listened to the conversation between an elderly woman, one of the uplanders, and an unprepossessing youth.

'I think that Kristina has gone out after Žiga,' the boy said, in a bitter tone.

Rubač's younger daughter, thirteen-year-old Kačka, tugged him by the sleeve to make him keep quiet. But he, seeing that Rubač's wife had not caught his words, repeated again more loudly: 'I think Kristina has gone out after Žiga.'

Now it turned out that Rubač's wife had heard him the first time after all.

'Let her go,' she snapped back caustically. 'He's a decent lad and why shouldn't they talk together outside when in here there are so many big ears and eyes that don't wish them well?'

'But that conceited Žiga will never marry her,' the youth retorted vehemently; 'I remember well what old Cádrovka said.'

'What was that?'

'That Žiga, when he felt like marrying, would get a girl with a hundred florins, and that he only talked to Kristina as a friend.'

'Cádrovka said that?'

'Upon my soul, I swear to God!' the boy assured her.

'Well, my dear Štefka, I won't try and turn her away from him,' Rubač's wife said in a sorrowful tone, 'let her find out for herself what the Lord has allotted her.'

'And you know,' said the lad in a sad, low voice, 'I have honorable intentions, I would give my life for her.'

'I know, Štefka,' Rubač's wife said gently, turning towards him. 'But what good is it, when there's only room in her heart for him? Believe me, she'll get plenty from us – scolding and even threats. She's well-brought-up and won't forget herself. That's why I tell myself: let her talk with him – if the Lord doesn't want her to have him, let her pay for it. I can't protect her any longer... all I ask is that you hold back and say nothing in front of her father. He beats her enough as it is.'

'I think he's already drunk again today,' said Štěpán with a sigh, changing the subject and staring into the corner where Rubač, with his hat on his head, had already given himself up to sleep in the straw.

'There you go, it's the last day, after all,' Rubač's wife replied. 'My God, I've got troubles enough even without Kristina.'

'I've never been drunk once,' the youth boasted gloomily.

'Well, neither has Žiga,' Rubač's wife noted by the way, and stood up from the wooden bench. 'I'm going to bed now,' she continued, clutching her back with her hands. 'Come on, Kača, come to bed as well,' she said, turning to her younger daughter. 'I don't want you talking back to me sleepily when I wake you tomorrow. We'll be rising at three o'clock...'

Kačka stood up obediently; they said goodnight to Štefka and turned towards the ladder. Eva moved out of their way and they climbed up the ladder – Kačka like a squirrel, Rubač's wife step by step.

Eva then looked at Štefka, who was hurrying out the door. A strange smile appeared on her lips. 'This foolish world...' she muttered to herself. Seeing that Zuzka was now alone, she went over and sat down by her on another basket.

'What are you sewing, Zuzka?' she asked her quietly.

'Town clothes for Aneša – they're easier to sew than the clothes we Slovaks wear,' replied the careworn girl, whose lad had abandoned her years ago. 'I'd like to finish them by tomorrow for the journey and I'm sewing without any measurements – just from memory. Every day when we get back from work, I forget to check and then in the evening, when I take up the sewing, she's already asleep. And mama says: don't disturb her from sweet sleep.'

'Your mother loves that child so much,' Eva said gently, 'almost as if you were married.'

'Well.' Zuzka smiled, unable to say anything more.

Then the mistress of the farm placed the larger bundle in her lap.

'There you go,' she said kindly. 'As I was packing, I found some clothes you can have – they're all as good as new.'

'May God reward you, Evuša,' Zuzka replied briefly, but with touching gratitude.

'And this,' said the mistress, edging the second bundle towards Zuzka's hands, 'I sewed at night for my daughter – a pretty camisole, a bodice and an apron – when she grows a little she can dress in things from her mother... And I stitched that banknote the baroness gave me for the apron into the corner of a tulle headscarf which I've never once worn... For the love of God, Zuzka, give it to Samko when you get back home – I hope he'll accept it from me

(150)

for the girl and forgive me everything – tell him I wish him all the best on this earth and the Kingdom of Heaven after his death – because he's a good man. Please give my warm greetings to my aunt as well…'

Startled and amazed, Zuzka looked at Eva and noticed some red flecks in those strange eyes of hers – they were not tears, but they touched Zuzka sadly. Up until then she had never mentioned the orphaned girl at home, or her husband. What was she thinking of?

'Aren't you going back home? Will you stay somewhere hereabouts?' she asked her, averting her eyes out of compassion.

All she noticed was that the mistress nodded before standing up and leaving her quickly.

The next day, before daylight, as they were all getting ready for the journey, they discovered that Eva, the boss's mistress, was suddenly missing. Mánek himself knew the least about her since the evening before when he had returned to his quarters tired and fallen asleep right away. Finally all of them – and Mánek too, with a kind of wistful annoyance – agreed that the mistress, who had always been strange, had probably secretly set out early for home empty-handed – or had gone out into the world to hide herself away…

But the next year, with another contracted farm manager in charge there for the season, they often remembered the sad story of how last year's mistress had hidden herself away for good in the cold, deep Danube. It was said that when they dragged her out one day near the ferry, all the color had washed out of her, so that they only recognized her by her clothes and distinctive eyebrows. And instead of the boss's mistress, they called her the boss's poor wretch…

Farmer Mešjany, who has since then grown serious and taciturn, lives a life of respectability with his wife Maryša.

The furrier Samko lives only for his daughter Katečka; to those who mention Eva to him he responds that everyone in the world makes mistakes, and before her death she had only him and Katečka in her heart...

THE TREAD OF FATE

JIŘÍ SUMÍN

They sat on the stoop under the tall, crooked pear tree that leaned over this quiet corner of the village; the dusty, white road running through the center of the village gave it a wide berth. The sociable mood of a Sunday afternoon had lured them out of the courtyards and stuffy rooms, and the conversation turned again and again to the same subject: the obligatory annual pilgrimage. Their ancestors had laid this duty on them decades ago, as an expression of gratitude for 'averting the divine punishment – the plague'. And there was no doubt that this year's pilgrimage expedition was meager. According to the pledge made in those difficult times, at least one pilgrim was supposed to set out from each house with a land registry number. And now they counted with indignation the numbered houses which had sent no one – not to mention those houses built subsequently, whose owners had the temerity to claim that the obligation did not extend to them. Old Belková's long, pale face peered out from under the black scarf, tied in a great swath around her head, as if she were looking through a crack. She wrung her knotted hands, insisting that God would send another scourge.

'But the priest didn't go either,' Borek, the retired farmer sitting next to her, objected with a knowing smile, lighting a fresh pipe with a spark from the old one.

The womenfolk were absolutely indignant at this bold remark.

'So what if he didn't go? At least he sent someone in his place!'

'A priest is a priest: one will do as well as another. He knows his duty... And besides: he's such an old man!'

'And has an awful lot on him to carry!' young Vacek commented in his deep, base voice; he was a lazy, young farmer with many debts, to whom no one paid much attention.

'Yes, it seems to me,' Borek put in soothingly, 'that somehow it isn't as solemn as it used to be...'

'If only everyone did his duty like the priest,' the womenfolk scolded.

'I know... I'm not saying that...' the old farmer equivocated, half routed already, 'I only wanted to say –'

'And the mayor didn't go either!' said Součková slowly; she was a stout, elderly widow whose cumbersome, harsh pronunciation seemed to crush every objection in advance.

Now completely routed, old Borek took the pipe from his mouth and looked at his daughter-in-law with shy, frightened eyes, as if seeking help.

But the young farmer's wife did not rush to defend her husband, who was not present. Sitting by herself in a chair near the door, as if enthroned above the others, who were content with sitting on the steps or a stone, she looked down upon her father-in-law coldly. This look reminded many present that the young woman was well aware that she had saved the farmstead for young Borek, and with it, of course, his respectability as well. She had been the richest heiress in the region. Either on account of her pride, or her cold, marble beauty, they nicknamed her 'the peacock'.

'He didn't go,' she repeated calmly, 'and I don't even know why... Maybe something came up.'

'I should think so! Certainly something came up!' old Borek chided her, dissatisfied with her defense. 'Of course it wasn't a trifle, but serious official business!'

'Maybe... I don't know for sure,' she replied in a reserved manner, and it was clear that some kind of sadness had cast a shadow over her dark blue eyes.

'But surely he sent someone in his place,' Vacek muttered knowingly.

'Of course he sent someone!' the old man railed, insensitive to the malicious barb. 'He even sent three people. Jíra the groom went, and a little girl and the farmhand Čajka. I'm telling you three people went!'

'Three,' Součková laughed. 'Only – as you were the first to say – it's not as solemn as it used to be!'

'No, it certainly isn't,' the womenfolk laughed.

The old man took the pipe from his mouth and blinked in embarrassment, not knowing how to defend the son who was his pride. But at that moment footsteps were heard in the hall and young Borek came out as if on cue. He appeared rather sleepy and it seemed that he wasn't thinking about defending himself. Having exchanged the usual greetings with those present, he leaned against the doorpost and lit a cigar. The old man grew so agitated that he sputtered:

'And you... you light a cigar for yourself and don't say anything!'

'What am I supposed to say?' the son asked with haughty poise.

'The talk here is that... that you didn't go on the pilgrimage.'

'On the pilgrimage!' he wondered, and surely would have liked to make a joke, but since they had chosen him to be mayor he acted with restraint and gravity in all matters. He was rather young for this office; indeed, there were even more serious objections. But his friends had spoken in his defense, saying that 'he had been to school' and finally come to his senses. Of course, he hadn't had much success in his education. He had studied at the grammar school. In the first year he had to re-sit an exam; he had repeated the second year; and in the third year he had been expelled. His father had then given up his ambitious hopes that his son would be a doctor. The son returned, satisfied and high-spirited; he had grown so tall that he had to stoop in all the doorways of the old family farmstead. He had a clever mind and a handsome exterior; he won favor and good fortune for himself.

Of course, there were times when he was declared incorrigibly frivolous, yes, he even seemed to be lost for good. But later it was generally acknowledged that he had changed; he had acquired some sense. Yes, acquired even dignity, correcting the lapses of his youth with a rich marriage.

Casually, he blew a ring of smoke, glancing surreptitiously down into the village. He almost forgot to give the explanation they were all waiting for in suspense. Only his father's repeated, sharp exhortation brought him around.

'What a thought...,' he said with a sneer. 'I'll make a different kind of pilgrimage... official business! Early tomorrow morning, or maybe even this evening, I have to be in Oseky.'

'That's what I said,' old Borek chimed in. 'Official business! My dear brothers, that can't be put aside, business is business! And what do you have to take care of in Oseky?'

'Well, military maneuvers, what else!' the mayor answered grudgingly, in a superior tone. 'As if you didn't know. The troops are already up there in the villages, all the way to Lidechov. The maneuvers begin the day after tomorrow. Three days now they've been in Oseky.'

The mention of maneuvers animated all of them. They began to thrash out everything that was already common knowledge, and to guess at what was still in doubt. The men spoke about their experiences and about events that were more or less believable; sometimes two or three – or all of them – spoke at once, depending on how good they were at attracting attention. Even lackadaisical Vacek, who was still lying on his stomach, stood up and began to mumble about the good times when he was a corporal. The womenfolk listened in silence, only showing their amazement with the usual interjections. Thus it was all the more startling when young Borková suddenly meddled in the conversation.[1]

---

1 Borková is the feminine form of the surname Borek.

'What do they need you for in Oseky?' she asked, turning to her husband. 'If you want to see the maneuvers, you'll have time enough if you go the day after tomorrow. You won't be needed to keep law and order there. They've got their own mayor in Oseky for that.'

Unpleasantly taken back, young Borek struggled to hide his irritation.

'You've got it all figured out, haven't you? As if maneuvers like that didn't concern us, but only the people in Oseky! So many troops all around, accommodation, distribution of supplies, the fall harvest and one thing after another... That's a woman's logic for you!'

She blushed a little, especially when the men loudly backed him up, and she did not speak again.

The conversation about maneuvers was finally exhausted and another subject taken up. A calmer, drier tone prevailed. Many fell silent altogether.

The old farmer Borek, who had just remembered something very entertaining, moved over closer to his sister-in-law.

'There's one thing I can't get out of my head. Did you hear the sermon today, sister?'

Součková emphatically affirmed that she had.

'And did you take note of the priest's words,' the old man continued in a muffled voice, 'did you take note of how he spoke about that woman... the adulteress, or whatever it was he called her?... He didn't even say it directly; he only suggested it somehow.'

'I certainly did take notice! The sermon's been buzzing in my head too. But I couldn't say now what his words were exactly. A chill ran through me, hearing him talk like that.'

'How did he put it? I've got a good memory. I still remembered it at noon. But now the beginning somehow escapes me!... "Let the woman," he said, "who advances before the husband of another, and seduces him with a fawning, fulsome tongue and brings ruin upon the family, let that woman," he said, "be forever despised by you; let all who are virtuous and honorable shun her; let..." There you are, now I can't remember the ending.'

'That's just the way it was! You've got a good memory, brother!'

'So what do you think, sister, would he have said that for no reason, or did he have someone in mind?'

'Who knows? It seems to me he wasn't talking to thin air. His voice was trembling. All of us in the back under the choir were set on edge. Boháček's widow said: Did you hear that? He's not thundering for nothing! That hit home!'

'Hit home, all right – but where was it aimed? There would have been some talk.'

'I say that before long something will come to light. The young people these days are so willful and spirited. It wasn't like that in our time.'

'It surely wasn't! Well, if only people noticed it. At least they've been forewarned.'

'Oh, they certainly have noticed. There's been a lot of talk about it. Some people think it was aimed at the Špýrs' maid, the one who got herself into trouble with the farmer. But I don't think that's right. Why would he mention old sins?'

'No, it wasn't aimed at the maid. It'll be something more serious. It was aimed higher up!'

'Then there's Drnkalka, that cooper's widow, who dresses herself up a bit too much. But I don't think anyone pays attention to her.'

'Well, we'll see sooner or later! The cat won't stay in the bag. It'll get out! He must know something if he talks like that. It's a good thing he gave this warning. At least we'll pay attention!'

All of a sudden they were interrupted by peals of laughter which sounded nearby and caught the attention of those chatting.

'That must be Kajta over there,' Bělková reckoned, laughing quietly as if even she had been touched by the wave of liberating gaiety.

'Who else but that babbler?' Součková commented gruffly.

But the old woman continued to laugh quietly, as if Kajta's very presence gave her pleasure.

'People always have fun whenever Kajta's around,' she went on. 'When we were plucking feathers in the winter at my daughter's, we had some good times with her. My daughter begged me: Mama, bring Kajta along! I'll gladly pay her, even if her work isn't worth much. As long as Kajta's talking, no one wants to go to bed. But when she's not there, they start to doze as soon as evening comes, and no work gets done.'

'I'm angry with her,' Součková declared. 'I'm her godmother, after all, and I have a right to remind her of what's proper. The other day she went past our house, and on purpose I ran out and called to her: Kajta, do go on the pilgrimage for me! – I'll go, godmother, I'll go, don't you worry. And there you are – she didn't go. I can't abide her chatter. Why, it's all lies from start to finish.'

'I don't think she'd lie. But she doesn't have any worries. Her husband is a good fellow, even if he likes to drink, and she doesn't have children, so it's as if she were still single.'

Meanwhile, the laughter across the way had died out and brisk footsteps crossed the road, accompanied by the audible squeaking of new, very shapely shoes.

The group under the pear tree fell silent in expectation, and all eyes turned instinctively in that direction.

A friendly, bubbly greeting was called out, and a small, spry, almost girlish figure flashed past; but the brisk footsteps accompanied by the squeaking of shapely shoes did not stop. Why, it even seemed they were hurrying away at a faster pace.

Dreary boredom threatened to descend upon the quiet corner under the old pear tree. Someone even sighed out loud.

Old Bělková couldn't bear the disappointment.

'But Kajta!' she called after the young woman, who seemed to bring gaiety with her wherever she went, like the spring brings flowers and the clouds moisture. 'Won't you even stop for a chat?'

Kajta turned her head; embarrassment flitted over her pretty, blushing face, like a little cloud over a clear sky. For a moment she hesitated. Something there curbed her bold and mischievous character.

'Oh but... I didn't see... God bless you, dear old Grannie! I'm in a bit of a hurry.'

The cloud vanished, the white teeth gleamed, but the mischievous, gray eyes remained downcast, like boisterous imps that should not be allowed to speak.

'Why are you in such a rush? It's Sunday, after all...'

'I want to get to mama's place in Oseky today. It's quite a way. My old man left on account of some job. He went all the way to Loukoť, where he'll make a roof for the new school.'

'To Loukoť? That's far.'

'Far, yes, and I don't even know where it is. He won't be home until next Sunday. What would I do here on my own? And poor mama has her hands full with work.'

The embarrassment had vanished completely, and sparks began to flash from the depths of her gray eyes, like when a fire threatens to flare up in a sudden breeze from ashes that are still warm.

'Will you stay there long?'

'Well, I don't know. If she needs me. They've got troops there in Oseky, haven't you heard? Poor mama is cooking for four men.'

'Well, you better hurry on then,' Vacek growled.

But Kajta didn't notice the biting remark because all of a sudden she sensed an approaching danger, visible only to her, and dropped her playful gaze. Yes, she even pulled the white batiste scarf further down over her forehead.

Old Součková coughed portentously.

'Do you remember, Kajetána, what you promised me not long ago?' she began, in her hard, threatening tone of voice. 'You promised that you'd go on the holy pilgrimage. I gave you money for prayers... I sent you a piece of bacon so that you'd bring me back a little of that holy water... I didn't want it for free...'

'But dear godmother... but...' Kajta sighed as if pleading for mercy. 'Those kreutzers, my goodness! I'll give those back to you, but the tomcat ate the bacon on me...' [2]

'For God's sake, forget about the kreutzers and the bacon! I don't hold it against you. It only bothers me that you didn't go! A young woman like you, with no work and no children...'

'Godmother, I couldn't! The Lord alone knows I couldn't. No matter what I did, it wasn't possible; it just wasn't possible! But godmother, I always go, year after year!'

'It's your duty, after all. You're the mistress of the house; you have your own property and you know the obligation laid on every numbered house.'

'I know... I know! It's true that we have a little cottage. But there's a hired man living on the farm – let him go for once. Why should I always have to pray and do penance for everyone else?'

2 A kreutzer is a small coin, formerly current in parts of Germany and Austria.

'You should have decided that amongst yourselves. No one went from that number, and yet you know what the obligation is.'

'Vrtek the cobbler lives on our farmstead,' Kajta defended herself energetically. 'It's true that he can't go; I'm not mad at him; but he has a wife after all. She could go sometimes too. She's been living at our place for five years and right before the pilgrimage, as if on purpose, she always lies down in childbed. But not this year... this year it came late. So couldn't she go this year?'

'It's hard for a mother to leave her little children behind, and you don't have children. You don't have any excuse. You have that sin on your conscience, no one else!'

Kajta stood there as if in the pillory, ashamed and helpless. Her restless, slender doe's feet stamped angrily, but her face grew serious and the look in her eyes went out, like cold, dampened ashes, under which, somewhere deep down, the last spark fades.

Old Bělková felt sorry for the young woman and hurried to her aid.

'Well, there was a mistake, but that's not so bad. You said you couldn't go. Maybe you were ill?'

But her good intentions were to no avail and Kajta foundered in even greater difficulties.

'Well... not exactly ill. It was something... I'm ashamed to say it.'

'What's the fuss?' objected old Borek, who had grown curious. 'Go on and say it!'

'It's the kind of thing,' Kajta protested, 'when it happens to a person, he'd rather not talk about it...'

'So what was it? Out with it!' Vacek shouted, 'the womenfolk are on pins and needles.'

'All right, I'll tell you: the cockroaches had spread all over our building...'

'Cockroaches! Those would have waited till you got back from the pilgrimage.'

'Yes, that's easy for you to say. But if you haven't lived through it, you don't know what a plague it can be. God knows what the cause of it was. I keep my place clean and yet I've never seen so many roaches in my life! They stretched like a dark cloud over the ceiling; they swarmed on the shelves, in the corners, behind the stove – everything was full of them. Under the table and benches one roach was crammed against the other. They fell into my pots; they ate from our plates; they swam in the milk... Well, I said to myself: this couldn't just happen on its own; someone must have set them on me to get revenge.'

'That could be,' Bělková agreed. 'Gypsy women usually take revenge like that when someone won't give them what they want. They know how to set a curse on a person.'

'My old man bit one in half in his bread and got very angry.'

'I should think so.'

'He started to curse and swear and finally he said: Take note, if you don't clear this vermin out by Saturday, then I'll clear them out myself and don't ask how: I'll set fire to this shack over your head! And you know, folks, it's his shack and whatever he says, you can swear an oath by it!'

Those passing by stopped to listen: chattering Kajta was in her element. With her godmother's preaching taken care of, she grew unusually cheerful. A kind of deeply buried, but poorly guarded, bright happiness glowed in her eyes. She used her entire body when she spoke. Her gray eyes sparkled; her white teeth flashed defiantly; her small, dark hands talked; her playful doe's feet stamped and danced about as if they wanted to underscore a point.

'So, folks, I cleaned and exterminated, and all for nothing. The more I exterminated, the more of them swarmed all over the place, and I had no idea what to do. But it happened that at that time my auntie fell sick, and I went by train to the city for medicine. In the train I met a strange woman from somewhere far away. She looked like a rich, respectable woman. She had a strange hat with gleaming ribbons and a double chin the width of your palm running from ear to ear. She was very wise and experienced. She read our palms and figured out everything about us as if it were written on our foreheads. She understood everything: diseases, court cases, crops, children and cattle. She could talk about everything like she was reading from a book. She gave everyone advice, but she wouldn't take anything for it. She was glad for the chance to show off her wisdom. So I also confessed my own troubles to her. "You silly creature," she said, "when there are so many cockroaches it's a waste of time to try and kill them. You've got a king there! Pay attention: the king is white and comes out at exactly twenty minutes past midnight; and when he runs you can hear a kind of tinkling, like silver spurs ringing. There's no other way but to catch the king – carefully! you shouldn't hurt him – and then slowly chase him to the crossroads with a willow switch. I'll teach you a kind of incantation; you'll say this incantation and when you've chased him past the crossroads, you'll lay nine straws across his way so that he can't come back. In three days, I guarantee, the roaches will move out, every last one! But make sure the king doesn't come back home with you, because then you'll never be rid of the roaches until your dying day." – So last night, folks, I caught that king... You're laughing at me under your breath, I know, but whether you laugh or not, it happened just like that woman said! I shut him up for the night in a little box, but I couldn't close my eyes for worry. Ten times at least I went to see if he hadn't run away on me. Early in the morning, before the cock's crow, I cut a willow switch, tipped the king out of the box, and, nice and gentle, I drove him on ahead of me. Was that a lot of work! You know how slowly a roach crawls –

if only he had crawled in a straight line! No, he went first to the left, then to the right, then he stopped and thought about something; it was enough to make a saint swear. If it wasn't for that incantation, I couldn't have budged him. But even so, it took a long while. I thought it would all be over by morning. I hadn't even dressed properly. Meanwhile, by the time the bells rang for holy mass we were only at the cross. And from there it was another two hours at least before we got to the crossroads. What anger and shame I had to put up with! People turned to look at me; they surely thought I was going mad. Even before we crawled up to the crossroads I was tired and sweating as if I'd been working all day. The poor thing, he couldn't move from the spot either. So I said to myself, that's quite a ways for a little creature like that, let him rest a bit and then he'll run on all the faster from the crossroads. I sat down on the baulk; the sun was blazing so hot I saw circles before my eyes, and the gadflies flew at me in a rage. There was nothing for it but to say the incantation again; I lashed the switch to the right and to the left, but the dear king sat as if nailed to the spot. Most likely he understood I was driving him on, and he didn't know, poor thing, where to turn. Once it seemed to me he was headed for Kozojedy, then again for Lidechov. But in the end he stayed put and refused to move. Oh, how I suffered! Many would still reproach me for not going on the pilgrimage, but believe me, folks, even if I'd gone all the way to Rome I wouldn't have endured as much as I did today! People went by, all cleaned-up and dressed in their best, and I sat there like a Gypsy on the baulk, unwashed, with my hair tangled, and I didn't know where to turn for shame. I hadn't cooked dinner, I hadn't heard the word of God. What was I to do? Where could I even begin? If I went back home with the king, I wouldn't be rid of the roaches for the rest of my life! Then it was midday; no one walked past anymore; everyone was at home resting in a cool room and eating Sunday dinner; and meanwhile my innards were twisting with hunger and regret. Then a kind of drowsiness came over me, I don't know how, and all of a sudden I woke up and – imagine my fright – the king was gone! I looked around; I crawled on my knees over the ground; I turned over every leaf, every pebble; in short, he was nowhere to be found! Despairing, I turned around and half-way back on the road I came upon him, almost stepped on him: he was scurrying back to the village! Just imagine, a little bug like that and how smart he was! He could outwit and get the better of a human being! Once again I began to say the incantation, only this time quickly, and I drove him back. As we came to the crossroads, he resisted a little, but I carried on, saying: Your Majesty, Your Majesty, they're cooking a feast for you in the distance...'

'Oh please, stop all this blabber!' old Součková burst out in annoyance. 'You can tell such tall-tales to children, but you can't fool us old folk.'

Kajta froze in shock; yes, she almost lost her voice.

'You don't believe me, godmother?' she asked, astonished.

'How can you even ask, you foolish soul!'

Kajta seemed crushed. But the men laughed so boisterously and irresistibly that little by little she gained her courage back.

'You don't believe me?' she asked more boldly. 'So come and see with your own eyes. It all happened like that strange lady told me it would. Even as I was going back home I met swarms of roaches. They were ours; why, I knew them, didn't I? They were supposed to move out in three-days' time, but not even half of them are left now. If you don't believe me, come and see for yourself. Now only a few are sitting around here and there...'

The strict old woman was piqued not so much by the tale as by Kajta's cat-like movements and lively gestures, which had something fawning about them and attracted the eyes of the men. She snapped high-handedly:

'Stop all this nonsense! "Your Majesty! Your Majesty!" Imagine calling a filthy insect: "Your Majesty!" Do you know, you simple soul, what majesty is? Why, you might as well be talking about the Emperor. If the gendarme hears you, he'll take you in.'

Kajta turned pale with horror and fell completely silent. She feared no one so much as the gendarme. For her, all earthly horrors and hardships were connected to this representative of official power. She was so bewildered that not even the new burst of laughter returned her to her former volubility.

Old Borek, who highly respected the authority of his sister-in-law, but also liked to listen to prattling Kajta, intervened to end the argument.

'Well, perhaps not the gendarme... He doesn't have anything to do with such things. Of course, you're right, sister, you've got a point there. Revolutions and uprisings are everywhere these days; people don't want to let those crowned heads rule anymore; it seems too high a price to pay. And if that incantation got as far as the authorities, the way they're always trying to ferret something out, they might think it wasn't meant for a cockroach, but for someone else.'

'Why, surely the authorities wouldn't believe such simple people still existed...'

'But, godmother, why does it seem odd to you?' Kajta defended herself in a fluster. 'Stranger things have taken place! You should hear what happened not long ago to my old man when he was going home late at night from work. You'd be amazed! My old man is no babbler or liar. He only says what he absolutely has to. Why, you know, after all, what a tight-lipped fellow he is... But when he says something, you can swear an oath by it.'

Kajta's storytelling talents revived as the crowd of listeners under the pear tree grew.

'Did something happen to him? Tell us!' they urged her eagerly.

'Did something happen to him!' Kajta wondered aloud. 'You didn't hear about it? I thought the whole village knew about it. If it had happened to someone with a big name, believe me, they'd have put it in the papers. But when a person is such a grumbler and so tight-lipped! – Well, folks, one time after pay-day – it was early in spring – he stayed on for a while talking in the pub. He doesn't drink, and only sometimes sits down there on account of his friends. So he was going home along the usual route from Lidechov to Vážce – maybe you know it – and when he came to the place where the Vážce woods begin, he looked around and said: "What's this? It all looks different somehow. There weren't so many trees here before." – Well, being what he is, he just walked on as if nothing had happened, until suddenly something startled him. "Damnation," he said, "why, these trees are kind of strange. Almost like they weren't even trees." He looked and looked, and sure enough, they weren't trees but enormous poles with black flags. So he went on, and all of a sudden, out of the blue, there was a great crowd of cats coming towards him. And they all walked on their hind legs. And the one walking in front carried a great book and read out loud from it. And when she saw him, she shut the book and said: Uncle Sotor, where is your tomcat? – Don't laugh until I'm done! You'll see, your hair will stand on end. – But my old man, as you know, doesn't scare easily. He went on his way as if nothing had happened and said: Well, where would he be? He's lying at home on the stove. – Tell him, said the cat that had been reading from the book, that the old governess died...'

Noisy laughter resounded all around, infecting everyone except – Kajta.

'Wait till I'm done, you won't feel like laughing then,' she admonished solemnly. 'Then they were carrying something like a body on a bier. In short, it looked like a solemn cat funeral. And the cats from all the surrounding villages were there; my old man recognized them. But being the way he is, he went on his way as if nothing had happened, until he saw the neighbor's tomcat – last year he used to come to our house for cream, and there was a lot of fuss because of him – and so my old man says: Aha, so you're here too, you old sweet-tooth? But the tomcat nodded seriously, and said in a deep voice: God bless you, Uncle Sotor! – Don't laugh, wait until I'm done: My old man came home, lay down and fell asleep as if nothing had happened. In the morning at breakfast the tomcat walked over as usual and started to rub against him. Just then my old man remembered the incident in the night and said to the cat: Wait, my boy, I have to pass on a message to you: Yesterday you were supposed to go to a funeral. Your old governess died. – Folks, the tomcat, as soon as he heard that, pulled his tail in between his legs and meowed in a grievous voice: Woe is me! I shouted and almost fell over in fright, but my old man said to the tomcat as if nothing had happened: Don't mourn, my boy, don't mourn! It all went off without you anyway. She had a solemn funeral, I saw it myself. – Before he could finish, the window tinkled, the tomcat flew out like an arrow and hasn't been back since...'

The last sentences were lost in the crazy laughter that broke out when Kajta imitated the tomcat's voice in a very realistic and faithful manner. Many wanted to hear it again. A vigorous debate started up; some declared that a cat would certainly talk like that if, by some strange chance, of course, it turned into Kajta; others, however, thought that Kajta would talk like that if she turned into a cat.

'So what's so funny?' Kajta repeated, elated by her success, which clearly didn't depend on whether or not every word she said was believed. A waggish smile tugged at her lips when she turned to her godmother with feigned gravity: 'There you are, godmother, my old man isn't a babbler or liar. He doesn't say much, but whatever he says, you can swear an oath by it. Well, what do you say to that?'

The old woman grew serious, as if ashamed to have joined in the general merriment.

'What I say,' she smiled contemptuously, 'is that this is even more filthy rubbish than the first story. Your old man must have been in his cups when he met that cats' procession.'

'My old man in his cups? Why he doesn't even drink!'

Amazement and anticipation followed this bold declaration of Kajta's. To begin with, they all thought she was joking. But Kajta put on a very serious face, stamped her feet and pounded her chest with her fists, insisting that she had never yet seen him drunk. Her behavior provoked a vehement protest from the women. To pretend and lie like that, as if people were blind! – He doesn't drink! Maybe not when he's building. – But the men clearly sided with Kajta, saying that Sotor was altogether a decent man who only drank once a week, after he received his pay. And if someone drinks 'from Saturday to Sunday', that doesn't make him a drunkard. But the women objected all the more passionately, insisting that he got drunk not from Saturday to Sunday, but from Sunday to Saturday. A young cottager with an honest, red face, small, mole-like eyes and a powerful, stentorian voice, shouted down the rest, saying that Kajta was an excellent, exemplary woman who wouldn't let anyone insult her husband.

And the crowd under the pear tree was having an excellent time at the expense of the poor carpenter.

'So maybe I was lying again!' Kajta laughed, turning around on her heel provocatively. 'Why do you listen to me if you're sure I'm lying? When I keep quiet, I don't get any peace: What's wrong with you Kajta? Why don't you say something? Go on – it doesn't cost you anything. Doesn't your mouth have to sing for its supper? Go on and tell us something! Then people say I'm lying. So let them give it a try! We'll see if anyone listens to them. Even when they speak the truth, their words aren't worth much.'

'You're bold, Kajta!' some woman shouted out.

Kajta tossed her head obstinately.

'Go ahead and say what you like about me. You won't be seeing me for a while anyway. I'm going to mama's, to Oseky…'

'Don't go to Oseky,' an old farmer tried to calm her down, 'the soldiers are there, and they can't be trusted.'

'I know, but people there are decent. The poor aren't envious, the rich aren't proud, and they all live there like one family. It's a pity I married into another village.'

'You haven't minded it much here until now.'

'I haven't. But in Oseky I'd be more content…' and chattering Kajta kept repeating that she would go – she was 'leaving right now' – but all the while she stood on the same spot, stamping her little feet. Not with the same vehemence, but rather in a kind of awkward indecision, as if she well knew it was time to go and yet stood there, captive to some other will, fixed by someone's gaze. Now and then she felt the sting of someone's spite, stirring a gloomy apprehension in her. She didn't feel like joking anymore, and yet her talkative lips did not stop. 'Mama sent me a message: Come by, Kajta, I've got an officer billeting with me and I'm not much good at cooking. I can't even play on the fiddle when they don't like the food, the way old man Vambera can.

'Old Vambera can really play,' a new tale started up.

'My Lord, and how sweetly! It could break a person's heart. God knows where he learned it. He never went about the world, and no one in the area can equal him. When he plays, half the village stands under the windows.'

'Who did he play for at dinner time?'

Kajta, still captive to some other will, still fixed by someone's gaze, was grateful for this question. Ignoring the stings that fell upon her in the form of muffled remarks, she started merrily on another story.

'Who did he play for? Why it was a soldier. Vambera's wife went off on a pilgrimage; the old man stayed home and cooked. At midday, a soldier came by and said: So where's dinner, old man? Old Vambera brought him meat and dumplings, but the soldier wasn't satisfied. He said: That's fine, old man, but where's the sauce? Plain roast meat and dumplings – they don't go together. – My young soldier, said old Vambera, don't be angry, it won't be so bad. I can cook well as long as I'm using just my two hands. As soon as I have to take up a wooden spoon, I'm at my wit's end. And you need a wooden spoon to make sauce. But you know what, little soldier: the food's not bad, so why shouldn't meat and dumplings go together? It's not for nothing that they say: What slips down the throat, goes on – like a breeze. So sit down and eat and I'll play something nice for you. The soldier agreed and started in on the food, and the old man picked up the fiddle and played song after song until people ran up to the windows to listen. When he'd finished playing, the soldier stood up and said: Thanks be to God for dinner, old man, it was good!'

This story of chatterbox Kajta's was also rewarded with praise and laughter. Now she stood there, supple and gay, angling for the flattering gazes of the men. It wasn't out of greed or conceit that she sought them, not for her own pride and happiness. For her they were worthless, empty trifles with which to adorn herself for the momentary pleasure of those eyes that still held her captive.

But the biting stings were more fierce than ever; and hostility and spite broke out openly.

'You foolish women! You listen to her devilish nonsense while she only makes it up to tempt your men away from you.'

Kajta noticed the sudden excitement, but she didn't hear the harsh words.

'Did you say something about me, Mother Říhová?' she asked, turning towards a square-shouldered peasant woman with a fat neck, swollen on one side, and glum eyes.

'Who else? I said you were digging a hole here. Why don't you go on now to Oseky, if you like it so much? What a pity! If that drunken old widower hadn't led you off, you'd still be sitting there today. You're in such a hurry, and yet you don't go. Surely you're up to no good.'

A chill fell upon the merry crowd in the icy silence. They were all rather offended. Součková, who claimed the right to scold Kajta now and then for her moods and high spirits, was outraged by this brutal invective.

'There you see, Kajta, what kind of reward you get,' she spoke in a mild manner in the absolute silence. 'You blabber nonsense to make others happy, and you only end up hurting yourself. You see, you see... and I always tell you for your own good: Hold your tongue! Don't talk so much! Whoever talks a lot either knows a lot or lies. And you don't know much, that's for sure. With your mischief and high spirits you make up silly stories so that people will run over, listen and laugh! That's your weakness, I know you! Now they've listened, now they've laughed, time has passed pleasantly and now – you've got your reward! Be sure and put it away safe in your pocket...'

'It serves her right! She had it coming,' some women cried out.

'There... there... you see! Remember that next time. Don't tell them anything, don't lie...'

'Damn it!' shouted the young cottager with the stentorian voice. 'Why go on about lies? Was she speaking under oath or something?'

'Or did she disgrace or slander anyone? Does that kind of talk hurt anyone?'

'There you see, she's got her defenders! They wouldn't stand up for an old woman, but for one like that...'

'It doesn't hurt anyone, only her... She demeans herself because she lies,' Součková argued.

'Who knows if she was lying!'

'She was. I wouldn't believe a thing she said anymore. Not even if she told the truth. To think that a soldier would let a man play for him, rather than give him good food – and on top of that say: Thanks be to God!... No, no, that wouldn't happen! Why, a soldier would simply beat the farmer, especially during maneuvers.'

'No, that story about the soldier doesn't seem right to me either,' old Bělková said kindheartedly, her thin, colorless face peering out from under the black swath of her scarf. 'I'd put more faith in the cats' funeral. Stranger things have happened. She didn't make up that roach king either. I first heard that cockroaches had kings when I was still a girl. Why shouldn't they? Even bees have queens. But about that soldier, that doesn't seem right...'

'It's a lie! I'll bet you anything!'

'You'll lose that bet, sister,' old Borek smiled. 'I'll tell you now. It's the truth. The public messenger talked about it in the pub when he brought a letter to my son. Isn't it so, my boy? You heard it, after all.'

Somewhat startled, the mayor glanced at his father in annoyance. But seeing all eyes fixed on him, he calmly blew a puff of smoke from his cigar.

'Yes, I think he said something of the sort,' he muttered through his teeth.

His wife, who had been sitting there until then cold and detached, looked up in surprise, and her pale face flushed slightly.

'And where did you hear the story, Kajta?' she asked in a voice which sounded like a taut string stretched to the point of breaking. 'You certainly didn't speak to the public messenger.'

'No,' Kajta said, rather uneasily, 'mama sent me the message.'

'The Lidechov limer brought you the message from your mama. I spoke with her,' Borková objected in the same ringing voice, which was already trembling a little.

'Well, yes... No...' Kajta stuttered. 'I'm not sure anymore who told me...'

The mayor, who had been listening to the jokes and quarrels with haughty composure, grew clearly restless. He laughed contemptuously and lashed an angry glance like a whip at his wife.

'Spying, that's what that is,' he sneered, 'why, her husband might have told her. He sits all day in the pub, doesn't he? No one makes a secret of it.'

The young farmer's wife couldn't answer. What had until then only spun darkly in her sad, uneasy soul, grew more clear and definite. Wasn't it suspicious that this very day Kajta was avoiding what every villager, and the village women in particular, regarded as a sacred duty – 'the divine services' – just when pressing 'official business' likewise prevented her husband from going to church? Had this urgent 'official business' of her husband's perhaps led along the path where pretty, roguish Kajta sat with her roach king? And now both of them were setting out for Oseky...

'It doesn't concern you, does it?' she said, looking firmly at her husband, who recoiled instinctively. There was something in her eyes that recalled the words which had slipped out of her mouth once in a volatile moment of their marriage, and had become generally known: 'If it weren't for me, you'd have been a farmhand long ago... yes, you'd have been a stableman rather than mayor!'

Certainly no one understood this look better than he did. With a helpless, sour smile, he slipped away unobserved into the hall and did not show his face again.

This silent struggle, with blows falling on both sides, had no witnesses. At that moment, Kajta had drawn all attention to herself; her success had flared up so suddenly and vigorously that it smothered all hostility and spite. For if one of her least plausible stories had found such splendid confirmation from trustworthy lips, the other stories could hardly be doubted anymore. So they thrashed them out again, and wondered at them, and even the most skeptical admitted that 'there could be something to them'. Many thought they had once heard something similar, which they recalled only in a fragmentary, incoherent form; the main filament of the plot had got tangled somewhere and then lost in the rush of daily cares and tasks. But Kajta had an excellent memory and maybe she knew something more about those half-forgotten cases. They all started talking to her at once, and some even held on to her dress, for it seemed that her restless, hopping feet were really and truly heading away.

And she really would not stay any longer. Laughing and chatting all the while, she left, supple and gay, turning around again and again to respond to one joke and then another. Her brisk footsteps, accompanied by the squeaking of shapely, new shoes, gradually receded. The others felt like she was carrying away not only the gaiety and good humor, but the Sunday peace as well. They began, automatically, to think of work and the worries of tomorrow. But from time to time Kajta's laughter and calling, in response to the comments of the people she passed, still disturbed them. To many it seemed like she was carrying away the remains of the day of rest, for although she had disappeared from sight, they sensed that wherever she went the day of rest followed.

Something like melancholy and a disgruntled reproach followed her brisk footsteps. Downtrodden malice timidly raised its head.

'You can't see her, but you can still hear her a long way off. What laughter and chatter.'

'It'll pass. She won't be like that much longer.'

'I don't see why not. She's a young woman after all.'

'Yes, like any other. Cares come, vexation, sleepless nights...'

'What sleepless nights?' muttered someone dull-witted.

'Well, after all...'

'What? The devil take you, speak up: what?'

'Well, who has to say it out loud? Everyone can see it anyway, that – she's with child.'

'Kajta? Kajta? And with...?'

The alarming, sensational question hung in the air. It stirred up malice and hatred and summoned them to speak. But in vain. Conscious of their recent defeat, they kept a proud, unapproachable silence.

'Why are you so surprised? After all, she's married... Isn't she?'

The simple, honorable souls, who see everything simply and honorably, started along naive lines of reflection.

'What do you know, old Sotor! Fifteen, sixteen years he was with his last wife – and nothing! He's been with Kajta seven years, and all of a sudden... what do you know, what do you know!'

But these credulous voices fell silent little by little, yielding to short, caustic remarks.

Old Borek sat, dejected, sunk in his thoughts, shaking his head.

'This is really a confounded business,' he muttered, 'why our women go about hand in hand with her, and they don't say a thing – they don't know a thing! She comes to our house every day; she's sincerity itself: grandpa here, and grandpa there, and we're the same way with her, as if she were one of the family. Confounded business! That would be terrible, indeed it would! What if the preaching today was aimed at her? She wouldn't be allowed to cross the threshold of my house! Not that!' And shaking his head more and more vehemently, he kept on asking in his fateful blindness: 'But tell me people – with whom? With whom?'

So they sat there a good while, stretched out on the grass or on the bank by the wall, debating in all seriousness and seeking – the culprit.

Only the young farmer's wife, sitting in the chair by the door as if enthroned above the others, pressed her pale, trembling lips together and kept quiet. She tried to stand up, but her legs refused to obey. Only when she had mastered her grief did she leave without a word, upright and proud, as if nothing had happened. But then she wandered about the house, undecided, despairing, with her eyes wide open, searching for all the objects that were mute witnesses of her love, as if she wanted to weigh the measure of the happiness experienced here against the bitter humiliation of the present moment. Suddenly she disappeared, as if the ground had swallowed her up, and the servants and children looked for her in vain. In a dark, out-of-the-way closet, cluttered with unused junk, she sobbed out her pain, and her sorely wounded heart groaned. Hidden and safe from the eyes of others, she gave way to her tears. She cried for the wasted happiness of her life and for the irreversible ruin of her husband, from whom she could not detach her heart. Kajta's playful laughter rang in her ears; it inflamed the pain, and she felt certain that the present moment would divide her path from his for the rest of their lives. There was no doubt that they would separate forever. Her heart, which could speak so clearly and urgently in this isolated refuge, would fall silent at once under his indifferent, aloof gaze, crushed by the shy pride of an honorable woman who could not beg for her husband's love, who was ashamed to rouse and fan the passion extinguished in him. Her just anger would then raise its voice, her contempt, pride and defiance.

Horrified by the possibility that she foresaw with such certainty, she sought deliverance from herself and from what was to come. A sort of a faint spark of hope shone from her memories. It seemed to her that once before she had been dying of this grief, once before she had been dying of this boundless despair. It was in the first bloom of her young love, in the full splendor of her happiness – two days before the wedding. At that time they had received unexpected, disturbing, but undoubtedly true, information about his reckless life, and the way he had squandered his property. Her parents, alarmed and outraged, sent word that he was definitely not to visit again. But he raced over that same day, despairing and determined, and he showered her with passionate words, appealing to her love: of course, her parents would not give their consent, that was obvious and clear. Why, her father was right to throw a groom like himself out the door. But was it possible for the two of them to part? Was it possible to live without one another? Why should their love be trampled underfoot on account of the contemptible money she was supposed to receive? Let them keep it, he wasn't interested in their money! They would both be poor like many other people, but happy as few had been. His farm was, of course, in debt, but it could still provide for a wife, even if he had to toil day and night. They might even sell the farm on him, and then he might have to work as a farm laborer or hireling! He could do anything, and bear everything, but live without her? Never! With surprising frankness he admitted to his lapses and faults, but what resolutions, what superhuman tasks he would set for himself, if only she would risk poverty, if only she wanted to be his. She wept and said 'yes' and her mother wept along with her. Her father was furious, denounced him and turned him away, threatened to evict him and yet did not. Then he gave his consent, but on the condition that his daughter would be disinherited. Before a year had passed after the wedding, the father himself brought the dowry, an even larger one than he had promised. She hardly cared at all about it, she was so happy at that time! His love was genuine, but his resolve disappointed her. She would endure even this impending disgrace with him, if only he would honestly and openly confess, as he had once before, if only he would promise to be different from now on. But he wasn't different, nor would he be.

She saw through the little window how he walked about the courtyard, hurrying in all directions at once, impatient, thrusting aside everything that forced him to think about the farm or the family. For a long time she had sensed that his mind was elsewhere, and whenever she had decided to disturb him from his thoughts with a vague hint, she encountered only despicable pretence.

When she heard him give the order for the horses to be harnessed, a recent, smarting memory rankled in her: Kajta's teasing words and playful laughter sounded in her ears and revived her pain. At that moment she left her hiding place, upright, proud, as if she had not felt the blows that had just fallen so heavily on her. When he saw her he was startled and tried to avoid her.

She stood watching the servant who was hitching up the horses. Then she turned to her husband.

'I'm going with those horses! You can take your own to Oseky!' she said, in a taunting voice, for she knew that he had no horses he could truly call his own.

Humiliated, undecided, feeble, he stood before her and stared rigidly at the ground. Slowly he lifted his head and, avoiding her gaze, asked quietly:

'Where are you going?'

She gave him a hard, defiant look; in that moment she did not feel the deadly blows under which her heart had groaned.

'For now, you don't need to know,' she said quickly, without mercy. 'But I will tell you one thing right away: I'll never come back to you again!'

Not surprised, but profoundly stunned, he bent his head, as if he had known and expected it all. Seeing her still standing there, defiant and spiteful, he walked rapidly away, fearing even greater humiliation. She laughed out loud at this rush, which seemed to her a cowardly retreat. There was so much offense and contempt in that laughter that he stood frozen to the spot. Measuring her with a cruel, flashing eye, he said, harsh and decided: 'Go on, go!'

A GREAT PASSION

RŮŽENA SVOBODOVÁ

I

Wedged between two slopes of the high mountains was a plain that was sometimes green, sometimes hidden in gray mist as if under ice. There were peasant dwellings scattered over it, as well as white manor houses on the borders of old parks, and red villas set between little forests, dark blotches shaded off from the green fields.

Along the road, cutting through the countryside and leading across the mountain ridge beyond the border, little cottages trickled over the common pasture in the narrowing valley, thickening finally in a village that was called the 'Fair Knolls'.

At the end of the village, right up by the tall pine woods, stood a handsome, imposing inn which was well known to the traders who carted their goods past it and out of the country. They lodged here with their servants and their wares; the lord's black huntsmen also frequented the famous roadside inn.[1]

It was an ancient village, with wood buildings, and right across the road from the inn stood a hundred-year-old elm tree with a hollow trunk. There was a legend about this trunk, according to which if a chaste maiden stepped into it the elm would not shut, but if an unchaste maiden stepped

---

[1] In the first short story in the collection *Černí myslivci* (The Black Huntsmen, Prague, 1908), the narrator explains that the twelve huntsmen are the servants of Bishop Rudolf, who controls a large estate in the High Mountains (Vysoké hory). The bishop always dresses in black and so do the huntsmen, who are famous in the region as dancers, drinkers and lovers. The bishop does not permit them to marry while they are in his service. Whenever one of the bishop's rangers retires or dies, the bishop promotes the eldest of the huntsmen to the vacant position, and finds a new youth to join his group of attendants. The story translated here is the second story in the collection. I refer to the bishop here as 'the lord'.

into it, the elm would embrace her and never release her alive from its darkness.[2]

This legend was linked to another very widespread legend according to which the rosemary would wilt, the stream would run foul, the milk in the cellars would turn blood-red and the rings would break in two, if a husband to his wife or a lover to his beloved would be untrue.[3]

The inn had been kept in the family for three generations and the present innkeeper managed it with his eighteen-year-old daughter, a graceful girl with high expectations – she might almost have been of genteel birth. They lived there with the old grandmother, who had long been incapable of work.

During the day hardly anyone appeared at the inn, but in the evening, when the covered carriages arrived with the merchants, coachmen, huntsmen and gamekeepers, the whole house came to life.

It was merry in the kitchen, full of work and bustle, and all evening long the old clog maker told merry stories which he had gathered on his travels over the world, and the young merchants and huntsmen came to pay homage to the young lady of the house, pretty Žofka.

Žofka's father kept a strict watch over her and often considered how he might marry her off to greatest advantage.

2 The word 'čistá' appears frequently in the short story, with different connotations. In the first instance, it is used to describe an innocent virgin girl (panna čistá), translated here as 'chaste maiden'. 'Čistá' also means clean, and it is used with reference to rooms: i. e. both before and after her marriage, Žofka keeps the inn in a state of 'čistota', translated here as 'pristine cleanliness'. The narrator also refers to Marjana's 'čistá světnička', translated here as 'clean sitting room'. After Jiří's betrayal, the narrator comments that Žofka's 'nejčistší víra' (translated here as 'purest faith') in man has been wounded.
3 According to popular superstition, rosemary has protective, lucky qualities; it is also a symbol of remembrance and fidelity at marriages and funerals.

He was most pleased by the thought that she would become the wife of a manufacturer who sometimes visited the inn for no reason at all and had long conversations with her.

The merchants, returning from abroad in the spring, brought her fine gifts: red shoes embroidered with gold, turquoise rings, fine gossamer shawls woven with silver, coral beads and fragrant soaps.

She did not honor a single one of them with her favor, nor did she ever accompany a single one beyond the doorstep.

She watched their figures disappear down the road between the tall pines; she heard the cracking of whips, the calls of the coachmen; she heard them recede into the distance in order to return six months later. But her heart did not ache for anyone.

They sent back pretty greetings for her through the men who had accompanied them over the mountain ridge with the draught team borrowed from the innkeeper – the 'buckle', as the mountain folk called it.

She did not even listen to the messages they sent.

It seemed that she liked the youthful huntsmen dressed in black much more, but her father protected her from them. Whenever he saw her chatting with one of them, he punished her with angry looks and immediately found some task for her to do in the ice cellar or in the larder, some useless task, and therefore boring, so that she preferred to avoid anything that might give occasion for such work.

He walked about the house, through the corridors and the kitchen, and was constantly peeking through the little windows which broke up all the walls to see what his merry, singing daughter was doing.

Perfect order reigned in the house; everything was scrubbed white and the polished brass rings on the wooden pots shone like gold.

Neat, supple, curly-haired Žofka, who always stood straight and tall, kept the house in this state of pristine cleanliness.

The mother of the house had died not long ago and the grandmother, as she herself said, 'could hear well and see well, but shook like a merry andrew'.[4] She had lost her memory and was amazed, for example, to hear that an eighty-year-old woman had died:

'She's died, has she? That young lady! Why, she was younger than me!'

When she was a girl she had served under the lord's chatelaine, *beim Hof*, as she put it; she had had a very good position, which she liked to recall, saying that she had lived *ein schönes Leben*.[5]

She once told the guests about her former mistress:

'She was a good woman. I respect her more than my own children, and I always think that when I die, if I still have my wits about me and am able to speak, my last words' (her wizened fingers played for a moment about her bluish, open lips) – 'my last words will be: "Frau Kastner."'

Žofka wanted to hear something from her about love, something about terrifying, burning love, but it had been such a long time since the old woman had known anything about such things, such a long time since she had forgotten everything, and now she did not even understand her granddaughter's questions.

Whenever the innkeeper had to go to the city on business, he entrusted his daughter to the old woman to guard.

And the daughter was radiance itself; as if she were on fire from her heels to her head, she trembled with a young, incandescent power.

---

4 A 'merry andrew' is a mountebank's assistant; a clown or buffoon.
5 Beim Hof – 'at court' or 'at the manor'; ein schönes Leben – 'a beautiful life'.

Her black eyes sought someone to captivate, her red mouth someone to kiss – not a peaceful, devout kiss, but rather the fatal caresses of a wood nymph.

II

When the black huntsmen came to the inn one very warm May evening, they brought along musicians and set to dancing.

The musicians played in the garden in the night darkness; those who did not dance sat drinking beer under the budding chestnuts, while the young people raced through one galop after another.

The huntsman Jiří came to ask Žofka for a dance. He was the most elegant of the huntsmen, a perfect dandy compared to the rest, and he had been the sweetheart of Slávinka, the ranger's daughter, for many years now.

They danced a mad galop, intoxicating like dark wine.

For a long time now Žofka had liked the huntsman Jiří, and he was not one of those boys who, for the sake of one girl, spoils things with all the rest.

Many times before he had set Žofka afire with his practiced, passionate eyes, and he was glad that she never dropped her eyes before him.

Now he embraced her in the gay dance; he touched her forehead with his warm breath and his hand trembled in hers.

For a long time now he had liked the fiery, radiant Žofka – ten times more than the mild, wearisome Slávinka, whose love was too morose.

Now he felt that Žofka's hands were also trembling. He gripped her more tightly in his arms. Her forehead touched his face.

Her hair fluttered against his lips and he kissed it gently. They flew about the hall in a tight embrace. The music came to an end.

He looked at her with eyes that pleaded, that professed the most blazing emotions, the flush of blood – and they demanded an answer.

She remembered Slávinka and avoided his gaze.

He leaned down to her firm, white hand and kissed it.

They went out of the hall.

They stood on the doorstep.

He said brusquely:

'I don't love Sláva anymore!'

'What do I care!' Žofka answered. 'It doesn't matter to me. Not a bit!'

'I just thought I'd tell you; I'm not trying to pique your interest...'

Her father emerged from the dark.

'Žofka! Go home!' he shouted.

She left the huntsman Jiří without a parting word.

She was angry and tears started in her eyes, the angry tears of an unfulfilled, uncertain longing.

Her father sent her to bed, while he remained in the garden with the guests.

Žofka went into the house, entered her little sitting room, stood still for a moment and thought for a while.

The eyes of the huntsman burned on her cheeks and throat; a chill flew lightly over her skin.

She stretched. She did not feel like sleeping; she did not feel like undressing.

'I don't love Sláva anymore!' she repeated and shuddered, recalling his passionate voice.

She could have danced all night long with the huntsman Jiří.

She sighed out loud and her teeth chattered... 'With the huntsman Jiří!' she repeated out loud, in a kind of fever. 'What strength the huntsman Jiří has! If he wanted to, he could crush a strong girl like me. He could lift me up with one hand like a little partridge. Of all his huntsmen the lord likes the huntsman Jiří best!'

She strolled to the door, entered the hall and from the hall she went out to the verandah. She did not know herself where she was wandering to.

Outside it was completely dark.

A soft hand gripped hers. She felt a scrap of paper in her palm. Quickly she turned back inside and lit the lamp. The paper was torn from a huntsman's notebook and on it was written:

Nor do I have people's blessing
when I come to court you.

She opened the window and said into the darkness: 'I'll give it to Slávinka!'

She did not wait for an answer, but quickly shut the window.

All night long she felt triumphant in her dreams and all the next day she sang and celebrated God knows what.

In the evening, she grew uneasy. The huntsmen did not come.

A rainy gale swept down from the mountains and a dense, impenetrable darkness covered the countryside.

The windowpanes quivered from the constant blasts of wind.

Žofka prepared to go to bed at ten o'clock. She walked about the house, putting out the lights, and then went out onto the verandah to put out the lantern. At first, she could not open the door because the wind was leaning against it with all its strength. Finally she managed to open it and the stubborn, wet, fresh wind, which had thundered over the woods, whipping them up into a kind of awesome, deadly chorale, struck her in the face.

Her skirts twisted against her sturdy legs.

She turned her breast to face the gale and inhaled the pure air in deep, ravenous breaths.

Everything exhilarated her, and the storm of her young blood was even stronger than the night thunder.

She had such a craving for life – heady, sweet and unfamiliar life!

In the darkness, without warning, a soft hand silently pressed hers.

She recognized it and kept quiet.

'Žofka!' the huntsman Jiří said eagerly. 'I came to see you.'

'No one called you!'

'I've been running two hours in this storm!'

'No one asked you to!' she answered, and her words were harsh, but her voice had an ardent, uneasy tremor.

'Are you ordering me to leave?'

'Go to Sláva!'

'And what if I never, never go to Sláva again?' the huntsman Jiří replied ardently, speaking right by her face.

From close up she saw his passionate, arrogant eyes and felt his warm breath.

'... never, never will I go to Sláva again. It's you I'll come to see!' he said to her in a thrilling whisper, in a voice which was intoxicated and intoxicating, which conveyed all that words could not express.

But Žofka, greedy to hear everything she dreaded and longed for with her entire being, protested:

'Why should you come to see me? There's no reason to!'

'Don't you know that I like you? You and you alone! That wherever I go I think of you? That I came for you in a storm like this?'

Žofka listened eagerly and kept quiet. Best of all she would have liked to say: 'Go on, go on – I can't get enough of it!'

The wind tore at her clothes and her hair. The lantern continued to burn; she did not put it out. In the dark she sought the eyes and lips of the huntsman.

Practiced, passionate, desirable lips came near to hers and kissed them feverishly.

'Žofka, Žofka,' said the voice, amazed at itself, amazed at the joy she brought, amazed at the first excitement of new love, one of life's strongest impressions.

'My Žofka!' he continued, and his words were a question, a confession, an assurance.

Instead of answering, Žofka's flushed face stayed close to his and she offered him her hungry lips.

He sheltered her in his arms and sucked at her naked throat, her fiery cheeks, her burning, greedy lips.

Someone tried to open the door. Žofka jumped away and pushed the huntsman into the darkness.

Her father appeared on the doorstep.

'I can't put out the lantern!' the daughter said, embarrassed.

'I'll put it out myself, but the minute I see you speaking with the huntsman Jiří, I'll send you away to Vienna to work and don't think you'll ever turn to me again!' he said, weighing every word and directing each of them with absolute certainty into the dark.

III

At the other end of the village in a tiny cottage lived a black-haired, robust old woman – a woman from the foothills – who was nicknamed Marjana Money Pots.[6] She was a herbalist, a rustic apothecary who collected herbs from miles around and sold them to housewives in the surrounding towns.

---

6   Svobodová uses the expression: 'Marjana, sedm centů dukátů', which means literally 'seven quintals of ducats'; I have used the phrase 'Money Pots'.

Often she was away from the cottage for days on end, leaving it empty. She had a clean sitting room, fragrant with mint, chamomile and other herbs.

Marjana Money Pots was dependent on the good will of the huntsmen.

If they had ordered her to keep out of the woods and mountain meadows, she would have had to sell her cottage and leave the countryside to eke out a living on some other estate.

The huntsman Jiří knew her well.

She always bowed down low before him and several times she invited him to her cottage.

Žofka was not supposed to speak to the huntsman Jiří, but she thought of nothing else but where she would see him next. She did not think of Slávinka, or of his infidelity; she thought only of her blazing happiness, her intoxication, her impatient longing for his embrace and his ravenous lips.

All night long she did not shut her eyes for fear that while sleeping she would not be able to think of him, and she called up in her imagination every quiver of joy from his kisses, every one of his passionate, coarse, ravishing words (all the more intoxicating for their coarseness) and every one of his mad, iron embraces.

'He would suck out my very soul if he could!' she said to herself, pleased and proud of his kisses.

In front of her father, they did not exchange a single word of greeting, and he was completely reassured.

Sometimes they all sat at the same table and the lovers, although they were scorched by passion, did not bat an eyelid.

Sometimes they only exchanged a little note under the table furtively – an arrangement for a rendezvous.

Twice they met in the woods.

The hillsides were turning green with little tufts of grass; the clover was opening up; in the rugged landscape only the alders and fruit trees still hesitated.

Žofka went a roundabout way through the forest to look at the fields. In the woods she found the huntsman Jiří. As soon as their eyes met, they ran towards each other.

They could not grasp all the happiness of their sudden love; they could not get their fill of kisses, could not stare at one another long enough.

One examined the other and both discovered unexpected charms.

'What a little mouth you have! As red as cherries!' he wondered.

'What beautiful eyes you have! Cruel eyes that are beautiful when I draw near,' she wondered in turn. No one was more beautiful than they.

Žofka, however, was not permitted to go far out of sight, and both of them had the feeling that they were always being watched, that Žofka's father would appear among the trees. Their embraces were constantly disturbed by this fear, and their kisses, in which they surrendered completely to one another, longed for greater solitude.

He kissed her little knees, wrapped in her fine skirts, her little ankles in white stockings, her arms all the way to her elbows; but she was constantly looking about, distracted, for fear she might see the strict, dark face of her father somewhere.

Marjana Money Pots loaned her cottage to the huntsman, gave him the door-key and went off to make the rounds of the stores or to collect herbs on the mountains.

The huntsman begged Žofka to meet him in Marjana's fragrant sitting room.

Žofka would run there to see her impatient lover whenever her father went to the city, or whenever she could use the excuse of visiting a girlfriend. The old grandmother was sleeping out her life and did not even notice that Žofka was gone, and the servants did not give her away.

The lovers made love in the clean, fragrant sitting room. No one knocked on the window; no one gave them cause for fear.

Žofka would return home in a state of blissful infatuation, exhausted from the kisses, enraptured with the life that had finally begun for her, with the love that fulfilled all her expectations.

IV

There was a blacksmith who often used to frequent the inn, a brawny, coarse, eccentric character, a brawler who had no equal in all the region. He could not tolerate an insult, and would immediately settle the score to the death.

In the taproom he always took a seat opposite the kitchen door and all evening long he would drink slowly and gaze at Žofka with dull, devoted eyes as she flitted about in the kitchen.

He would always sit without a jacket in a colorful shirt, his chin resting on his hands.

Sometimes for months on end he was peaceful, as long as no one offended him personally.

But whenever he got in a temper, they would leave him alone in the taproom, and if he fell upon someone anyway, the victim had to be defended by all present. Otherwise he didn't escape from the blacksmith's hands alive.

None of those who knew that the huntsman Jiří waited for curly-haired Žofka in Marjana's cottage said a word to the innkeeper.

But one time the innkeeper drove off, entrusting the inn to his daughter and his daughter to the old grandmother. In the evening, impatient for kisses, Žofka ran off into the dark to meet her lover.

The blacksmith-brawler saw her running over the meadows and set out after her. He wanted to find out whether she had a lover, and if she did where she was rushing off to meet him, and who that lucky person might be. She ran on ahead of him, happy, glowing and light-footed. The brawler saw her disappear into Marjana's cottage. He took up a position in the bushes across the road and waited. He suspected something was wrong. He heard his own heart beating. A moment later he saw the huntsman Jiří enter the cottage...

He waited until long after midnight. He lay in the wet grass and chewed on it in pain. They came out, yet they still had not had enough of each other. They kissed again – sweet, tired kisses – right by the bush behind which the blacksmith-brawler was hidden.

Only when they could no longer be heard did the brawler howl like a wolf and fall back again into the wet grass.

V

The next day, when the innkeeper returned from the city, he learned that the brawler had been carrying on all day, that one of his bad days had set in. He drank plum brandy, shot after shot, and muttered threats to someone or other, saying he would kill him; they could not understand who.[7]

In the evening, the huntsmen arrived in two carriages. They had had an *Amtstag* in the city, and returned in good cheer.[8]

The innkeeper asked them to be seated in the little room because the brawler might, in his moodiness, annoy the gentlemen.

'He's as savage as a wild beast!'

7   Plum brandy – slivovitz.
8   'Amtstag' (office-day) means a day when the huntsmen had to be in the bishop's office, an administration day.

The huntsmen were not afraid of the brawler and laughed at the innkeeper. There were eight of them against one man, and he had often amused them before with his furious outbursts. Many times they had torn a man from the brawler's grip so that he would not beat him to death.

The huntsman Jiří ordered a bottle of red wine.

He wiped the neck of the bottle with a napkin, poured the wine slowly into his glass and admired it with pleasure.

Everything in the world pleased him; his gaze was proud, self-confident, and he carried his head high.

The blacksmith-brawler stood up from his place, staggered a little, wrinkled his low brow, came reeling over to the huntsman Jiří and without a word insolently dropped down on the seat next to him.

The huntsman knew that the brawler wanted to provoke him.

He acted as if he hadn't seen him. He wanted to have a drink and he raised his glass.

Narrowing his eyes in a suspicious and sinister manner, the brawler snatched the glass from his hand with a quiet swoop, like a bear, and downed it in one gulp.

The huntsman did not lose his composure.

He poured a second time and was about to drink it himself.

But again the arm in the colorful shirt reached out for the glass and the blacksmith-brawler downed it once more.

The gentlemen at the table began to be amused. Their rough laughter and deep voices mixed together in wonder and curiosity.

Undisturbed, the huntsman Jiří poured a third time, pushed aside the brawler's outstretched hand and said soothingly: 'Now you wait. I want to drink now!'

But hardly had he raised the glass to his lips when the brawler jumped up, knocked him over, seized his genteel throat with both paws, kneeled on his chest and tilted his head back.

Just in time, the huntsmen rushed to help him.

The blacksmith-brawler would have broken his neck.

The black huntsmen were not sparing with their blows; they beat the blacksmith, and because he had spoiled their fun, they did not sit back down to their glasses.

They conferred and then ordered the grooms to tie the brawler to one of the coaches with a chain. Then they drove off. This act of revenge was the huntsman Jiří's idea.

The blacksmith-brawler had to run behind the carriage of the huntsman Jiří. When they were going uphill, he was able to keep up; but whenever they came to a flat surface and the horses started to trot, the blacksmith could not keep up. He would fall down and his strong, muscular body would bash about behind the carriage over the rough road.

They untied him after a two-hour drive, battered and bloody, with one broken foot, which had to be amputated a week later, never to heal again.

VI

Night descended upon Žofka's life, a night during which she knelt in prayer before the image of the Mother of God. She had not consulted her before; but now she fled to Mary when the world suddenly went dark in front of her, when she had to recite the prayer of St Margaret.[9]

The hundred-year-old hollow elm, in which she had hidden a hundred times as a child and as a girl, the hundred-year-old hollow elm would have shut behind her a long time ago and never released her from its embrace. She had not even thought of the elm before, but by now she knew

9   The 'prayer of St Margaret' may refer to St Margaret of Antioch, a legendary virgin martyr. She attracted devotion in the Middle Ages and later. She is the patroness of women in childbirth.

that if she did not become the wife of the huntsman Jiří immediately, she would utterly ruin her anxious father, she would have to go abroad, give up her free life, her friends, everything that tied her to the mountains where she was born. Joy at the thought that she would have a beautiful son, beautiful like the huntsman Jiří, a being similar to him, with the same brown eyes, and similarly passionate, graceful and brave; joy at this thought was battered down by the torment of those slights which awaited her as the mother of a child out of wedlock, whose father would not be tied to her by any law and could go away and abandon her, despised by all, left with the orphan child and poverty.

In her torment she pleaded with the Mother of God not to let it happen; she promised to live a life of renunciation from now until death. But with her entire loving being she passionately wanted it to be true that she would have his son, a new being similar to him; even if he parted from her and abandoned her as he had Slávinka, the ranger's daughter, she wanted to have his son at least.

Mary did not listen to her.

Pale, confused, distracted in her work, Žofka now considered how she would tell Jiří. She was afraid sometimes of men's love of comfort; she was afraid that Jiří would leave her in order to rid himself of the responsibility; she dreaded that this confession would also be a parting.

But the huntsman Jiří reassured her. He promised her that she alone would be his wife, that everything would be concealed for the moment, that she would go away for a while to the city so that no one would find anything out, that he would take care of and pay for everything. It would be easy to find an excuse for her departure; in three years' time it would be his turn to serve as the quarter-ranger, and then they would take back the child, whom, in the meantime, they would send off to be raised somewhere else. He reassured her.

She left in time for the city, in order to learn how to cook, and she returned happy and smiling. She left behind a handsome, strong little son with a nursemaid in a village and she continued to live as she had before. The huntsman Jiří still loved her bright, graceful, charming being; all the while they continued to meet in Marjana's fragrant sitting room and no one betrayed them to her father.

After three years Jiří was appointed quarter-ranger in a distant region. Before he left, he asked the innkeeper for his daughter's hand in marriage and begged to be able to take her away as soon as possible. The innkeeper was impressed by his quiet, modest and constant love and promised to give her to him.

He bought two cows and a set of furniture for his daughter's dowry and made arrangements for the wedding.

Žofka was ecstatic; she pestered the entire household, not sparing even the aged grandmother her crazy little songs.

On the day when everything was ready, the cakes baked, the clothes sewn and decorated with myrtle,[10] when the groom was supposed to drive up, an important message addressed to Žofka arrived by post.

It was the wedding announcement of the huntsman Jiří and Slávinka, the ranger's daughter, whom he married that same day in the lord's royal city. Slávinka's father announced the marriage and the address was written in an unknown hand.

The lame blacksmith-brawler was sitting in the taproom; the innkeeper was standing at the counter. Both of them saw how Žofka's hands shook, how the blood rushed to her face, how she turned pale and put her hand on her tortured,

10   Myrtle is a symbol of purity, love, peace and happiness; it is customary at weddings, either in the bride's bouquet or worn on her person.

defeated heart. Both of them saw how she staggered, but they were not quick enough to catch her.

She tumbled over in a faint.

They revived her.

She came to and immediately remembered the horror in all its entirety. She broke into tears – loud, heart-breaking weeping – without caring who heard her, who was present in the inn.

'My God, my God, what will I do, what will become of me?' she moaned.

Her father tried to console her and said:

'Never mind, you're not going to cry over a groom! Surely all is not lost because of one man!'

Žofka was sitting on the bench behind the table, where they had led her after she had recovered from the faint, and she beat her forehead against the table.

Her father's words unleashed her bitter despair, which had been building up over the past few moments.

She lifted her curly-haired head, her face, full of red blotches, disfigured by tears, and she said in a voice which had matured over the past few moments and which would always be tinged with sadness:

'Papa, if you only knew how wretched I am, how worthless I am, if you only knew, you would kill me, and that would be a good thing! For years, I went through life and never thought about anything, never drew back from anything! Not once did I ask myself what kind of person he was, what kind of soul, what kind of character he had. Like a blind woman I believed him; at a word from him I followed him. Everything about him was precious to me. Every harsh word of his, every sweet word of his. Everything pleased me. Not for one moment did I doubt that he was an honorable and truthful human being. He told me that he and Sláva had separated for good, that he didn't love her, that she had hurt him, and I believed every word. I never deceived him myself, not even with a glance. For three years I did not look at another man. I belonged to him – I was his sweetheart, his wife. Up to this moment, I had considered myself a human being. But now, papa, now that I see that I belonged to a liar, to a base and deceitful human being, to a fraud, I realize that I too am base, deceitful and fraudulent. I wasn't his wife; I was a whore, and you should have me driven out of the village with whips!'

Her father leaned on the counter and listened. The veins on his forehead were swollen and he breathed with difficulty.

'What – what are you saying?' he hissed, afraid to understand.

'Yes, papa, I will tell you everything,' Žofka said in a hoarse voice. 'There is no longer room for me in the world because there is no just punishment for me. I lived with him; I was his wife for three years; we met in Marjana's cottage; grandmother did not keep an eye on me! I did not go to learn to cook; that wasn't why I went to the city. I was at the maternity hospital; I left a son out there in the world and I'm expecting another child! I am telling you this because I cannot bear to live: I'm horrified by myself, and by the thought of what a deceitful father my children have. Do what you want with me, beat me to death if you want. My life doesn't matter to me – nothing matters to me! But for the love of God forgive me for bringing you such grief, for bringing filth into your life!'

She slid down from the bench and bowed her head all the way to the ground.

Her father slowly drew near. He was filled with disgust at life, from which his one pride had been taken. The suffering of an evil passion, revulsion, anger and helplessness against Fate grew in him and raised him from the ground. He chattered and hissed as if in a fever; he had no idea what he would do or what he would say, but he wanted to kick aside that pile of clothes which lay on the beaten earth of the taproom. He looked around to see if he could find something with which to strike her. He looked for a knife; he even looked in his pocket for his pocketknife.

'Damn you!' he said, his lips pale with rage, and finding nothing, he shut his eyes. He could not bear the light, he could not bear to look at her, he could not bear to look upon life.

He took a heavy wooden chair in his hands and raised it.

The blacksmith-brawler, who had seen everything, jumped up and grabbed it from his hands.

The innkeeper might have picked up another chair; he might have shoved the lame blacksmith aside; but he did not do so. The tension of his first outburst was spent.

He collapsed onto his chair, hid his face in his hands and lamented in a bitter, rough voice, breaking into tears:

'I was a proud man. I set store by my honorable family. I worked; I saved money; I carried on business; I aimed high, so that my daughter could be a lady. And for what? So that they can stone me and drive me out of the village, so that everyone can point a finger at me! All because of you, you ungrateful viper! I'll drive you out!' he shouted. 'I'll whip you! I won't share in your shame. Let everyone know that I disown you publicly. Let none of your shame remain with me!'

The blacksmith-brawler stood in the middle of the sitting room, somewhat embarrassed, softened, steeling himself for some act. He swallowed his words, seeking new ones. He did not look at Žofka, collapsed and sobbing on the ground, or at the innkeeper. He looked into himself, into his most sacred emotions. His heart ached from the surge of noble intentions.

'Miss Žofka,' he said finally, still faltering. 'Don't cry, Miss Žofka, get up; no one knows anything about it and no one will find out, and I – if you want it – I will marry you. His child will be my child and no one will be allowed to insult you! I can still crush any man!'

Žofka was not listening. She was indifferent to his words. She too was looking only into herself, into her passionate memories, and she could not find a single one she could linger over and not turn away in disgust. Everything that had intoxicated her before, all the moments spent with him, all the odd, caressing words which had previously intoxicated her, came to mock her in the very center of her soul, came to humiliate her and fill her entire existence with disgust.

'How many times did he repeat them?' she asked herself.

She did not realize that they were hackneyed, that he had not even invented new words for her. The words wandered forlorn from one love to another, long ago stripped of the magic of their birth. He repeated the same thing to all of them, probably at the same time. He was not the one man in life from whom she had expected everything, all degrees of wisdom and good advice, all degrees of happiness. He was a good-for-nothing, an ordinary, empty swaggerer, who was only trying to seduce. He knew how to dazzle with his eyes, nothing more. And that was the man for whom she had sacrificed herself, her entire future, her father's life. That was the man she had trusted.

The innkeeper shook hands with the blacksmith.

'I hadn't intended to give my daughter to a blacksmith-brawler; I had greater plans for her. But now that this has happened, go ahead and marry her, as soon as possible. Today is Thursday; there's a feast day next week. The marriage banns will be announced and the wedding ceremony will be on Monday. If you beat her, it's all she deserves! But don't stay here in my sight. You know how to work; you'll find work anywhere. Go to the ironworks, I don't want to see either of you!'

Before Žofka had risen from the ground, her fate was decided. She made no objections. If they had driven her through the village, if she had had to kneel through the night on burning coals in front of the house of Marjana Money Pots it would have been all the same to her. Her purest faith in man had been wounded, her soul had been scorched by humiliation and disgust, and nothing else mattered.

She married the blacksmith-brawler. On the day of her wedding, someone or other brought a portrait of the newly married couple, Jiří and Slávinka, to the inn, so that Žofka would remember all her terrible torment, so that his betrayal would remain intact in her soul, tattooed with a fiery needle, so that all the rosemary would wilt forever, the streams would run foul, the milk in the cellar would turn blood-red, and the rings would break in two.

VII

Žofka, the curly-haired young lady, went out into the world to work with her husband, the blacksmith-brawler. Even when he tried to be most gentle, she suffered because of his coarseness. Her scorched soul did not open up into blossom. She suffered, she changed, she fell silent. Her little daughter was born dead and Žofka was glad that it never even looked upon the bitter world.

Jiří wrote to her; he begged her forgiveness; he explained everything to her, admitting his own guilt.

Some time ago, he had seduced Slávinka too; he had destroyed her too. And she had driven with her father to the lord and presented her cause to him. She was the first, her claim was greater. The lord had ordered him to marry her immediately, or else he would be released from the royal service. The lord himself had had the marriage announcements sent out from his office. The marriage was misery. They tormented one another. He hated Slávinka and he even told her so. When she lamented her forlorn life, he said to her, 'You insisted on it yourself!' Everything depressed him and he begged Žofka for one thing, to be able to take his son into his own home – the son who was still being raised somewhere in the world and for whose keep he paid himself. If he couldn't have her, he wanted to have her son. In order to please him, his wife had said she would be kind to the boy. But he would not trust Žofka's husband.

Žofka was moved, and because her husband had reproached her several times on account of the child, she agreed that the blacksmith would only beat him. Because she did not have the power to make her son's fate more beautiful, she consented.

But not even the little boy brought Jiří peace. There was one thing he could not understand: why he had not thanked the lord for the position and simply left, why he had allowed himself to be bound, why he had submitted, why today he had to live under the power of the lord's will.

He neglected his duties; all over the woods they stole wood from him; the gamekeepers could be bribed; wagons slipped away from the clearings and he didn't know anything about it. Everything, everything, oppressed him. He received a reprimand from the lord's forest authorities. He pulled himself together somewhat, but the work simply gave him no pleasure. His good, suffering wife complained to their relatives. They sent some old aunt to go and speak to him. He sent her a message that he would shoot her if she came near the gamekeeper's lodge. And so they dragged their brutal, poisoned life on.

Žofka, the brawler's wife, heard about it all. She was able to bear her hard, coarse existence with the crippled brawler only because she knew that they were both suffering, she and her beloved, because she could cherish his image again in her saddened soul, because the memories grew sweet again and subsided. Only then, only then. In the factory city, black with coal, she missed the woods where she was born. Sometimes she would sit alone with her face in her hands, her eyes covered, and she would imagine everything, everything from years past: the rustling of the woods, the wind that flew through the tops of the trees, the scent of the wilting, mown grass, the sharp sounds of the swinging of the scythes, the old elm, the house, the mountains, the famous high mountains and the dales, the widow-herb and foxglove, the meadows in the valley with the well-trodden footpaths and Marjana's wooden cottage, the scrubbed, fragrant sitting room. Dear God, dear God! And somewhere in the world a little son, a black-haired boy, with skin like brown silk, whom she could not call to her side. Dear God, dear God! Her husband never let her go to him. And before her lay a life which, in the way it took shape, was incomprehensible to her – a life which was by now set, unchanging, ugly, measured to her death! Tears trickled down between her fingers; moaning convulsed her chest. And it all began in a dance hall on a warm evening in May; yes, yes, it all began with a passionate galop. And look at how it all turned out. Her husband comes home, the same man who wanted to strangle her beloved; he drags his lame leg, the one her beloved had maimed during that ig-nominious ride. Her husband is often gloomy, drunken, but he never beats her; he only threatens to. He has never yet struck her with a blow. But his words fall even more heavily on her, and he wants her to love him. It would be better if he beat her... The fragrant sitting room is lost forever and there are moments when every last nerve of her fiery be-ing trembles for it. But that's all past, all of it; she has no one to kiss; she does not have the one under whose kisses she swooned. So much water has flowed by since then, so much water has flowed by. She has a blacksmith-brawler for a husband, and somewhere in the world a child, a pretty, nut-brown little orphan.

After sometime, she received news. Her little boy had fallen ill. They summoned her. The blacksmith would not let her go. The child died. She was not permitted to go to the funeral. For a long while she grieved, then gradually she grew calm and listless.

VIII

Empty, dusky years passed by. The memories faded; in time they did not hurt so much; they returned less and less frequently.

Her father died; the blacksmith, whose crippled leg hindered him in his work, returned to the roadside inn in the village with his wife.

Dull, pointless years passed by. Žofka grew indifferent. Her face was fresh, full and rosy; her curly hair turned gray and silver. She still dressed elegantly, in a black dress with a narrow, white collar at the throat. She welcomed the gentlemen, the merchants and the huntsmen, with dignity, and she kept the house in a state of pristine cleanliness. The floors and the pots were white, scrubbed; the brass handles always shone like gold.

Once again she heard the rustling of the woods where she was born, she heard the wind flying through the tops of the pines.

Her tamed, anxious husband stood behind the counter or repaired something in the house. He walked about noisily, without a jacket, in a long-sleeved undershirt, and was constantly delivering cantankerous monologues about the work he was doing.

IX

Thirty years passed.

One day people saw a stranger in the village, an old man with a gray head of hair, a gray beard and flashing eyes. Deep in thought, he walked towards the inn. He could not make up his mind to go in. He returned to the village.

A short while later he appeared again on the footpath.

He wore a gray, flannel suit and fine linen, and his hands, too, were fine.

He hesitated a moment. Finally he went in.

The old lover had come to look upon his beloved of long ago.

After thirty years.

All those who remembered the old heartbreak thought she would lock the door in his face.

But Žofka led him into the little room; she laid out the table for him graciously and made her guest feel at home. Her husband the brawler, dragging his lame leg, maimed on that infamous night, carried the food to the table and served him. A long time ago he had ceased to be jealous.

The lover from years gone by spoke with his beloved of long ago. For a moment their eyes grew moist; yes, at moments their cheeks even blushed.

'Žofka, my dear heart, how are you?' he asked her.

'How else, Jiří? I'm fine now, I'm fine now!'

'How long has it been since we saw each other, dear heart?'

'It's thirty years now!'

'The last time we spoke was at the crossroads at Trojický.'

'I walked along with you there for the last time when you left to take up your new post. To this very day I never go along that path.'

'And I went by the cottage and looked everything over. How life has gone by, deaf to it all!'

'Yes, it has gone by.'

'Will we see each other again some time?'

'We'll hardly see one another again; life rushes on. And anyway, what now, what use is it now, when life has flown by so pointlessly?'

Žofka, the blacksmith's wife, wept. Tears squeezed their way through her fingers, pressed against her eyes.

Her beloved looked at her quietly with moist eyes. They stood once more on the doorstep, as they had long ago. They shook hands in parting, but could not say a word because of the pain.

What could they have said to one another now anyway, when their lives had blossomed and wilted in vain, without leaving a trace?

They separated, in order to live out the rest of their days in quiet – days which had begun for them a long while ago with a kiss in the evening – a victorious, radiant, fiery kiss.

A SAD TIME

ANNA MARIA TILSCHOVÁ

That first morning was terrible. It was only a few days after the Feast of St Wenceslas.[1] The day before, during the annual autumn fair, a frantic, icy wind had raged, shaking the windows, twisting the poplars, raising a loose, white dust on the road as high as a man and even higher.[2] On that day, if anyone had called out in fear for help, no one would have heard him. During the night, the wind calmed down and then came that morning. At six o'clock a cloud covered everything; there was no shadow, no light... only the same heavy gloom lay on the earth in the fields and on the sparse grass. The musicians had just carried their instruments out of the pub and behind them the drunks were carousing on the road, when Vincka, paler than pale, ran up to the sexton's garden where they were getting ready to go dig potatoes in the fields. Her old fingers, half-crippled from toil, were shaking as she held onto the fence and described how she had seen her daughter off and then, when she was returning through Dvořák's woods, had seen something on the ground, but for horror and fear she could go no closer – no closer.

So the sexton himself went off to have a look with his eldest son. They went up along the stone path to the fields, until they both saw two waxen, clenched fists rising against them from the trampled grass as if threatening – and they turned around. On the way back they met frightened people who had run out of their homes just as they had risen from bed – women with their hair down, and men just as they

---

1 The feast day of St Wenceslas is 28 September.
2 The word 'posvícení' (German 'Kirmes'), translated here as 'fair', refers to the village celebration held on the anniversary of the consecration of the local church.

were, half-dressed. 'Someone was killed in the night,' they said, and ran here and there, alarmed, aimless, like people do when lightning strikes a place where there is no water. No one knew what had happened... only the word 'misfortune' was carried about faster than the wind scatters seeds. And only when they had gathered together in a large crowd did they set out – men and women, a blind grandfather with a cane, children with goats trailing behind them on red ropes, young men, and all the way at the back a solitary, strange dog, which did not belong to anyone in the village and which had one clouded blue eye and one brown eye. In disarray and confusion they went past the half-finished building site and the pile of crude bricks to the brambles on the edge of the woods. There were hairs caught on the bush that protruded across the path – long, individual strands of a woman's hair torn out – strands which clung to the rough weave of women's skirts like soft calipers or withered fingers. Oh – by the furthest bush – there a young woman's body lay in blood. They recognized Štefa only by her sick, red eyes. She had just turned eighteen at the time of the second hay-crop. Both corners of her mouth had been cut with a knife so that her clenched teeth grimaced in her gums between dangling lips. Her head had been smashed with a rock and the white bodice she had worn to the dance the night before her death was all red. Simple-minded Štefa, the one the girls made fun of because she was almost blind but still had eyes for the young men – someone had killed a pitiful cripple like that!

'God have mercy!' the old tobacconist said, raising her mottled hands, brown from the sun, to the heavens. 'Whoever murdered like that deserves to be murdered too!'

They were all silent; only Antonín Novotný said hurriedly:

'He was a torturer or a tiger!'

And he stood right by her in his fireman's uniform; his trousers were so white it looked as if he hadn't even worn them dancing the night before.[3]

At the back, the girls clasped each other about the waist and quietly whispered together, while the strange dog sniffed at the blood on the ground. But how odd! It didn't make a sound, didn't bark. The girls recalled that it was Toník who had put his arm around Štefa's neck that night and said to her: 'You'll go with me, won't you, Štefka?' And three o'clock was chiming in the windows when those two left the hall together.

They had even shouted after her because she was so obliging to the handsome youth – she, who hardly ever danced and yet had to stay while the band played, from the first song of the night until dawn. But who could have known that instead of going to a comfortable bed Štefa was going to her death? Now, when she lay there dead and cold in the chilly air, they asked one another as they stood before the dull face of the girl from the poor rented cottage – why?

It didn't occur to anyone, aside from the gendarme, to suspect Antonín Novotný. They only asked him if he didn't know more than they did, considering that he had led her home from the dance and considering that they lived so close together that only the blacksmith's forge stood between them. Toník didn't want to know a thing about it – he'd slept – with his brother – in the shed – until waking! And old Psovina, when he'd passed by the courtyard at six, had seen him still sleeping soundly with his face turned up. No one could recall hearing anything bad about him; he didn't get into fights, didn't quarrel, didn't drink and in the religious processions he sang to God in a clear voice. The only thing they held against him was that he wouldn't

3 In the cities, fire-brigades sometimes had paid employees; in the smaller towns and villages they were made up of volunteers.

give up those devilish cards, that he, a single man, played with married men – what a shame! As for the rest, he had one brother and old parents. And no one in truth could say of those three that they were immoral people, and they all took it badly when the gendarme insisted and bound the boy's hands with a rope even before the commission arrived.

'What do you say to that, old father?' a cartman from somewhere else asked him – and he frowned. And someone else came up and asked the same question. Only then did the old man answer calmly, as if he didn't want to judge anyone:

'May the authorities punish whoever did it!'

All day long Štefa lay there, just as she had probably fallen to the grass when she was struck, with her skirt hiked up over her coarse stockings from the fair, green, blue and pink-striped. All day long slow crowds from other villages and townships, from the woods and the clearings, even from the factories in the city, passed by in single file. It drizzled from morning on, as if sharp, cold needles were falling from the sky to the earth, and in the distance the hills and white groups of two or three houses, straggling over the sluggish slope, disappeared in the gray vapor. Ceaselessly, from every corner, crowds of people thronged; they argued about the misfortune and they pitied both, murderer and murdered alike, and in the next breath they cursed them both. It had never been this sad before – people didn't cook, didn't work, didn't tend the cattle, and only asked: Why? Who? They supposed it was dissolute boys from some other place because they thought that if someone who lived among them had done it, they would have been able to tell from his uneasy, evasive eyes. They didn't even suspect Toník when the commission opened the fists of the dead girl and found a tangled clump of chestnut hair like Toník's trapped in them – neither hatred nor love could have guided his knife, so why would he have done it, the foolish man? Only in the evening did they carry away Šte-fa's body to the communal shed, where drunken, shameless, epileptic Anka lived, and where beggar women spent the night on the straw and died. Those who weren't local left before twilight and the straggling village seemed abandoned. That first evening no one, not even grown men, went out of doors; everyone was afraid. Not of the dead, but of the one who killed her. Children cried out in their sleep – the Lord God knows what a gloomy time it was, not one of the people could express it in words!

The next day when the gendarme, following regulations, pushed Toník over to the corpse so that he could look at it again, he hunched up his shoulders and resisted going inside.

'Why are you taking me to her?' he shouted. 'Do you really think I did it? I didn't do it, I didn't!'

They pushed him inside anyway and when he came out a minute later, some girl noticed that his eyes were wet. But what could be easier than to throw words around?

The sun rose, the sun set, but it was still sad until they buried her. Štefka's mother, who hadn't gone up to the woods when it happened, now, after the court examination, carried home the remains of the body, covered with a blanket, to lay them in a coffin. Two gendarmes walked through the village with fixed bayonets, going for a while along the road, then suddenly dropping in on the cottages, so that people didn't know what to say from fear. One gendarme guarded the door while the other inspected and turned upside down whatever came into his hands – a cupboard, a chest, a closet – but there was never anything there. It was disquieting. They all felt like convicts – like people who had brought hardship and shame on the village. And crowds of strangers continued to inspect the silent place soaked with blackened human blood in Dvořák's woods.

Now some people began to say that they didn't like Toník's vehement words or his sneering eyes, but those white trousers were his innocence and virtue. On account of those parents of his, no one believed it – except that now there was talk that had been hushed up before. The prettiest girl, the Nejedlýs' Manča, recounted how he had rested his chin on her shoulder while they were dancing and mused: 'I'd kill you, girl, I would, but that would be a pity!' All the girls admitted that not one of them would have left the dance with him; they were all afraid of him. When their mothers stood by as the girls worked at the looms, he wouldn't even speak to them, but as soon as the mothers left, he would snatch and grab at the girls. They all agreed – that was no violent love but an evil frenzy. But the poor wretch – why would he have killed her?

People came from all over for Štefa's funeral, and it was a splendid one, as if they were putting a bishop in the ground and not a wretch beaten to death with a rock. They couldn't all fit in the little church. The women spread their skirts over the graves, as they did on pilgrimages, and knelt on the steps under the lindens all the way to the road. There were people everywhere, but they didn't talk out loud, only murmured like water in the distance. Behind the priest, young men in black clothes carried the strange, small coffin with the remains of Štefka's body, which looked like a child's. The brother of the one locked up was among them and it was painful to watch how he staggered. After the ceremony, when the priest prayed for the murderer, the whole church wept.

It was all over; the grave was filled in, but the colorful crowds were still standing about the village as if waiting for something. Suddenly, one of the gendarmes, with a mysterious look in his small, deceitful eyes, pushed through the dense group of people. He stood up on the step before the Jew's shop and held above his head the bloody pair of fireman's trousers that he had found stuffed inside a fireman's helmet under the straw at the Novotnýs', at the very moment they were putting Štefa into the earth. He waved them up and down like a flag and shouted at the top of his lungs:

'This is the virtue, this is the glory of Antonín Novotný!'

At first they didn't understand, but then suddenly a buzzing started up, like the sound of spring water spraying and rushing over rocks. They all shouted:

'Skin him!' – one louder than the next – 'Beat him to death!'

The seething was indescribable. If he had been among them, the people would have judged him on the spot and beaten him to death. And in that mad crowd, furious that it had been deceived, that it had mistaken a murderer for a good man, his old parents cowered. They stared stupidly; they still didn't understand until the raging gendarme pointed a finger at them:

'Those are the murderer's parents!'

Only then did the mother cover her eyes with her apron. From all sides they gathered round the old couple, seized them and asked, or demanded: Had they known anything? People remembered that the week before, the gendarme had noticed yellow, rusty stains on the sash of a shirt that had been washed. And they asked the mother: Had she washed it? She had. And she had even asked him, 'What's this from?' 'None of your business,' the son had answered. Don't bother your head about it. And for God's sake, how could a mother tell on her own child, even if she had known or suspected?

The parents had to go with the gendarme right away – they weren't even allowed to change their clothes. The father beside the mother, in her worn coat and short skirt for wearing at home, so that it looked like the gendarme was leading two tramps to the city. The gendarme had lost his head; he struck the dumb woman down into the mud, the woman who had made soup from ground ivy and chicken feet, and he shoved the parents on.

'They won't be citizens in your township anymore!' he shouted furiously. 'They'll die in prison!'

If it hadn't been for the old, sensible people, the crowd would have thrown itself on him – everyone felt so anxious seeing the parents walk together on the road, with their heads down and hands bound, just like sheep, and walking just as slowly. They even had to carry the trousers, stiff with dried blood – what did they feel like then? They thought – they thought they had a good son and all the while he was like that!

All the same, there were some who found it in their hearts to shout after them: 'Serves them right! Why did they raise him like that?' But the parents walked on by the fence, which was red in the sun, to the woods, with the bloody clothes in their hands. They walked on as if they couldn't hear, couldn't see and couldn't understand anything anymore. And – even those people fell silent.

But – no one knew why – the parents were released the next day. People found reasons, they found reasons, as people always do – but the sun and moon never meet, nor can man understand the will of heaven. People were intimidated, startled, confused, sad and wistful, and they were afraid because they kept thinking that he might have killed someone else, just as he'd killed Štefa. Why, he might have killed anyone. And what did that foolish man say, in his confusion? That he had stuck the knife into his sleeve while still at the pub, that he hadn't been drunk, that he had knocked her down with a rock from the stream – and instead of explaining why, he only said: 'Silence is eternal!' Only later, when winter followed autumn and the black night was twice as long as the day, did people decide that Death had probably led them and that both had only followed where they had to go.

BIOGRAPHIES

BOŽENA BENEŠOVÁ (née Zapletalová, 1873–1936) was a writer of short stories, novels, poems, literary criticism and plays. She came from an upper-middle-class family; her father was a lawyer. She had little formal education. In 1896 she married the railway official Josef Beneš; they were divorced in 1912. Her one son, Roman, was born in 1897. Her first poems date from 1890, and fragments of prose and drama have been preserved from 1895. She published her first short story in 1900. In 1902 she met Růžena Svobodová and F. X. Šalda; under their influence, she began to write more systematically and to publish. She traveled to Italy with Svobodová in 1903 and 1907. In 1907–1908 Benešová edited the supplement 'Žena v umění' (Woman and Art) for the Brno journal *Ženská revue* (Women's Review). She moved to Prague in 1908 and began to work closely with the journal *Novina,* as well as *Česká kultura* and *Lípa.* In the 1920s she supported herself by writing for *Večer* and *Tribuna.* During the same period, she became friends with Anna Maria Tilschová and Pavla Buzková. From the mid-1920s on, she suffered from the heart disease that finally killed her. Her first literary works depict young women revolting against the environments in which they have been raised (e.g., *Nedobytá vítězství,* Incomplete Triumphs, 1910). Her best known work is *Don Pablo, don Pedro a Věra Lukášová* (1936), which treats a young girl's encounter with a child molester. The story published here is from the collection *Tři povídky* (Three Stories, 1914).

RŮŽENA JESENSKÁ (1863–1940) wrote poems, short stories, novels and plays. She was the oldest daughter in the large family of an official who later became a businessman. She taught for two years at an elementary school in Mladá Boleslav and then at various schools in Prague. She was forced to retire from teaching in 1907. She also worked as an editor of journals for children and anthologies for women. For a short time in 1921 she worked as a theatre critic for *Ženský svět* (Women's World). She traveled extensively in the Baltic countries, France, Italy and Russia. She began to publish regularly in the mid-1880s. Her first novellas were published in the journal *Světozor* under the male pseudonym Martin Věžník. Her style was influenced by the Decadent writers. She published three biographical novels. She also published a novel about a child prostitute: *Román dítěte* (A Child's Romance, 1905). Some of her work was aimed at a readership of adolescent girls: *Jarmila* (J., 1894); *Jarní píseň* (Song of Spring, 1902). The collection of short stories *Mimo svět* (A World Apart) was published in 1909.

MARIE MAJEROVÁ (née Bartošová, 1882–1967) came from a working-class family. Her father died when she was quite young and her mother moved to Prague and supported herself with sewing. Her mother's second marriage was to Alois Majer, and Marie took his surname for her literary pseudonym. After finishing school, she worked as a maid in Budapest and as a typist in Prague. In 1902, she gave birth to a son; the father was the Social Democratic journalist J. Stivín. She married Stivín in 1904; in the same year they both went to Vienna, where they worked for the Social Democratic newspaper *Dělnické listy* (Workers' Mail). She lived in Paris in 1906–1907, where she attended the Sorbonne as an external student and became acquainted with the anarchist commune there. She later returned to Prague and wrote for Soc. Dem. periodicals. She divorced Stivín in 1920, and in 1922 married the graphic artist S. Tusar (divorced in 1931). She joined the Communist Party in 1921 and worked as editor for its periodicals. In 1929 she was expelled from the Party for criticizing Gottwald's leadership, but was allowed to join again after WWII and was honored officially in the post-1948 period. In the 1930s she wrote for a broad range of newspapers and journals. Her first collection of short stories, *Povídky z pekla* (Stories from Hell, 1907) was influenced by anarchism. Her first novel, *Panenství* (Virginity, 1907), depicts a working-class heroine who struggles to preserve her financial independence and virginity. In the 1920s Majerová was attracted by the program of revolutionary art; her later work, particularly after 1945, is tendentious. Her *Havířská balada* (Ballad of a Miner, 1938) was translated into English. Several of her works were made into films and others were presented on radio. She translated from French and German. She also traveled a great deal, visiting the United States, the Soviet Union, North Africa and China. The story published here is from the collection *Plané milování* (Illicit Loving), published in 1911.

HELENA MALÍŘOVÁ (née Nosková, 1877–1940) was a journalist and a writer of short stories and novels. She also translated from German, French, Bulgarian and Serbo-Croatian. Her first collection of stories was *Lidská srdce* (Human Hearts, 1903), followed by *Křehké květiny* (Fragile Flowers, 1907) and *Ženy a děti* (Women and Children, 1908). During the First Balkan War (1912), she traveled to the south to work as a reporter and nurse. She later became a Communist and published tendentious plays for proletarian youth. In 1920, she traveled to Russia incognito. Her first political essays were published in the collection *Rudé besídky* (Red Meetings, 1922). She worked for the Communist newspaper *Rudé právo* (Red Justice) and the women's weekly *Rozsevačka* (The Sower). The story included here was first published in *Křehké květiny*.

GABRIELA PREISSOVÁ (née Sekerová, 1862–1946) was a Czech dramatist and prose writer. Her first work was a short story at the age of 16. She married Jan Preiss, a clerk at a sugar refinery in Hodonín, in 1880. She spent several years in Moravian Slovakia and is most famous for the tragedies she wrote set in that location: *Gazdina roba* (perf. 1889, published 1890), and *Její pastorkyňa* (Her Stepdaughter, perf. 1890, published 1891). The play *Gazdina roba* was made into the opera *Eva* (1899), with music by Josef Bohuslav Foerster. Leoš Janáček used the drama *Její pastorkyňa* for the libretto of his opera called *Jenůfa* in English and German (1904). The short story included here was written before the play with the same title, and was published in the collection *Obrázky bez rámů* (Unframed Pictures) in 1896.

JIŘÍ SUMÍN (pseudonym of Amálie Vrbová, 1863–1936) was the fifth child of a miller's wife. She boarded at a convent school as a girl, but otherwise was self-educated. She read German, French, Russian and Polish. She did not have a happy childhood; her mother divorced her father. She entered early upon a literary career, writing verse and plays, as well as short stories and novels. She traveled a great deal. She has been compared with the Czech writer Josef Šlejhar, both in terms of the themes of their works and the difficult experiences in their lives. She was interested in negative social phenomena, such as divorce and the hypocritical upbringing of girls. Her other works include the collections of short stories *Z doby našich dědů* (From the Era of Our Forefathers, 1895) and *Příčina rozvodu a jiné povídky* (The Cause of the Divorce and Other Stories, 1913), and the novels *Zrádné proudy* (Treacherous Currents, 1904) and *Spása* (Salvation, 1908). The short story included here was published in *Kroky osudu* (The Tread of Fate) in 1912.

RŮŽENA SVOBODOVÁ (née Čápova, 1868–1920), a Czech writer of short stories and novels, moved to Prague when she was six years old and lived there until her death. She was educated at a convent school, and pursued independent study of literature. In the 1880s she worked as a governess. In 1890 she married the poet, dramatist and prose writer F. X. Svoboda. She ran a salon, attended by the foremost Prague artists, including F. X. Šalda, H. Kvapilová, Benešová, M. Pujmanová, and others. She also edited the journals *Lípa* (The Linden, 1918–1919) and *Zvěstování* (The Annunciation, 1919). Her other works include *Přetížený klas* (The Overburdened Ear of Grain, 1896), *Milenky* (Lovers, 1902), *Pěšinkami srdce* (Along the Paths of the Heart, 1902) and *Posvátné jaro* (Sacred Spring, 1912). The collection *Černí myslivci* (The Black Huntsmen), from which the present story is taken, was published in 1908.

ANNA MARIA TILSCHOVÁ (1873–1957), a Czech prose writer, grew up in a wealthy family, and patrician Prague families often figured in her works. She attended a secondary school for girls and was an external student at the Faculty of Arts of Charles University. She spent most of her life in Prague. In the 1920s, she edited the women's journals *Lada* and *Nová žena* (New Woman) and the Social Democratic *Pestré květy* (Bright Flowers). In 1947, she was named a National Artist. In literary handbooks, her writing is described as Naturalist. The story included here (published in *Na horách,* [In the Mountains] 1905) would tend to confirm that label; her works from *Fany* onwards are Realist. Her works include: *Fany* (1915); *Stará rodina* (An Old Family, 1916); *Synové* (The Sons, 1918); *Vykoupení* (Redemption, 1923).

SOURCES FOR BIOGRAPHIES

Vladimír Forst (ed.), *Lexikon české literatury,* vol. 1 A-G, Prague, 1985; vol. 2, part I, H-J, Prague, 1993.

Květa Homolová, Mojmír Otruba and Zdenek Pešat, *Čeští spisovatelé 19. a počátku 20. století,* Prague, 1982.

Pavel Janoušek (ed.), *Slovník českých spisovatelů od roku 1945,* vol. 2, Prague, 1998.

Jaroslav Kunc, *Slovník soudobých českých spisovatelů,* Prague, 1945.

Jan Lehár et al., *Česká literatura od počátků k dnešku*, Prague, 1998.

Josef Polák, *Česká literatura 19. století*, Prague, 1990.

Gabriela Preissová, *Jiří Sumín,* Prague, 1937.

R. B. Pynsent (ed.), *The Everyman Companion to East European Literature,* London, 1993. Entries by R. B. Pynsent and Karel Brušák.

MODERN CZECH CLASSICS

Published titles
Zdeněk Jirotka: *Saturnin* (2003, 2005, 2009, 2013; pb 2016)
Vladislav Vančura: *Summer of Caprice* (2006; pb 2016)
Karel Poláček: *We Were a Handful* (2007; pb 2016)
Bohumil Hrabal: *Pirouettes on a Postage Stamp* (2008)
Karel Michal: *Everyday Spooks* (2008)
Eduard Bass: *The Chattertooth Eleven* (2009)
Jaroslav Hašek: *Behind the Lines: Bugulma and Other Stories* (2012; pb 2016)
Bohumil Hrabal: *Rambling On* (2014; pb 2016)
Ladislav Fuks: *Of Mice and Mooshaber* (2014)
Josef Jedlička: *Midway upon the Journey of Our Life* (2016)
Jaroslav Durych: *God's Rainbow* (2016)
Ladislav Fuks: *The Cremator* (2016)
Bohuslav Reynek: *The Well at Morning* (2017)
Viktor Dyk: *The Pied Piper* (2017)
Jiří R. Pick: *Society for the Prevention of Cruelty to Animals* (2018)
Views from the Inside: Czech Underground Literature and Culture (1948–1989), ed. M. Machovec (2018)
Ladislav Grosman: *The Shop on Main Street* (2019)
Bohumil Hrabal: *Why I Write? The Early Prose from 1945 to 1952* (2019)
Jiří Pelán: Bohumil Hrabal: A Full-length Portrait (2019)
Martin Machovec: Writing Underground (2019)
Ludvík Vaculík: *A Czech Dreambook* (2019)
Jaroslav Kvapil: *Rusalka* (2020)
Jiří Weil: *Lamentation for 77,297 Victims* (2021)
Vladislav Vančura: *Ploughshares into Swords* (2021)
Siegfried Kapper: *Tales from the Prague Ghetto* (2022)
Jan Zábrana: *The Lesser Histories* (2022)
Jan Procházka: *Ear* (2022)
A World Apart and Other Stories: Czech Women Writers at the Fin de Siècle (2022)

Forthcoming
Ivan M. Jirous: *End of the World. Poetry and Prose*
Jan Čep: *Common Rue*
Jiří Weil: *Moscow – Border*
Libuše Moníková: *Verklärte Nacht*

*Scholarship

MODERN SLOVAK CLASSICS

Published titles
Ján Johanides: *But Crimes Do Punish* (2022)

Forthcoming
Ján Rozner: *Sedem dní do pohrebu*